Along the River Road

Along the River Road
A Novel

Isaac Morris

Along the River Road

Charleston, South Carolina

ISBN-13: 978-1466469747
ISBN-10: 1466469749

This is a work of fiction. All of the characters, names, incidents, organizations, and dialogue in this novel are either the products of the author's imagination or are used fictitiously.

Front cover image: CreateSpace Cover Creator
Title page image: Illustration from a *Map of Mississippi* by cartographer Jean-Baptiste Louis Franquelin, ca. 1682. The image of the death of the Piasa is based on a description given in a journal by explorer Louis Joliet, ca. 1673. The image is displayed at Pere Marquette State Park, Grafton, Illinois. Library of Congress.

Acknowledgements

I will never forget the first time I drove the stretch of highway between Grafton and Alton, Illinois. I could not believe I was in Illinois. That stretch of the Great River Road has to be among the most beautiful places I have been, and I have returned to the area many times since. The communities of Grafton, Elsah, Chautauqua, and Alton, near where the Piasa Bird can be seen, are all well worth the drive and perhaps a weekend in one of the area's fabulous bed and breakfasts. I couldn't find a better setting for my novel, and I trust the residents of the area will be forgiving for the liberties I have taken with my presentation.

There is no "Fast Tony's" restaurant in Springfield, Illinois. There is, however, a "Jungle Jim's" which serves the best breakfast and lunch anywhere on Route 66. Its owner, "Jungle" Jim Davison, served as the inspiration for the fictional character "Fast Tony" and for this I make no apologies. Jungle and his crew have made my days brighter for years. I hope this returns the favor by bringing them a smile.

Thanks to my friend Jim Cox for enlightening me about life in the jungles of Viet Nam and for his service to our country, for which he paid a high price.

My thanks to all of the usual suspects: Carol, my wife and editor in chief, for putting up with me all these years; and my four children whose combined efforts produced six grandchildren and two great grandchildren. There are undoubtedly more to come, God willing!

Isaac Morris

If I had rhymes both rough and stridulous,
As were appropriate to the dismal hole
Down upon which thrust all the other rocks,

I would press out the juice of my conception
More fully; but because I have them not,
Not without fear I bring myself to speak;

For 'tis no enterprise to take in jest,
To sketch the bottom of all the universe….

Dante (Longfellow Translation)
Inferno, Canticle XXXII

––––––––

"This is a beautiful river," he said to his companion.
"Yes," said the ferryman, "a very beautiful river, I love it more than anything. Often I have listened to it, often I have looked into its eyes, and always I have learned from it. Much can be learned from a river."

From Siddhartha, by Hermann Hesse

––––––––

"I see that I am floundering around in the dark, and need to pray and meditate a great deal. And that it is true that this summer I have done some very foolish and dangerous things."

Thomas Merton

Prologue

August 19th, 1968
8:30 a.m.
Rural Jersey County, Illinois

CATHERINE BARSTOW RAN OUT OF the house through the back door. Melvin was screaming and throwing things in the kitchen and she was terrified. She had told him she couldn't live like this anymore. He wasn't taking it well.

She heard the screen door burst open and, from the corner of her eye, she saw him reach down to pick up something that was standing at the bottom of the stairs. Her heart nearly exploded when she realized what it was that had been leaning against the steps. She had to get to the car. The keys were in it.

Her leg got tangled in her bathrobe causing her to lose her balance in the wet grass and fall on her face. How many seconds had it cost her? She righted herself and ran desperately toward the gravel driveway.

When she reached the black and white Chevy Impala she grasped the door handle, jumped into the driver's seat, and slammed the door.

That was when she saw it coming.

The axe blade crashed through the window before she could get her arm up all the way. Part of her hand came off, blunting the blow somewhat as the blade struck behind her ear. She blacked out for a moment, regaining consciousness only to see blood—lots of it—sluicing down the inside of the windshield.

Responding with super-human effort, she pushed violently on the car door with her body weight and the hand she had left, surprising Melvin for a moment, knocking him off balance. She was a fright as she climbed out of the car with part of her hand missing, blood pouring out of the side of her head. The world was spinning. She was afraid she couldn't remain conscious for long but she had to get out of there. Her life force kicked into high gear, compelling her to overcome the threat of extermination any way possible.

Her legs couldn't sustain her lunge forward; she lost her footing and went down hard into the gravel. She was crying.

Catherine looked up in time to see Melvin, the man she fell in love with three years earlier, raise the axe in the air.

That was the last thing Catherine Barstow saw in this life.

August 2009
Grafton, Illinois

IT WAS EARLY EVENING AND the summer sun still glowed brightly—and hot—above the limestone cliffs

Margaret Donovan sang along with Rick Nelson to "Fools Rush In" as she drove her red Hyundai Elantra along the Great River Road north of Alton.

Rick, or "Ricky" Nelson wasn't of her generation, but when she **was** a kid one of the first movies her dad rented after they got a VCR was *Rio Bravo*, a John Wayne western that featured Dean Martin and Ricky Nelson. In the movie, Nelson and Martin sang a duet—"My Rifle, My Pony, and Me." It touched something in her, so she walked downtown the next day and bought a Ricky Nelson album. Now, some 23 years later, she had several of his albums loaded on her iPod.

Looking back at former teen idols like Nelson, with their fresh-faced innocence, she wondered what changed in the world to create superstars out of criminals and drug users whose songs amounted to little more than paeans to violence, sexual and otherwise.

Margaret smiled now as she remembered her father. Her dad, who had been the Sheriff of Morgan County, loved John Wayne. As he grew older, he even resembled Wayne somewhat, especially when he smiled. Her dad and John Wayne—like the fresh-faced, gentle Rick Nelson—were from a generation that was fading quickly.

As she left Alton on Highway 100, she passed a limestone cliff on which was painted the Piasa bird, a mythical creature first depicted by the prehistoric residents of the place where three rivers meet. The first European to record the Piasa was Father Jacques Marquette when he explored the region in 1673. The painting seen by Marquette of the Piasa—or "PIE-uh-saw"—bird no longer exists, but was recreated several times in different locations, the most current restoration dating from 1996.

The fantastical bird had the face of man, shark-like teeth, a rattler-like tail, horns that resembled antlers, and red, giant wings. Such symbols were frequently found among the Mound Builders, a prehistoric people who had a huge settlement in the vicinity of modern-day Cahokia. It may have served as a warning to outsiders coming into the area. For Margaret, this depiction of a beast, designed to inspire fear in the midst of such natural beauty, served as a reminder that the devil lurks in Eden.

As she rounded a curve, she again encountered the beauty of the McAdams Highway between Alton and Grafton. When she had first seen it, she couldn't believe she was in Illinois. The waters of the Mississippi and Illinois rivers come together near Grafton, where the Mississippi flows from west to east. On the road along the river bend can be seen some of the most beautiful sights anywhere.

The beautiful cloudless blue sky arched over the ancient limestone cliffs that were hundreds of feet high. On the Mississippi River, speedboats, pontoons and a tug pushing four barges, each the size of two football fields, moved at varying speeds. One shirtless speedboat driver a hundred feet away from the road passed her and waved. The water was high and lapping against the white gravel on the other side of the guardrails; a heavy downpour could easily send water across the road. She passed dozens of bicyclers who were out on the Vadalabene bike trail, some alone, others in groups. She noted several families—father, mother, and varying numbers of children—riding on bikes rented from a fudge shop at the edge of Grafton.

As she passed the Elsah turnoff, Margaret turned off the iPod and allowed the glorious day to saturate her soul. As she gloried in the beauty surrounding her, she was grateful that she took advantage of the opportunity that presented itself several months earlier. The decision brought her to this place, this ancient place with its natural wonders, this place where her soul could find its moorings.

She needed that.

She entered the city limits of Grafton, turned off of Main Street and drove into the garage of a residence near the limestone structure of St. Alban's Catholic Church. Margaret Donovan was home.

Several miles behind her the giant Piasa grinned, its incisors pointing upward, its black eyes surveying the River Road.

MARGARET'S ALARM WENT OFF AT five in the morning. Her head felt like someone had wrapped a belt around it while she was sleeping, and her mouth tasted like a troop of girl scouts had tramped through it during the night. Before going to bed she had poured herself a tumbler of merlot to help her sleep. She must have poured another at some point, and another one after that, because there was only an inch of wine left in the bottle by the side of her bed. She padded into the bathroom and popped two Tylenol and brushed her teeth.

She put on a pot of coffee and then returned to her room to put on her running gear. She jogged every morning, weather permitting. It was an extension of her prayer life. She lived in an earthly paradise, and God was on the river, in the clouds, on the bluffs and everywhere else she looked. On mornings like this, it also helped her clear her head.

After downing a cup of coffee, she left the rectory at a sprint, headed towards the main road, then turned east and headed out of town. The sun was leaking light over the two-hundred-foot limestone bluffs and steam was rising from the river to her right. The air was clean, and it wasn't too hot yet. It would be before long, but now it was perfect.

She stopped at one point to adjust her iPod. Then she selected an album of antiphons that had been composed by Hildegard von Bingen, a 12th century nun whose reputation as a philosopher, musician and *avant-garde* thinker was unparalleled at the time. She was probably the first woman in history to write about the female orgasm. The *a cappella* voices of a choir of nuns gave apt expression to the essence of this morning on the timeless river. She started to fasten the iPod in its case, but then she took it out again.

She looked at the slender, brushed instrument with its white click wheel and stroked it lovingly. She thought of the woman to whom it once belonged. The woman she had bought it for. The woman who had loved Elvis Presley and had hundreds of his songs loaded. They were all still there.

The woman was Mary Frances Hohmann, who lived her adult life and died as Sister Theodora.

Theodora rescued Margaret from a life of isolation, and led her to a new life as Sister Margaret. Margaret's mother died when she was too young to remember her, but Theodora had appeared at a time when she was lost in a dark wood to help her find her way. She loved her as much as she might have loved her own mother. Margaret brushed a tear from her eye, and then resumed her trek along the Vadalabene trail that paralleled the River Road. She was the only one on the trail at this hour, but she was not alone. Theodora was with her. She always would be. And someday, if Margaret succeeded in living her life the way she should, Theodora would greet and hug her again on the other side of life.

COME OCTOBER, IT WOULD BE *two years since Theodora died. Margaret had left Springfield in May, and so missed the hours of walking and talking with Theodora. She wrote her faithfully, and the prioress sent e-mails regularly to keep Margaret informed of Theodora's declining health. Theodora had cancer of the liver, and her time was marked.*

Near the end, Margaret sat by Theodora's bed, brushing her hair, talking whenever Theodora felt like talking, and reading whenever she slept. She was there to the last.

Shortly before Theodora died, she woke up and saw Margaret dozing off in the chair next to her bed. Margaret heard the bedcovers rustling and opened her eyes.

"Could I have a drink of water?" Theodora asked in a raspy voice.

Margaret picked up the glass, placed the straw between Theodora's lips, and supported her head while she sipped.

"Thank you," Theodora said.

"You're welcome."

"It's time."

Margaret wiped a tear from the corner of her eye. "I know," she said.

"It's the way it must be. I am ready."

Margaret knew that if anyone was ready, Theodora was. She also knew that the beatific vision awaited her friend, with no stopover in between this world and the next.

"Have I ever told you how much ..."

Theodora waved her arm weakly to stop Margaret. "You have a thousand times. You need say no more. You have said it sufficiently."

"I will miss you."

"You won't need to. I will be there."

Then Theodora closed her eyes and went to sleep again.

It was just past midnight when Mary Frances Hohmann went to her reward. Margaret was still sitting next to the bed.

MARGARET SPENT AS MUCH TIME as she could kneeling at the casket before the wake. Theodora looked as beautiful as she ever had, and in her hands was clasped the letter of commitment that she had signed when she took her vows more than 50 years before. She had kept her promises.

Hundreds came to pay their last respects. Former St. Dominic's faculty, former students, community leaders, other sisters of the order stationed elsewhere, priests, and members from other religious orders who had, at one time or another, been touched by Theodora. Three lay teachers from Louisiana drove up to honor the woman who had served as their principal for several years.

Margaret was sitting in the front row when she saw a group enter wearing the dress uniforms of the Sangamon County Sheriff's Department. She choked up when she saw Sheriff Jim Hargrove in front of the pack. There were only a few threads of red in his hair, which was now otherwise white. She stood and walked over to him.

She hugged the sheriff and thanked him for coming.

"She was a grand lady," Hargrove said. "And a good friend to you. I wouldn't have missed coming for anything."

She kissed him on the cheek and then looked over at the tall figure of Ernie Jones, Hargrove's chief of detectives.

"Ernie, thank you."

The tall, black man hugged Margaret tightly. "I am so sorry about your friend, but I have no doubts about where she will be spending her time from now on."

Margaret smiled. "Yeah. I'll be lucky if I ever see her again!" Ernie laughed, and so did Margaret. Then she turned and found herself face to face with Bill Templeton.

A flood of feelings swelled up in her as she looked at the man she hadn't seen since she said good-bye to him months earlier in St. Alphonse Church. He looked handsome in his dress uniform, and as she looked at him now she remembered the moments she had spent in his arms, the smell of him, and his heart beating beneath her head as he stroked her hair. This was a man she had almost thrown over her vocation for.

For an awkward moment, she didn't know what to say, what to do. Finally, she gave in and simply walked over and put her arms around him. He hugged her back tightly. She held him for several moments, longer than was wise given the fact that the prioress was watching from the front row. Finally, she let go, stepped back and looked at him once more.

"I am so glad you came," she said.

"I was hoping you wouldn't mind," he whispered.

"I would have minded if you hadn't. Come and see my friend." With that, she took his hand and walked to the casket.

"She was a wonderful woman," Bill said.

"That she was."

She turned back to talk with the sheriff and Ernie, letting go of Bill's hand. They talked for several minutes, and then they left. She watched Bill walk out of the room.

The next day, as she drove from Springfield to Grafton with Theodora's iPod plugged in, Elvis' rendition of "It Keeps Right On A-Hurtin'" playing. Margaret wondered if she would ever stop feeling what she felt in her heart for Bill Templeton.

MARGARET REACHED THE ELSAH TURNOFF and went into the village. Unlike the village of Chautauqua, a mile north, Elsah was accessible to the public. The homes, many of which were built in the 19th century, were privately owned and not open for viewing. There were many homes made of limestone, but various architectural styles—from Greek and Gothic revival to Italianate—also drew admiring glances from visitors. Several bed and breakfast inns welcomed lovers, old and young, who sought to escape from modernity and experience the quiet of this riverside town. It was a place straight out of a storybook. *Midwest Living* magazine once featured the community—which it dubbed as "The Town that Time Forgot"—as a must-see for anyone traveling the River Road.

She ran the circuit of the village, turning past the structure that was her favorite, the small, white Methodist Church. Elsah tourist information described it as Gothic, but it was of white clapboard with tall, rectangular windows (no pointed arches), simple shutters, and a belfry that was reminiscent of a New England chapel. It was picture-postcard perfect, and Margaret couldn't wait to see it lighted for Christmas.

The sun was bright and hot by the time Margaret walked up on the porch of the rectory. It was eight-thirty when she stepped into the shower. When she finished, she prayed in the church and then started her day.

THE RECTORY, LIKE THE CHURCH, was constructed of limestone, as were many older structures in Grafton. Limestone was readily available and quarrying was at one time a major source of employment in the area.

The interior had woodwork that could never be duplicated today, taken from the trees that lined the hills of the town. High ceilings and large windows helped keep the building a bit cooler in the summer. Margaret tried to keep the air conditioning units in the office and in her bedroom shut off as much as she could. In the winter, however, the high ceilings contributed to drafts, and the heating system relied on gravity. Still, Margaret loved the old house.

The message lights on the phone were blinking. A pre-recorded message had been placed on the main line giving the time for Sunday mass; so many calls—though there were never that many—were intercepted without necessitating a return call. The other was the unpublished number, the one the chancery usually called on. Father Thomas, the Parochial Vicar she had replaced at St. Alban's, called it the "bat phone." She hit the main line.

Claire Fogarty called to inquire whether she would like to come to dinner sometime over the weekend. Margaret loved the dinners at the homes of parishioners, although a steady diet of meat and potatoes was not doing anything to enhance her figure. She had to run twice as long in the morning to compensate, and now—catching a glimpse of her profile in a body-length mirror that graced one of the doorways to the office—she was noticing a bit of a paunch. Of course, vanity was something that was supposed to be beyond her. Somehow it wasn't.

On the bat phone, Ann Fisher, the Bishop's secretary in Springfield, had left a message asking Margaret to call her when she had a chance. Ann could wait, she decided, so she sat down at her laptop to finish the Sunday bulletin.

St. Alban's Catholic Church
Grafton, Illinois
Father Michael Kennelly, Moderator
Sister Margaret Donovan, O.P., Parish Life Coordinator

Parish Life Coordinator. Such was now her title and her life.

After leaving Springfield, she had been assigned to a collaborative Dominican novitiate house in St. Louis, the same house she lived in for a time during her novitiate. There were more than twenty religious communities around the country that sent young women there so they could experience a sense of community, so important to a religious vocation. In this time of shrinking vocations, religious houses could not provide a sense of community to only one or two novices, except with older nuns. Providing a place where novices could experience fellowship with peers, where friendships could flower, and vocations could blossom was very important for novices. Margaret loved working with the women at the novitiate. As a former deputy sheriff, she brought valuable insights into personal development and provided a strong shoulder to lean on for those who experienced doubts about their vocation.

Unfortunately, there were fewer and fewer women entering the Dominican order. When Margaret arrived, the class consisted of only six women, ranging in age from 24 to 47. Most had finished college, some had worked, and one was a childless widow. For the coming year, the class would have only three women—all from New Orleans where recruitment efforts were yielding greater results. There were concerns that the novitiate could continue with such low numbers. A one-year hiatus was being contemplated.

Margaret had received a phone call one evening from the prioress in Springfield, Sister Agnes Ann Carpenter. Sister Agnes asked if Margaret would be interested in an opening that was coming up in southern Illinois.

Canon Law, the ecclesiastical code that governs the Catholic Church, allows a bishop to appoint a person other than a priest to work in the capacity of a parish administrator when priests are in short supply. In the Springfield diocese, as in many others, there was a shortage of priests that grew more alarming every year. The bishop had contacted the prioress to see if she could recommend anyone to fill the role. Of course, a priest would be appointed as Parish Moderator, as Canon Law required, to fill the sacramental role; but, practically speaking, Margaret would run the parish.

She loved the novitiate, but feared that it might have to close its doors soon. Grafton was familiar to her. She had visited the area several times with other sisters on weekend outings. She had fallen in love with its charm, its history, and the beauty of the place where the two rivers flow together.

Margaret gave the prioress a resounding "Yes!" and within two weeks started her new job.

Margaret's duties were actually more time-consuming than that of a priest-pastor. Most priests would not be caught dead fixing the plumbing, cleaning the rectory, or working in the yard; but all that was part of what she had to do since there was very little budget to hire anyone.

The parish did employ a younger man named Vergil Atkins to do some odd jobs, but it was more out of charity than necessity. The arrangements were in place when Margaret took over, and Margaret never questioned them—although she found it strange that neither Vergil nor his mother attended church. Vergil had mental problems, the nature of which was not clear. He never looked up at you when you spoke to him, although he was always very polite when he replied. He was paid a pittance, and she knew that simply having something to do was all that really mattered; if not to him, then to his mother, Rachel Atkins.

She finished the bulletin and hit print to send it to the printer and waited for the bulletins to accumulate in the tray. She had learned that during the winter months 75 bulletins were more than enough. The parish had one hundred and eighty-nine members, about seventy families, but only about a third attended regularly. In the summer—tourist season along the river—she printed one hundred bulletins. A few summer people came to church. She suspected that the vast majority of them spent Sunday mornings recovering. But she was happy to see anyone who stopped in—even the ones with hangovers.

While the bulletins printed, she checked the schedule for the rest of the week. There was a funeral scheduled for Thursday morning for Mrs. Agnes Cutworth, a long-time parishioner. Mrs. Cutworth had been in a nursing home in Jerseyville for several years, so Margaret only knew her from her weekly visits. She doubted that Mrs. Cutworth even knew when she visited. Margaret made a mental note to check with the cemetery caretaker, and perhaps run by to see if everything was in order.

Overseeing St. Alban's cemetery was another of her duties. It was not difficult because the caretaker, Eli Barstow, did such a fine job. Father Thomas told her that Barstow, who lived in a small house adjacent to the cemetery, had been caretaker since the mid-seventies. He still dug graves by hand whenever possible.

The printer stopped and Margaret grabbed the stack of paper. She decided that she might as well fold them now and be done. Margaret was about to return Ann Fisher's call when she looked out the window.

Vergil Atkins was standing in the yard.

VERGIL WAS A GROWN MAN in his 30s, possibly into his 40s, but he was in appearance an attitude quite like a child. Vergil's mother had apparently dropped him off to work and hadn't rung the doorbell. Margaret knew that Vergil would stand in the yard until kingdom come unless and until someone told him something that needed to be done. Once he had a direction, he would carry it out to perfection. She got up and walked to the front door.

"Good morning, Vergil," she said, smiling.

"Good morning, Sister," came the characteristically polite reply.

He was looking down at his shoes.

Vergil stood about 5 foot 6 inches, had a slight build, dark hair cut close, and eyebrows that almost grew together. He might have appeared normal but for his halting reticence around other people. She was never able to make out the color of his eyes, as he seldom looked directly at her. He was wearing old blue jeans, a blue short-sleeved work shirt and dirty sneakers. His face and hands were always clean, however, at least before he started working. There was an overwhelming sense of sadness about his person that always touched Margaret.

She walked over, touched Vergil lightly on the arm, and said, "Come around back."

He flinched slightly to her touch. His face reddened briefly, illuminating a long, white "S" that streaked through his short hair. He followed her to the back of the rectory.

Margaret pointed to the yard.

"Vergil, do you see all those branches?"

"Yes, Sister."

"The wind and rain the other night has made quite a mess back here. Could you please gather all of them up and take them to the front of the rectory? Here, let me show you."

She walked back to the front of the rectory and pointed to a spot at the edge of the yard near the driveway. "Just stack all of them here," she said. "Mr. Fogarty will come pick them up next week."

Fogarty was a retired farmer whose wife, Claire, volunteered him to do little things around the parish whenever Sister needed them done. He always came when called.

"Can you do that, Vergil?" She knew he could, but always felt better eliciting a response that reflected understanding.

"Yes, Sister."

"Good. Bless you Vergil."

"Sister?"

"Yes, Vergil."

"Then can I work in the garden?"

Margaret smiled, reached over and gently touched his arm. This time he did not flinch, although he still did not look up. The garden was next to the garage, and contained tomato plants, peppers, zucchini, green beans, onions, and a variety of other vegetables all of which Vergil had planted in the spring, some from seedlings he had grown himself. It was his special mission, according to Father Thomas. Yet, Vergil always asked permission.

"Of course you can, Vergil. It is your garden, and I admire how well you care for it."

She thought she saw the beginnings of a smile, but it quickly faded.

"Thank you, Sister."

"Thank *you*, Vergil.

"CATHOLIC DIOCESE, OFFICE OF the Bishop."

"Ann. This is Sister Margaret."

"Hello Margaret." There was no smile in Ann Fisher's voice. "What's up?"

"I wanted to inform you of a decision that the bishop has made regarding Father Kennelly."

Father Kennelly, the parish moderator, lived in Jerseyville where he was pastor of Holy Trinity Church. He sometimes said mass at St. Albans, but Margaret had to get other priests to come when he could not. Father Kennelly's health had been precarious for some time. He had suffered a TIA some months back, and his health continued to fail.

"The bishop has decided to replace Father Kennelly as moderator, given the state of his health."

"Oh? Who with?"

"Father Seamus Corrigan."

"I don't know that I have heard his name," Margaret said.

"He is in his early seventies," Ann said, "and strong as a bull. He is a former chaplain for the Marine Corps, and served in Vietnam. Interesting man."

"So, he's going to be at Holy Trinity?"

"No. He will travel, when necessary, from Springfield. He is at the Cathedral."

"Where was he before that?"

Silence. Ann Fisher was not chatty, and took her position with the bishop seriously. As far as she was concerned, information was always on a "need to know" basis. Margaret guessed this was something she didn't need to know.

"He wants to come this Sunday for mass," Ann said, ignoring Margaret's question.

"Actually, I have Father Jim coming from Hardin this Sunday. It's already been scheduled," Margaret said.

One of the tasks Margaret had was to ensure the presence of a priest at Sunday mass. The Moderator was not necessarily that priest, and lately had seldom been since Father Kennelly was in bad health. Father Jim Clancy was in Calhoun County, and his morning mass was at eleven. Calhoun County was squeezed between the Illinois and Mississippi Rivers, and the nearest bridge was in Hardin, twenty miles north of Grafton. Fortunately, there was a ferry a few miles upriver at Brussels that operated 24/7. A nine o'clock mass in Grafton was no problem. Clancy, a forty-something man with an infectious sense of humor, was one of Margaret's favorite priests.

"You'll need to notify him," said Ann. "Father Corrigan feels it is important to get to know the people who are placed in his charge."

Just like that. Margaret pondered this for a minute. She envisioned the new priest requiring everyone in the church to stand at attention while he walked through the congregation, row-by-row, ensuring that they were dressed properly. *She* was the parish administrator, and for a moment she thought about challenging Ann on this, but only briefly. Her vow of obedience kicked in. This was coming from the bishop after all.

Get a grip, Margaret.

"Of course. Is there anything I should know about Father Corrigan?"

"He is a priest who has served well and faithfully through the years. That should be sufficient," said Ann.

"Thanks," said Margaret.

I can hardly wait.

Vergil

MOTHER TOLD SISTER THAT WE had vegetables at home and we didn't need any more. We do have vegetables at home. I planted them. All of them. I started with seeds in little pots in the shed behind the house before the cold went away and watered and fed them and then put them in the garden and now they are growing all over. I love to dig in the dirt. I take them to mom when they are ready to come off and she doesn't even thank me. Sister thanked me. Sister is nice. Sister is pretty. Mother isn't nice any more. She isn't pretty any more. Is that my fault too? I wonder why mom doesn't thank me. Is she still mad at me because of my head? I am sorry. I tell her that every day but she doesn't say anything at all. But she uses my tomatoes and peppers, radishes, melons. No cucumbers. I don't plant cucumbers. I just wish she would thank me. Take them and thank me. Use them and thank me. But she just takes them.

It wasn't all my fault mother. Why did you stop loving me?

But she didn't really. It just seems that way sometimes. At night, after I go to bed, I can smell her. She walks into my room and stands by my bed. I steal a peek through the slits in my eyes and she never suspects I see her. One night she put her hand on my head and lightly rubbed it across my hair.

Then she bent down and kissed me.

I just wish, sometimes, she would smile more and show me those feelings when I was awake. I think my mom is in a lot of pain. Could it be because of the cucumbers? The priests used to talk about this bad thing that made people unhappy. I wasn't sure how to say it. Cucumbers is as close as I could get.

Concup— there's that word I could never say that the priests used to mumble about. So I just say cucumbers. *We must fight cucumbers, the attraction of cucumbers. It will drag you into hell.* They are bad. They make a person bad. No cucumbers.

I'm okay most of the time. I just can't remember some things. Like the pretty Sister. I can't remember her name. But I remember other things, things from a long time ago. Things I don't want to remember.

I remember the night we crashed. But not much more. I was in the front seat and Billy Armstrong was driving his dad's car. Mike and Steve were in the back. We had been drinking beer and smoking pot. I think Billy was using heroin. Heroin. That grows in the ground too. We had crossed the highway four times without stopping. We were invulnerable.

I remember the faces in the car looking at us. Little kids. It was a black four-door. That's all I remember.

I broke thirty bones and my head went through the windshield. Or so mom told me later. I have trouble remembering. Billy, Mike and Steve didn't make it. Mom says I was lucky.

I don't look at it that way. I plant vegetables. You put them in the ground and they come back up. Billy, Mike and Steve are in the ground. They won't come back up.

Those kids. I wake up screaming and sweating sometimes because I see them looking at me. They are in the ground too, along with their parents.

I feel something. I guess that's good. I was drunk most of the time, or high, or sometimes Billy would give me heroin. I didn't feel anything then. That was what I wanted. Not to feel. When I started to feel I lost my temper. I still do, and mother is afraid of me when I do. I don't mean to. Then I meant to. Now, it just happens. Not much. I am on medicine. I used to take drugs to stop feeling, now a doctor gives me medicine so I can stop feeling.

I like planting things in the ground. I know they will come up again.

That's good, isn't it?

IT WAS ALMOST 90 DEGREES by ten-o'clock as Margaret drove down the narrow road to St. Alban's Cemetery. She always ran by to see Eli Barstow before a funeral, not to check up on him—he was very reliable and things were always in order—but only to see if she could be of assistance in any way. She knew she couldn't, but she felt it important for Eli to know that she was there if he needed anything, to make him realize that he was valued.

The sun striped the road through tall trees on the hillsides as she passed the old St. Agnes church, long abandoned, and found the gravel road that led to St. Albans. A mile or so down the road she could see the iron fence surrounding the twenty-acre necropolis. She pulled up in front of the main gate, which lay across the road from the small, one-story frame house where Eli lived alone.

The house was sided with simulated brown brick asphalt rolls. It had stood on the property for years, judging by the look and style of it. The front porch was newer, made of treated lumber. Several outbuildings, some very old, sat on the property and a large garden sat off to the side. Eli had lived there for years, getting up every day to care for the cemetery and, when necessary, to dig a grave. He still dug graves by hand most of the time. A backhoe sat idle in one of the wooden buildings, probably to be used only when the ground was frozen.

She got out of the car and walked down a long, narrow lane that was partly covered with gravel and bordered by monuments of varying sizes and shapes. A large statue of the Virgin Mary topped one monument, but most were simple stone markers inscribed with the names of those who rested beneath them. Some of the stones were bleached and dated from the nineteenth century. The sun was shining full on the stones, and Margaret felt perspiration begin to slide down the side of her face. About one hundred yards away, she could see a grotto that had been built many years before by the faithful at St. Albans. Most of those who worked on it and dedicated it were probably beneath the ground now. But the grotto still welcomed family members when they came to pay their respects.

About fifty feet off the path she saw the huge pile of dirt and a young man picking up tools and walking away. Vergil sometimes helped Eli, but not today. The other boy was Jerry Crowe, a tow-headed youth who lived in the area and made a few extra dollars finishing graves.

As she neared the grave—she first thought it empty—a huge man suddenly hoisted himself out and up onto the ground. She started at first until she realized that it was Eli Barstow.

Eli wore no shirt, and perspiration was running down his chest. His chest and arms were huge, muscular, and intimidating. His six-foot-four-inch frame was equally daunting. He wore a Cubs hat and was drinking now from a large plastic bottle of water. His hair was thin and gray, and his face was shadowed by what appeared to be at least a two-day growth of hair. He turned when he saw her coming, and his eyes widened. They were eyes that reflected alertness and intelligence.

"Good morning, Sister," he said. His voice was deep and

commanding.

"Hi, Eli. You done already?"

"Sure enough. Started early so the sun wouldn't kill us."

Margaret walked over and looked down into the hole that, this time tomorrow, would welcome Agnes Cutworth. The sides were remarkably straight, and the walls of the grave were such that a plumb line would probably show them to be nearly vertical. A large pile of dirt sat on a tarp next to the grave, and a vault sat in a crate nearby. He still had some work to do, but what he had done—with only one helper—amazed her.

"I never cease to be amazed at your workmanship, Eli."

"Well, that's my job, Sister."

Laconic. That was Eli Barstow.

Margaret looked down at the grave again. "So, they really do go six feet down."

"Well, close to it. Five and a half will do; but I usually go six. Just to make sure no one comes crawling out."

Margaret smiled. Eli didn't.

"Anything I can do for you, Sister?"

"Nothing, Eli. Just wanted to make sure there wasn't anything I could do for *you*."

"Nope. We got it covered. But thanks for asking."

"I see that. And, as always, I appreciate that."

"Good to know." He picked up a large shovel and started to walk towards the vault.

"Eli?"

He turned around. "Yeah?"

"We're getting a new priest?"

"Father Kennelly getting worse?"

"I am afraid so."

"Humph."

"Thought you would like to know."

"One's the same as the other. I don't see much of them anyway, unless they come out here to pray over one of these poor souls." Then he walked away again.

Margaret knew the visit was over. "Well, thanks Eli. I'll see you again."

He turned again to look at her. "Reckon so." He threw the shovel down and took another swig of water. "Who they sending?"

"A priest from the Cathedral. A Father Seamus Corrigan."

Eli's eyes flashed. For a moment he just stood there.

"Young kid, I would guess."

"Actually no. He's in his seventies I believe. He's been around."

Eli wiped his face with a dirty kerchief he had taken out of his back pocket.

"Corrigan?"

"You know a Father Corrigan?"

"Don't think so. What's his first name again?"

"Good Irish name. Seamus."

Margaret could swear that his face took on a darker color, which was amazing given that he was well bronzed from years of backbreaking labor in the hot sun. He stood there for about thirty seconds, and then turned back toward the crate containing the vault.

"Can't say," he said.

"Well," Margaret said, "I will head back. Take care"

"Will do," he said, ripping the side of the crate away with his bare hands.

AS MARGARET DROVE BACK, THE empty grave was much on her mind. Some day—a day known only to God—one very like it will welcome her. These thoughts had occurred to her many times when she visited her parents' graves in Jacksonville. And the grave of Eric Thompson, a man she once loved whose life was cut short on a lonely stretch of highway after a routine traffic stop. Still, actually seeing an empty grave, one that was freshly dug out of the earth, left her uncomfortable. We do not miss consciousness before we are granted it; now, in possession of it, we cannot conceive of having to lose it.

She remembered how the ancient Greeks spoke of the deaths of warriors. It was something about how they "ended their days in the sun." Margaret loved the light. The way the sun was illuminating the beauty that now surrounded her on the McAdams highway. She knew that she would so miss the sun.

Her studies had made her aware of the peculiarity of her faith's teachings on resurrection. The philosopher René Descartes had done an injustice to our view of humanity by separating us into two substances, body and soul. She smiled when she thought of how

Descartes, once he had made that theoretical separation, spent the rest of his life trying to figure out how the two interacted. The "mind-body" problem, her professor had called it.

Saint Thomas Aquinas didn't see the problem. He wrote that body and soul were inseparable and that, once the soul departs, the matter of the body becomes matter of a wholly different kind. A brain is a necessary condition for mind; a body is a necessary condition for a soul. Both combine to form each of us uniquely. As for their recombination, he leaves that to faith. Scripture tells us we will be re-personified on the last day, our bodies and souls reunited. Only faith could account for this. Aquinas knew his limitations and accepted them. Science can't see beyond its limitations, and accepts nothing outside of them.

There was something else about the morning's visit to the cemetery that bothered her. As she neared Grafton, she experienced an uneasy feeling in the pit of her stomach.

It was clear that Eli Barstow was upset by something she said.

She thought of the Piasa, and how the beast almost seemed to smile at times.

Eli

THE GRAVE IS READY. THE vault is in place and the crank is set to lower the casket. The rug is placed on the edges so that they show green and people don't have to realize that it is dirt that the old lady is going into, or think about that it is dirt the old lady is going to be again someday.

Jesus, it's hot. I sent Jerry home. Jerry is a good worker. Vergil is when he decides to come. Vergil is—well Vergil is Vergil. Damn shame. Too many drugs, then going through a windshield. Because of too many drugs probably. But he does okay when you tell him what to do. Rachel hasn't had it easy. She lost Jake when the kid was in high school, and then this. Boy she was a looker back in the day. Now she looks like hell.

Sister was making over the grave. Why shouldn't it be well dug? It's what I do. It's taking somebody home for the last time. They deserve that.

First grave I dug was in the jungle. The guards made me dig a grave for Arnie Kingman from Little Rock, Arkansas. Arnie and I went through basics together, and we stayed together right up until the time we were captured when a mortar attack took out half our platoon, including the lieutenant. The gooks could tell me and Arnie was close, and they figured it would be a nice touch making me put him in the ground. They were real thoughtful like that. Arnie died hard, with shrapnel in his gut, but the place he was going was better than the cage he had been kept in.

They led me two or three klicks into the jungle, threw his body down and said, "Bury. You. Bury." One of them threw me a field shovel and then they all sat down with their rifles, drank water and laughed at me. I was a kid, but I'll be damned if I was going to let those gooks get to me. They'd bloodied me up plenty when I first got there, and damned near beat the hell out of me. There was still some shrapnel in my calf. I had dug out most of it. They hadn't seen too many guys my size in there, and they seemed to take special pride in bringing me low. But they didn't. I still can't see good out of my right eye after the beatings they gave me, but I can still see good enough out of the other one. So, I picked up the shovel and dug.

I worked on that grave for four hours, without stopping. I was so goddamn thirsty my tongue was swollen. I dug straight down, and then shaved the sides as neatly as I could. When it was over, I crawled out and looked down. I went more than four feet, and it was a damned near perfect rectangle. They looked at it and said something to each other, and then laughed. Then one of them picked up the shattered body of the poor kid I dug it for and threw him in. Arnie landed like a rag doll, one arm twisted beneath his body, his legs all tangled, and his face in the dirt.

Then one of the gooks handed me a canteen. I drank until he pulled it away. Then he picked up the shovel and said, "Finish."

I finished. They left no marker. One of the gooks put Arnie's dog tags around his neck.

I noticed a smell in that part of the jungle. Others were out there, none buried as deeply as this one, some just thrown there and left to rot. Their people back home would never know what happened to them. At least Arnie had a decent place to rest.

I told them about it after I made it out of there. Did the military ever search? Did they ever bother? Of course, by the time they got around to it, the jungle was probably completely different and most of the bodies had probably been eaten or dragged off by critters. It was one moment in a jungle far away and it was probably a different jungle by the time they went looking. If they ever went looking.

The gooks must have liked the way I worked, because they came and dragged my ass out of the cage every time they had another job. I must have dug twenty graves for guys and every one of them I dug with care. I didn't know any of those kids, but I figured I owed them that. They went into those holes without ceremony, but the holes they went into were dug with respect.

Hate? There aren't many humans I can ever say I hated. One of them was that short gook that sat on a log, drinking water, and wearing dog tags from the guys he had me bury, like they was jewelry. He always smiled at me. Even when he was spitting on me or bashing me with his rifle butt. He was the coldest son-of-a-bitch I ever saw. I always wondered where that bastard ended up. Hopefully in hell. He seemed at home there.

The other was a guy I never saw. I only read his name. *Father C. Father Seamus.* Surely it couldn't be. I first read that name forty years ago. I'm sure that's what it was. This guy's in his seventies. Maybe it's not the same. How in hell could it be? If it is, how in hell did he show up here and where the hell has he been?

I cleaned up the site and took my tools to the shed behind the house. Didn't have to worry about Vergil today. About this time he would be standing in front of the house waiting for his mom to pick him up. He could probably drive himself. Problem is, you never knew where he would drive. He might end up in Williamson County. Or in the river. Oh, he could drive.

I always wait around a bit until Rachel picks him up. The car pulls into my drive, and Vergil walks over and hops in. He waves but says nothing. Rachel looks at me from the Jeep, and gives kind of a wave. I wave back. There are a lot of memories tied up in that woman. Life has a way of tearing the flowers off the stem. Her flower has been long gone, but I remember when it wasn't. She was the prettiest girl in Jersey County once. She always could set me on fire.

Those days are over. The gooks took care of that with their electrodes and their crank box. They never got a thing out of me, but they made sure I wouldn't stick my porker in anybody later. I sacrificed my balls on the altar of democracy. Still, I remember. Rachel was something. I sometimes dream about her. I don't worry much about what might have been, though. Would've, could've, should've. Don't do anybody any good.

I'm sure people wonder how I could live in an old, run-down house next to a cemetery. There are lots of reasons. Guess part of me feels at home with the dead, for one. For another, you can't ask for better neighbors. And, of course, this part of the world is where I came out of, and where I'll go back. I know better than most what "dust to dust" really means. In fact, the only time I ever set foot in a church is on Ash Wednesday. I walk out of there, my forehead blackened with soot, and I understand. That part, I really get.

I showered, popped a beer, and then cooked up a couple of hamburgers on the outside grill. I sliced an onion and a tomato, and put a cold slice of cheese on each one. Grilling hamburgers was another thing I got proficient at in base camp. Got so the guys wouldn't have anyone but me do it. I didn't burn them they said. Somehow there was something about charred meat that left me nauseous, so I am always careful not to burn the meat. It took me a while after Catherine and Melvin for me to eat another hamburger.

The sun was reflecting through the trees as it began to set, but it wasn't bringing the temperature down much. It was almost 100 degrees by four o'clock, and the humidity was drenching. I swatted half-dozen mosquitoes on my arm while those burgers were cooking. Nasty little fuckers.

The air conditioning felt good in the kitchen. I miss mom.

She was with me until around 1999. It made things a little more habitable around here. She was good company too. I think she always felt like she was responsible for the way dad treated us boys, but I never blamed her. He treated her just as bad. Maybe it's a blessing that the gooks took care of my reproductive possibilities. They say a kid who got beat will beat his own kids. I can't imagine that but I guess I'll never know.

Teri stopped by for a little while after supper. She is good about that. We weren't that close as kids, but ever since Melvin and her mom died we have shared a blood bond of sorts. We wrote letters back and forth when I was in Nam—until I couldn't write letters any more, that is. She was the first to welcome me home, and helped me find this job and this place to live afterward. She managed to overcome the horror of it all, and has done well. She has been very loyal to me. She has been married for twenty years or so, but I don't think she is that happy. She lost a kid. I have tried to be as loyal to her. That's about all the family I have now. Same with her. Her brother died some years back. Killed himself.

Seamus ... *Connery*? Was that it? Christ, I forgot. Seamus was the name that hit me.

I walked back into the bedroom and pulled some stuff off the top shelf of the closet. After a few minutes, I found an old cardboard box that I hadn't had out probably since I moved in here. I walked back into the kitchen and opened it. There was a bunch of old photos of me, mom and Melvin, and an old notebook. I pulled out the notebook and opened it up. The pages were yellow, and darker around the edges. Some kind of bug was crawling across the page. I squashed it with my thumb. Then I opened the diary again.

That day, after I found Catherine and Melvin, I went back in the house and sat in a rocking chair that was in the living room to wait for the sheriff. I was nervous, so I got up and started wandering around. I found this notebook sitting on a chair by the corner desk where Melvin did his schoolwork. After I opened it, I started to read. I didn't want the sheriff to find it, so I closed it and ran out to the driveway and stuck it in my car.

I read it once, a week later. Then I put it in my room at

home. There it stayed until after I came back from Nam. When we sold the home place, and mom and I moved here, I brought the box with me.

Every time I think of that day, something comes up from my bowels and works its way through my stomach, into my head and behind my eyes. It gives me the same horror that I felt later when I would hear the gooks coming to get me. I knew that I had another soldier to bury.

Yet for all the horror, I remember something funny. KXOK out of St. Louis used to play a silly show called *Chickenman*. I still remember hearing, "He's everywhere, he's everywhere," and hearing the superhero—played by the guy with the voice you always hear on radio commercials—say "I'm looking for a uniform. Something that will strike tear-roar into the hearts of criminals everywhere." It was on the radio that day.

I had graduated in May, and in order to avoid being drafted I had signed up after school got out and was scheduled to leave in September. I was spending the summer doing odd jobs, drinking with my buddies, and chasing tail. Rachel was my favorite, but I wasn't settling in with anyone. Vietnam was in my future, and I had no idea whether I would ever come back. The way I figured, after what Melvin and I had endured growing up, Vietnam would be a walk in the park. I had no idea what was in store for me, or what my older brother had endured that I didn't know about.

It was hot, I remember that. I had been trying to call Melvin since around seven in the morning but there was no answer. I called again around ten. Nothing. I was getting worried, but for some reason waited and decided to call back.

It wouldn't have made any difference, come to find out.

Melvin was my older brother, older by twelve years. I love him. He always protected me when our dad came home drunk. On more than one occasion, Melvin ended up bleeding and badly bruised. All I got were memories that wouldn't go away. Memories of my mom with a broken nose, or Melvin and my dad grappling with one another on the kitchen floor and memories of the screaming and the yelling.

The old man died when I was about seven and things quieted down. I remember Melvin going to seminary after high school. He came home after a year or so—I never knew why—and went to college in Edwardsville. After he got out, he got a job teaching at a Catholic school in Alton.

As time went by, it was obvious that Melvin had problems. No shit. Who wouldn't have had problems? But Melvin's were so bad he had to take medicine. He took Lithium for years. I can't imagine what that stuff does to a person. Years later, I read that they started using it in batteries. The batteries those little shits around the country are stocking up on to make their meth. It seemed to help him—when he took it.

I went to Alton and picked up some parts for my F-150 and got home in the early afternoon. I tried Melvin again. There was still no answer. Now I was really getting scared. Melvin had been crying the day before when I talked with him. We were supposed to have gone fishing that morning, but he never called. We fished whenever he was feeling okay. We hadn't fished much that summer.

I remember, at one point, Melvin started banging the receiver against the wall phone. It was badly cracked, I noticed later when I was in the kitchen.

He said that Catherine was going to leave him. Jesus, why was I not surprised?

I popped another beer and started going through Melvin's diary one more time.

Looking for some priest named Seamus who was once at Holy Trinity

From Melvin Barstow's Notebook

Sept 8. 1967

When Doctor Engfresch first told me to keep a journal I thought it was silly. But the more I thought about it, the more it made sense. I have been to a lot of doctors and none of them ever told me anything like this. But I like to write. Always have. I like to write poems. He told me it helps focus my thoughts and helps me to think about things that bother me. So when it's quiet, when she is asleep, I will write. It isn't easy. My hand sometimes shakes. Tremors. The Lithium. Sometimes I stop taking it and it gets better. But that causes other problems.

The doctor said to write about any memories, from the earliest to the latest. One of my earliest is of a bird. I must have been about two years old, because we lived in Mt. Olive at the time—not that I knew that, but I pieced it together later. Dad worked the mines there and it wasn't until I was three that we moved to Jerseyville. I remember sitting in a high chair. It was a sunny day—the sun always comes into my earliest memories. The days I remember are the days that were bright. Light coming into my consciousness. The light awakens us. It awoke me to life. I was looking out of a window and I saw a bird fly straight into the window and it must have been open because, in my memory, the bird did not hit the window or crash but came right through it because it was open and into the house. That's it.

Another memory is of Grace. She must have been my baby sitter. I remember that she had brown, curly hair. She wore a white blouse with frills down the front and bright red lipstick and I remember it was the first time I became aroused physically. I must have been three, but she brought out a part of me that I didn't understand. A part that I have spent the better part of my life fighting against.

My mother was a devout Catholic. My earliest memories involve being in church. The experience of church was for me a many-layered thing involving most of the major senses. The smell of incense and candle wax, the sound of Latin incantations and responses, the voices of nuns singing 'Gloria in excelsis;' light coming through panes of many colored glass. Years later, in high school, I came upon a poem by Shelley that really spoke to me. I didn't understand a lot of the poem—Adonais, I think it was—but these words I got.

> The One remains, the many change and pass;
> Heaven's light forever shines, Earth's shadows fly;
> Life, like a dome of many-coloured glass,
> Stains the white radiance of Eternity,
> Until Death tramples it to fragments.

The interior of Holy Trinity stained the white radiance of my eternity. Stained.

Until death tramples it to fragments.

ALICE WHITAKER POURED TWO CUPS of coffee and walked them over to the table near the window. Sam Watson and Pete Crawford, a couple of locals, were sitting there waiting.

"The usual, guys?" she said.

"You bet," said Sam.

Alice wore a white cotton shift and a black apron, and white tennis shoes that were showing a great deal of wear. She wore her brown hair in a ponytail, and it was evident that she didn't spend too much time on it of a morning. She wasn't exactly what one could call pretty, and she wore very little makeup, but she was not a bad-looking girl. She was getting a bit heavy on the bottom and her thighs were thick. Although she smiled for customers, one had the impression, overall, of a young woman with very low self-esteem.

Sam Watson was well into his seventies, wore a ponytail and a St. Louis Cardinals cap. Pete was a few years younger, balding, with glasses. An aging hippie and somebody's kindly grandfather. They had been friends forever, and frequently lunched at Maybelle's.

"How're those boys?" Pete asked.

"They may not live through the summer," Alice said. "They're pushing every button I got."

"Boys are good at that, Alice," said Sam. "Should have had girls."

"Like I had a choice in that, Sam. Test tube babies haven't come to Grafton yet."

"No, we get them the old fashioned way," said Pete with a grin.

"Haven't figured a way to improve on *that* yet," said Sam.

"Oh, they're fine, really. They're just full of shit. Onion and pickle only, right Sam?

"Right."

"Be right up."

The chimes over the front door rang, and an elderly couple came in. Tourists.

"Sit anywhere, folks," Alice said on her way to post the order.

Alice took the drink orders for the couple and left them with a menu when Margaret walked into the restaurant.

"Hey, Sister! Be right with you. Cop a squat."

"Will do, Alice."

Margaret spoke to Pete and Sam as she walked to the table near the corner. They weren't in the parish. As far as she knew, Sam worshipped in his own universe. Pete and his wife were Methodists. But they were friendly, like most folks in Grafton.

"You hungry today?" Alice said as she walked up to the table carrying a glass of iced tea, Margaret's regular drink at lunchtime.

"Actually, I am," Margaret said.

"Out running again this morning, I hear."

"Yeah. Where'd you year that?"

"Couple of guys came in for breakfast asking if I knew the hot chic that was running along River Road this morning. I said, 'Yeah. That's the nun from St. Alban's.' That shut them up. But then, what do you expect in that running outfit? Converts?"

Margaret smiled. "God understands."

"Then he must be a man, honey. Roast beef sandwich and mashed potatoes on special today."

"That works for me, Alice." As Margaret looked up, she noticed a large bruise on Alice's arm. It appeared to be shaped like fingers. Alice must have caught her looking at it because she turned quickly and headed back to the kitchen.

"Be right up," she said.

Margaret read the Alton *Telegraph* and sipped her tea in the corner seat that gave her a clear look at Main Street. The lunch hour was past, and the restaurant was clearing out. On the street, tourists were making their way into the buildings that lined Main Street. Storeowners sat in chairs outside of their shops hawking their wares. Dozens of motorcycles were parked in front of the Reubel Hotel down the street. Margaret smiled when she remembered that the hotel was supposed to be haunted. *Bikers weren't easily intimated*, she thought to herself. She watched as Clark Watson, who owned the fudge shop that stood directly across the street, outfitted a young family with bikes for a trek down River Road. Traffic on Main Street was heavy today, which was good for Grafton.

"Here you go, Sister," said Alice, returning with a plate piled high with roast beef, bread, mashed potatoes and gravy.

"How you been, Alice?"

"Okay. Same old, same old."

"I miss you at church. You used to come every now and then."

"Yeah, well, you know how it is. Sometimes Sundays aren't just what they should be. But I come when I can. People treating you okay there? Lot of people still aren't used to having a nun there instead of a priest."

"It's slow," Margaret said. "But, all in all, it's going okay. And I love being here."

"Yeah, it's a little slice of heaven around here," Alice said. Margaret heard something in her tone that relayed a different message. Alice, like a lot of people who lived in Grafton, no doubt got a kick out of the fact that visitors saw something very different in the town than they did.

"Be right back," Alice said, as a customer walked up to the counter to pay his bill. The man—probably a truck driver—looked over at Sister Margaret and winked. Margaret smiled at the man and wondered whether it might be a good thing to start wearing a veil. Then she focused her attention on the roast beef that was spilling over on her plate.

People in Grafton were slow in accepting a nun in the parish. The women, for the most part, were fine. But the men were slow to come around. The lack of vocations to the priesthood—complicated by the scandals involving child abuse that the church was pedaling furiously to put behind it—was truly dispiriting. Attendance on Sundays was half what it was before she came, even with a priest officiating. Her work was cut out for her. She had to keep her hand to the plow.

"Well, I'm out of here!" Alice said, taking off her apron.

"Here," Margaret said, reaching into her purse for a five dollar bill. "Take this before you leave."

"Aw, leave it for Tracy," Alice said, referring to the young girl who had just come in to start her shift. "She just got married."

Margaret smiled. "I'll leave one for her too. Take it!"

Alice said, "You're nice, you know that?"

"I'm just desperate for someone to talk to. Got a minute? Sit."

Alice slid into the booth opposite Margaret. "I'll bet you are desperate. It must get awful lonely in that big old house."

"Actually, it's not that bad. I am pretty busy keeping things scheduled and keeping the place up. And it's peaceful. I like that.

Every now and then, I like to find someone to talk to. So I come downtown, or drive to St. Louis to see some of the other sisters. I'm not complaining."

"I hear old Mrs. Cutworth died. She's been dying for years."

"Yeah. I was just at the cemetery. They're burying her tomorrow. Father Jim is coming over."

"You see old Eli out there? He still digging those graves himself?"

"Well, he has some help. But he still digs them by hand. He's really something. Doesn't talk much."

"No, I don't suppose he does."

"He got a story?"

"Yeah. He's got a whopper. He grew up around Jerseyville and went to school about the same time as my mom. He had an older brother who killed his wife and then himself. Eli apparently found them. Then he went to Vietnam, and I heard he was captured. Spent some time as a POW. Mom said he came back here in the seventies, long before I was born, and went to work as caretaker at St. Alban's. Been there ever since."

"I can't remember seeing a more imposing man," Margaret said. "He's huge. His arms look like they could squeeze the life out of a bear."

"Yeah, but mom always said he was a decent guy."

"We're getting a new priest in charge at St. Alban's," Margaret said.

"Thought you were in charge."

"Well, not officially. Father Kennelly is officially the Moderator. The church has to have a priest in charge."

"Father Jim usually said mass when I came."

"Yes. Father Kennelly couldn't come much. They're sending someone from the Cathedral."

"Well, guess it doesn't matter much," Alice said.

"His name is Corrigan. Father Seamus Corrigan."

The name obviously meant nothing to Alice. "Well," she said, "hope he's easy to work with."

Margaret did too.

BY 4:30, MARGARET WAS FINISHING up her work in the office. She saw a red Jeep Cherokee swing into the drive and pull up in front of the church. She knew Rachel Atkins' automobile by now. Vergil's mother was coming to take her son home.

She watched Rachel get out of the Jeep. The woman was in her late 50's, perhaps as old as 60, and her weight seemed to have concentrated in her stomach. It protruded in such a way as to tent the short-sleeved blue work shirt that she hadn't tucked in. She wore blue jeans and tennis shoes. Her legs were not heavy. They looked strong. Her arms were slightly puffy, as were her hands, but she walked with a swagger that suggested she was a woman to be reckoned with. She wore her hair short, and it wasn't very stylish. Although her face showed signs of developing jowls, when you spoke directly to her you could see that at one time she had been a very attractive woman. She might still be if she would smile. But Margaret never saw her do that.

Margaret watched as Rachel looked around for her son, and then crossed over toward the garden.

As she passed, Margaret stepped out the front door.

"Hello, Rachel."

The woman stopped, and then looked up at the porch.

"Afternoon, Sister."

"You shouldn't have any trouble finding him," Margaret said.

"Nope. The garden. I think he dreams about that garden at night."

Saying no more, Rachel turned and walked back to the garden. Margaret watched as Vergil stood up, picked up a basket filled with peppers and tomatoes, turned and slowly followed his mother to the front.

"Good night, Vergil. Thank you for all you did," Margaret said,

Vergil placed the basket of vegetables on the porch. Rachel kept walking.

"Please, take some of those home," Margaret said.

"He's got a garden at home," Rachel said. "We sure don't need any more vegetables."

Margaret would end up placing them in the vestibule at church, and knew they wouldn't last long. Of course, she would take a few tomatoes and peppers for the kitchen. Vergil stood for a moment between the nun who had addressed him and the mother who was moving closer to the Jeep. He was momentarily uncertain of what to do.

"Vergil, you have a lovely evening," she said.

Then Vergil looked up—yes! He actually looked up!—and said, "Thank you, Sister."

Then he walked around to the passenger side of the Jeep, got in, and waved as Rachel backed up and turned toward the street.

THAT EVENING, MARGARET WENT TO the funeral home to lead the prayer service for Mrs. Cutworth. As she knelt at the coffin leading the rosary, she thought of other coffins she had knelt before. Her dad's. Theodora's.

Halfway through the rosary, she smiled when she thought of Theodora's wake, and she remembered how Elvis Presley's *In the Garden* played softly in the background.

When she got home, before going to bed, she poured a tumbler of merlot and listened to the song on her iPod. She fell asleep with it on repeat. It was still playing when she awoke next morning.

THE MORNING COMMUNION SERVICE WAS sparsely attended, as usual, and by more women than men. A few older men were with their wives, and there were several couples she didn't recognize. Probably tourists.

The communion service was like a mass, except there was no consecration of the host. It consisted of the same introductory rites, then the readings, but when communion time came Margaret simply took hosts from the tabernacle that had been consecrated the week before by Father Jim and distributed them to the congregants, who walked up one by one to cup their hands and receive the small, white wafer.

"The Body of Christ"

"Amen."

For some, a communion service was something they just couldn't get used to. Many felt that a service without a priest was not a service at all.

Others, however, barely noticed the difference. She smiled one Sunday morning when she heard a woman comment to her husband, "I like Sister's mass better."

All in good time, Margaret reminded herself. The Church was in transition, and either the vocations would step up, or churchgoers would have to become much more accustomed to communion services.

FATHER JIM CONDUCTED FUNERAL SERVICES for Mrs. Cutworth and gave a nice homily to the 12 or so people who attended. Not many people remembered her. Father Jim was close to Margaret's age, probably about 36. He had a full head of black hair and a nice smile. He was a good-looking man, with dark brown eyes and a Roman nose. He wore trendy Silhouettes, eyeglasses that you had to look twice at to even notice they were there. He was clean-shaven, well groomed, and he had a voice that soothed.

Margaret rode with Father Jim to the cemetery. She enjoyed his company. He was a quick study and was a very pleasant conversationalist. He also had a great sense of humor, and—like Margaret—he loved literature. They frequently had very interesting discussions about poets and books most people don't bother to read any more. She told him that his services would not be needed on Sunday. She explained that Father Corrigan would be coming. His only comment was somewhat cryptic.

"Father Seamus, huh? There's a blast from the past."

"You know him?"

He was quiet for a moment. "No. Just heard about him."

She wanted to ask if what he heard was good or bad, but decided not to inquire any further.

It was hot, nearly 90, and very humid. But the service was brief, and soon she was back at the rectory working on the fall schedule.

Every now and then she would look outside and see Vergil mowing the lawn. The intense heat didn't seem to bother him, and the lawn didn't really need mowing. But he was doing it anyway and— as always—doing a nice job.

MARGARET HAD COME IN FROM cleaning the sanctuary Friday morning when the bat phone rang.

It was Ann from the bishop's office.

"Morning Ann."

"There's been a change in plans."

Oh God, what now? Margaret thought.

"Father Seamus has decided to come tomorrow and hear confessions, and then to stay over. Is that acceptable?"

No, that is not acceptable. Father Jim is coming for confessions, and how am I supposed to entertain a seventy-something priest?

"Of course," Margaret said, realizing that it was not really a request. "What time will he arrive?"

"Well, now, confessions are at four, so it will be prior to that," Ann said in her unique way of making you feel about two inches tall. Again, Margaret bit her tongue.

"That will be wonderful."

"Of course, you will be able to accommodate him?"

Margaret added straightening the guest room to her "To Do" list on the pad in front of her. Also grocery shopping since she would have to feed him.

"Of course, Ann."

"That's wonderful. I'll tell him you will be ready."

Margaret hung up and swore under her breath. Then she picked up the phone and called Father Jim.

THAT EVENING MARGARET HAD DINNER alone at the Fin Inn, a two-story limestone structure northwest of downtown Grafton on Main Street. She was seated next to one of the four aquaria in the building, and a large, ugly blue catfish was watching her eat one of his distant relatives. It was an eerie experience, one that can only be had on the river. At one point she turned and blew him a kiss. He seemed impervious to her charms, and slowly turned and moved to the other side of the tank.

"So, you like them over there better, huh?" Margaret said.

She remembered the conversation she had at Maybelle's with Alice. Margaret did, occasionally, get lonely. It was worse than that, actually. At times, she struggled with her desires. The technical term was *concupiscence.* The church must have believed that by describing it in such a way would make it more academic and less threatening. She had been sexually active when she was younger, and still remembered her ill-advised interlude with Detective Bill Templeton when she was in Springfield. It was hard to turn away from Bill; she had actually started to love him. Still did. Her dreams were sometimes erotic. The relief for that—forbidden as mortally sinful even to those not committed to celibacy—was not available to her even though it lay at her fingertips. She knew she couldn't give in to that. She found herself resorting to a large glass of wine whenever the feelings would come up; and, of course, prayer.

Lately, she found herself drinking more and more merlot.

Before retiring, she went to the church and prayed for God to help her in her struggle to overcome concupiscence. Somehow, saying that word made her want to giggle. But the problem wasn't funny—just the word. This was, after all, the life she had chosen. This was one of the major battles she had to win if she was to keep her vows.

Then she returned to the rectory, undressed, set her alarm for the early run, and spent the night dreamlessly. She'd had another large glass of wine before falling to sleep.

She woke up sobbing around three in the morning. Her mother had appeared to her in a dream. She saw her mother's face—it was the same face she remembered from the black and white photo her dad had on his desk at the jail, the only face she knew—and she felt her warmth as she reached down and hugged her while she slept. She told her how sorry she was to have left her before she got to know her and then she looked very sad and spoke very seriously. "Look to me," she said. "Look to me to understand you. I don't want you suffering."

Margaret sat on the side of the bed for half an hour before going back to sleep wishing it had not been a dream. Wishing that the mother who died when she was too young to remember had lived and helped her grow up.

"DADDY, TELL ME ABOUT MY mommy."

For years, that was the last thing that Margaret said to her father after he read to her from The Cat in the Hat and Goodnight Moon. Her father would tell her stories about what her mother looked like, how much she loved Margaret and the fact that he loved her so very much.

"Tell me how you fell in love with her," Margaret would say. He had told the story many times before, but she loved hearing about how her mother and father fell in love.

"I was in the service, and your grandfather owned a restaurant near the base. I used to stop in for lunch, and one day this beautiful young woman waited on me. She asked

what I wanted and I couldn't answer her. I was so caught up in how beautiful she was. She asked me if I wanted more time. She must have thought I was stupid or something. Finally, I blurted out, 'No. I know what I want. I want to go out with you.'

"She laughed and said, 'You and everyone else who comes in here.' And I said, 'But I'm different.' She said, 'How.' And I said—"

"Because you are going to go out with me," Margaret said, finishing his sentence. Then she would giggle.

"That's exactly what I said. Good memory, peanut."

"When did you fall in love with her?"

"As soon as I saw her. It took her longer to fall in love with me. I'm a work in progress."

"What's that, Daddy?"

"I'm harder to love."

"No, you're not. I loved you from the start."

It was then that he would kiss her on the forehead, and hold her close. Sometimes she noticed that he was shaking a little as he held her but if he cried he wiped the tears away before he looked at her again. He was smiling as he said goodnight and warned her about the bedbugs biting.

"Mommy's in heaven, right, Daddy?"

"Yes, dear. So you have to live a good life so you can get to heaven too."

"I wish I could see her now."

"Someday, peanut. But not now. You have a job to do here first."

"Being your little girl, right?"

"Right. And that is a long-term proposition."

"What's a popostion?"

"A really big job that takes lots of time. And I need you."

"I'm here, Daddy."

"And I'll be here as long as I can."

And he was. He was a great dad and a good friend. She loved him dearly, but there had been a hole in her heart from the first moment she realized that she was different. That, unlike other kids she new, she went places with only a father. The rest of the kids had mothers. Pat Donovan was the best father any man could have been, but there was always *something different about Margaret.*

She knew that her daddy missed her mother. For years, all Margaret knew of her mother's visage was the black and white photograph of her that Pat Donovan kept on his desk at the County Jail. She wore a turtleneck, and her face was slightly inclined in the photo the way some photographers used to angle their portraits. Her hair was shoulder-length, slightly curled, and her eyes—her eyes were the most beautiful things about her. Margaret's dad always said that she had her mother's eyes. Her mother was never far from them, but she was not where Margaret needed her. Where other kids had mothers present, she had only her absence, a stark photographic shadow, and the memories of her father to keep that mother a part of her life.

And, of course, her dreams. That was where she visited often with the mother who left her before she ever got to know her.

VERGIL SAT ON A CHOPPING BLOCK behind the rectory weeding his garden.

It was overcast, but the heat and humidity hadn't abated. Rain was in the forecast.

A black Crown Vic traveled down Main Street and turned north toward St. Alban's. Margaret had been sitting at her desk, tapping a pencil, her eyes fixed on the front window. Waiting. She saw the car pull up in front, and walked over to the door.

She watched as the man reached over and picked up something, and then watched the door to the Crown Vic open. Out stepped a tall man, dressed in black. He was broad shouldered and had his hair cut close in a military style. He shut the door and began walking toward the porch. Margaret stepped outside.

"Father Seamus, I am Sister Margaret."

The priest smiled, and walked up to shake her hand.

"It's a pleasure, Sister. I haven't been down here in years. The place hasn't changed much."

"Please come in," she said. "It's cooler inside."

"I hope so," he said, walking through the door that she was holding open.

"Have a seat in the office," Margaret said. "How about a glass of iced tea."

"Sounds great."

He walked into the office, and Margaret walked through into the kitchen and poured a large glass of iced tea. When she walked back into the office, she saw that Father Seamus had, indeed, taken a seat. The one behind the desk. Her seat.

Well, he is the parish moderator.

She placed the tea on a coaster and set it down in front of him.

"Many thanks," he said. "Please sit down."

Margaret walked around to the front of the desk and sat in one of the chairs.

"I will be hearing confessions in about twenty minutes," he said. "Do you want to go first? We can do it here."

Margaret hadn't considered this, although it was quite reasonable to assume that she—an avowed religious—would be expected to make confession. She looked at the man sitting across from her. She had just now laid eyes on this man, and would no more have thought to confess to him than to a stranger on the street. Unfortunately, she didn't know how to get out of this gracefully.

"That's very kind," she said. "Of course."

Father Seamus took out his purple stole, kissed it, and placed it around his neck. "I will do this however you like. The old fashioned way, if you prefer, or you can simply talk. Or a combination of the two. I'm real flexible like that."

He laughed. She had the feeling she was expected to laugh as well. She just smiled.

"Very well. Bless me Father, for I have sinned. It has been two weeks since my last confession."

Margaret recounted the times she had shown impatience in her role as administrator, and recounted times she had used foul language—something she frequently did when she lost her cool (a holdover from working with a lot of foul-mouthed law enforcement types or even more foul-mouthed lowlifes she encountered in the field).

"I ask forgiveness for these and all the sins of my past life," she concluded.

Father Seamus was quiet for about a minute. Then he looked up at her and said, "No impure thoughts?"

Margaret could feel her face turning bright red. She couldn't believe he asked her that question! Never, in all her years as a Catholic, had a priest—after hearing her recount her various failings—gone on a fishing expedition. But the problem was this was one thing she deliberately had not mentioned. She must have taken too long to respond.

"Sister?"

"Occasionally," she said haltingly. She was recalling the feelings she had been having only the night before. "I sometimes struggle with them, but I manage to overcome them."

"Only with the grace of God, Sister, can you overcome them. That is why confession is so important. Can you be more specific?"

Now she was really getting flustered. What was he looking for, a play by play? "Not really, Father. Only, at times, I feel as though I am fighting with what I can only think to be natural urges. I shall continue to fight them."

"*Natural?* That's another word for *sin*, Sister. If you don't recognize that, then the battle is lost. You must fight concupiscence, every day of your life; or at least until you get too old to have it be an issue any more. If you don't, it will win. Your salvation is at stake here. Are you sure that's all, Sister?"

Margaret swallowed. "Yes, Father." She wasn't sure why, but she was beginning to feel dirty somehow. She wasn't going to continue this line of discussion. She had confessed what she knew to be sinful. Granted, she had tried to avoid it—he had a point there. But there was something wrong, at least in her mind, about being asked to go into more detail. Something very wrong.

He just looked at her. Finally, he told her to make a good Act of Contrition, and performed absolution.

"Well, that was easy," Father Seamus said as he took off his stole.

"Thank you, Father." Margaret thought it anything but easy.

"The church is open?"

"Yes, of course."

"I will go and hear confessions. I left my bag in the front seat of the car. Would you have someone get it and put it in my room?"

"I'll take care of it," Margaret said, standing and turning toward the door.

"Oh, and Sister?"

Margaret turned back.

"What time will dinner be served?"

Humility. Obedience. Margaret kept saying those words to herself as she watched the priest walk across to St. Alban's. Remember your place.

God, grant me the strength, Margaret said to herself.

She had no idea that it was going to get a lot worse.

THE FIRST SIGN THAT THERE was something dreadfully wrong occurred after confessions were over.

Margaret had just taken a chicken casserole from the oven and was placing it on the dining room table. She had found an easy recipe that called for chicken breasts, chicken broth, tomatoes and green peppers (both of which she had in abundance, thanks to Vergil). She was just about ready to retrieve the dinner rolls from the top rack when she noticed Father Seamus close the side door of the church and begin walking toward the house.

At the same time, she noticed Vergil carrying a basket of fresh peppers toward the house. She didn't think anything of it. Not until she looked up after retrieving the dish and noticed that Vergil had stopped dead in his tracks.

Father Seamus smiled and spoke, but Vergil didn't speak. He just stood there.

"Oh, dear," Margaret said to herself, and realized that she should have warned Father Seamus about Vergil. Or Vergil about Father Seamus. The priest was a stranger, and one didn't know how Vergil would react to strangers.

She placed the rolls on the counter, dropped the potholders and went to the front door and out on the porch.

When she walked to the side of the house, Father Seamus was there. That's when she noticed Vergil. He was still standing there.

"I should have told you about Vergil," Margaret said to Father Seamus. "He works around the rectory sometimes."

Then she watched in horror as Vergil dropped the basket of

vegetables on the ground, turned and began throwing up. He then walked over and leaned against a tree, and threw up some more.

"Oh, my," Margaret said. "Excuse me." The priest watched as Margaret walked over to the young man who was obviously in a great deal of discomfort.

She placed her hand on his shoulder, and he turned quickly—almost viciously—and placed his hands up in the air as though to ward her off.

"Vergil?"

"No cucumbers," he said. He actually screamed it.

"Vergil, I know. We don't have cucumbers. It's all right."

"No. It isn't." He backed away further, and then started off down the hill to the street. Margaret looked at her watch. Surely, Rachel should be coming along soon. But she saw that Vergil was walking down the street now toward Main Street. She quickly followed.

"Bad. It's bad. *I'm* bad," he was saying to himself, over and over. Then, at one point, he stopped and threw up again. He was standing up as Margaret reached him.

"Vergil, please. Let me take you home."

"No cucumbers. No cucumbers."

Margaret was reaching for her cell phone when she saw Rachel's jeep turn off of Main. Thank God.

Rachel pulled up alongside Vergil and got out. "What's wrong?"

Vergil just stood there, rocking from side to side.

"I don't know," Margaret said. "He was working in the garden and began throwing up.

"Come on, Vergil," Rachel said, taking his arm gently. He didn't flinch at his mother's touch. "Let's go home."

"Let me know if there's anything I can do," Margaret said. She was feeling quite helpless.

"He'll be fine," Rachel said, starting up the car. Then she noticed the priest standing by the porch.

"Different priest?" Rachel said.

"Oh, yes. We have a new parish moderator." Rachel never came to mass, so it hadn't occurred to her to mention this to her.

"Oh," Rachel said. Then she reversed and executed a three-point turn in front of the rectory.

She stopped before finally shifting back into drive and looked at the man standing on the porch. Margaret noticed her staring. She stopped next to Margaret and rolled down the passenger side window.

"What's his name?" Rachel asked.

Margaret looked up at the porch, and then turned back to Rachel. "Father Corrigan," she said.

Without saying a word, Rachel put the window back up and sped toward Main Street.

Margaret walked back up to the rectory where Father Seamus still stood. He opened the door, and then turned to her.

"There's something wrong with that boy."

Brilliant, Margaret thought. "Yes, I should think so."

THE CASSEROLE WAS QUITE GOOD judging by the way Father Seamus wolfed it down. He enjoyed talking about himself and his life as a priest and didn't seem at all concerned that Margaret might have something to bring to the conversation. He also loved talking about his career in the Marines.

"It's a damned sorry thing that Nixon listened to all those commie hippies. It drained the juice out of our commitment. We should have nuked those North Vietnamese and ended it. Our boys came back dispirited, and Communism was left to infect the rest of Southeast Asia."

He had a particular fondness for Ronald Reagan. "Best President we ever had," he noted at one point between bites. "He stood up to those commies, and you know what? That wall came down."

Margaret had no desire to get into a political discussion with a man whose leanings were somewhere to the right of Attila the Hun. She just smiled most of the time.

She couldn't help but notice that, for a man in his seventies, he was in remarkably good shape. His arms were showing a bit of flab but his hands were still strong, his knuckles well defined. He looked the kind of man who could choke the life out of a person with very little effort. A slight paunch stretched the front of his black clerical shirt and his white collar appeared a bit snug on his short, thick neck. Overly large seemed the head, which sat upon his neck squarely like a block on a cylinder. White hair shorn in military fashion covered his head and his face was clean-shaven. A prominent Roman nose protruded boldly from the center of the face, and a few stray hairs peeked out from within it. He sported dark framed glasses that accentuated deep blue eyes. He would occasionally squint when he spoke, particularly when he wanted to emphasize a point or when he delivered a punch line for one of his many jokes. Then a brief smile would erupt on his face, quickly to disappear. The Cheshire cat from Lewis Carroll's Alice in Wonderland came to mind. He clearly thought himself a loveable, comic figure and expected others to laugh with him. But his smile wasn't warm as much as it was disdainful; it seemed, when the muscles in his face relaxed, that he didn't want you to know what or who he really was. You were not worthy. The overall effect was of a man with a sense of humor that, at first glance, would draw you to him but leave you feeling like you were the butt of the joke, not a fellow human being with whom he was sharing it. He was not convivial, but condescending. He was never wrong, always right. In short, in spite of his jocular persona, he was not a man who made you feel easy in his presence.

At least Margaret didn't. She wondered if men had this same reaction. Some priests didn't feel comfortable in the presence of women. She got the impression that Father Seamus was one of those priests.

Margaret's reverie was cut short when Father Seamus asked if he could have some more iced tea.

She dutifully poured it from the pitcher that she had placed on the table, very near to her visitor.

Father Seamus made it very clear what her place was here.

After dinner, he spoke with her at length regarding her duties in the parish and what was expected. He ran down a laundry list of things that she was to do—all of which she had been doing for some months now—and what her limitations were. She sat patiently, listening and assenting to his various suggestions.

This too shall pass, she thought to herself. Where did that expression come from, she wondered? It wasn't in the Bible, in spite of what a lot of people thought. Wherever it came from, she hung onto its wisdom while gritting her teeth through the rest of the evening. Finally, she had had enough.

"Father, with all due respect, you must know that I have been here for some time now and that I am fully aware of what my responsibilities are. I really only need to know if there are any changes that you might envision. For example, will you be saying mass and hearing confessions regularly? When you cannot, I will need to make other arrangements. A schedule might be in order. As to other changes, I can only surmise that you would want to be around a bit longer in order to assess where changes might be needed."

Margaret could feel the temperature in the room dropping. Seamus' smile disappeared. Two minutes passed with only the sound of the antique mahogany grandfather clock in the foyer ticking. Ticking. TICKING.

"Very good, Sister. I can see you are a take-charge sort of person. I like that."

He didn't like it one bit.

"I think I will retire now. I gather my room is ready?"

That's what I am here for, thought Margaret.

"Yes, I will show you."

"No need. That's one thing I can do myself. I have been here before."

He stood and turned toward the foyer, but then turned back.

"Oh Sister? As for changing things, you're absolutely right. I will take my time. However, one thing needs to change right now."

"Yes, Father. What would that be?"

"That retarded kid. What's his name?"

"Vergil Atkins."

"How is it he ended up working around here?"

"He has been here since the late nineties. The pastor then—Father Schmidt, I believe—brought him in. I'm told Father Schmidt felt for the boy. He doesn't get paid much. And he's *not* retarded. He suffered a brain injury in an automobile accident many years ago."

"Details. We can't have a retard like that working around here. Too much of a liability, unless St. Alban's has resources beyond what I think it does. He's got to go.

"Pleasant dreams, Sister."

From Melvin Barstow's Notebook

Oct 15, 1967

Haven't been very faithful to this. I took some time to read what I wrote last time. My white eternity was fragmented early on. I suppose kids are sensitive to chaos surrounding them, but I didn't remember a lot until I saw my mother crying and bleeding. I must have been five or so. I didn't connect the dots right away. It took me a while to realize that my dad had done that to her. It took seeing her a few more times like that for me to connect it.

I must have been six the first time he hit me. The first time I remember him hitting me. He was screaming at my mother. The familiar smell of Falstaff was all over him. He hit her in the stomach, and I ran up and pushed him. His hand caught me on the side of the head and I went flying across the living room. My mother ran, flew over and picked me up and held me close. I don't remember whether I was bleeding or not. That time. I remember she picked up a glass that was on the coffee table and broke it and held it out and told him if he hit me one more time she would kill him. I looked up and saw him laugh. Then he waved her off and walked out the door.

He didn't come back that night. But he eventually came back. Over the next several years, I was privileged to be his whipping boy. I managed to take that blessing away from mom for the most part.

I couldn't believe it, but when I was around 11 or 12, my mom got pregnant. I was furious at her for bringing another kid into the family. Not because I wasn't lonely, or didn't want a brother or sister. But I knew what was in store for that child.

I made up my mind, then and there, that my dad wouldn't bother that child. He would have to kill me first.

Oct 28, 1967

Mom had taken me to church since I was a baby. I wrote already about the experience. But the church was one stable element in my life, and no doubt in my mother's life. My little brother, Eli, went with us, but he never seemed to take to it the way I did. He wasn't the studious sort; I was reading all the time. He wasn't given to reflection; I was always meditating, either in the pew or out in the back yard at night when the stars were out. He was always working with something, putting it together or taking it apart; I was always studying. I always wondered which of us took after which parent. I always thought Eli took after dad, and that I took after mom.

Lately, I wonder whether there is more of my dad in me than I care to think about. Catherine might think so too. I am so sorry for her sometimes. Other times, I don't want her near me.

I'm not ready to write about the other thing. I need some more time.

The lithium is helping. Most of the time. The doctor says I suffer from manic-depressive disorder. I haven't had a real bad episode since a few weeks ago. I felt so energized. I remember chopping an entire cord of wood without stopping. Then I painted the shed out back. I had painted it a couple of months earlier but I figured it needed it again. Then, I found that I couldn't get out of bed. Catherine begged me to be more regular with my medicine, but I dismissed it. Until one day when she screamed at me to stop what I was doing and come in to eat. I picked up the axe and swung it against the side of the house. After seeing what I did, I cried. The next day I started the Lithium again. Maybe the medicine is helping. Now I have the tremors again. I guess everything comes at a price.

But give me some time. I am not ready to talk about some things yet.

I am not sure I am ready.

Rachel

JESUS CHRIST. I CAN'T BELIEVE it. It took me hours to get Vergil settled down. He finally went to sleep. What in hell is going on?

Later, I went through an old junk drawer and pulled out the old black and white photo I took behind Holy Trinity one morning after Vergil had served mass. We lived in Jerseyville at the time. The glass was broken from when I threw it in the incinerator. Why I retrieved it I don't know, except I never wanted to forget that face.

Vergil was about 12, and the three of them—Vergil, Corrigan, and another boy named Frank Wright—had just finished the morning mass when I asked Corrigan if he would pose for a picture with the boys. They still wore their cassocks and surplices, and Corrigan wore his black cassock. He was a good-looking guy back then. He stood with his arms on the boys' shoulders. Vergil and Frank were smiling. They adored him, just like all the other kids in the parish. Especially the boys. How in God's name could he have done that to them? I didn't know whether he ever bothered Frank—his mother took a long time to admit it—but I know what he did to Vergil.

We didn't figure it out until Vergil was about fourteen. Jake and I mistook his acting out as adolescent rage. Christ, teenagers are hard to figure. Then one day I found him crying in the garage. I went in and he flew into a rage, damned near scared me to death. I told Jake, and Jake went out and talked with him. Next thing I know, I heard Jake yelling and saw Vergil running down the street.

I asked Jake what in the hell was going on. He just stood there, white as a sheet. "I'm gonna kill him," he said. I asked him what Vergil had done to make him so mad. He said it wasn't Vergil.

"I'm going to kill that god damned priest," Jake said. Then he jumped into his pickup truck and took off.

I jumped into my car and followed him. I pulled up behind the truck at the rectory, just as Jake ran up to the door. He started out ringing the doorbell, and then proceeded to pound on the door. No one was there, or I am sure Jake would have killed Corrigan right there in front of God and everybody. I ran up and grabbed his arm.

"Vergil told me the whole story, Rachel. That fucking priest has been fooling with our boy. God knows how many others."

I stepped back. I was in shock. It couldn't be. Priests don't do those kinds of things. No. Not Father Corrigan. Everyone loved him. Not Vergil. He was my son. I told Jake there must be some mistake.

"There's no fucking mistake," Jake said, and then he bounded off the porch and back to the truck.

THERE WERE OTHERS, INCLUDING FRANK. I telephoned half a dozen parents, and several called back over the next few days to confirm my worst suspicions. We should have figured it out. Corrigan had fixed up the basement of the rectory with his own money and had pinball machines, television sets, stereos—all designed, he said, to give kids a place to go where they could be comfortable. It was a den of iniquity. None of the kids ever told their parents because they thought we wouldn't believe them. Finally, we went to the police.

There we learned that someone had complained once before. The police chief told us he went to Springfield personally to talk with the bishop, and was assured that the problem—if there *was* a problem—would be addressed. Chief Harkin was Catholic and was not of a mind to take on the bishop. He trusted him.

Big mistake.

Meanwhile, Corrigan stayed at Holy Trinity and went on to molest Vergil and God-knows how many others.

I told Jake at the time that we were making a mistake.

We and seven other sets of parents went to Springfield to meet with the bishop and his lawyer. It was finally settled. They paid us each ten thousand dollars and assured us that Father Corrigan would be removed.

Removed. I didn't know for sure what that meant. So imagine my surprise, almost thirty years later, to see the bastard smiling at me from the porch at St. Alban's.

I challenged the bishop, saying that Corrigan needed to be thrown in jail, not "removed"—whatever that meant. The bishop, a portly man with a warm, well-practiced smile, said that he understood how I felt but that surely as a good Catholic I would want the matter settled in a manner that would not bring opprobrium to the church. I told him I didn't know what in the hell 'opprobrium' was and asked him to speak English. I will never forget his words.

"Mrs. Atkins, scandal to the Church must be avoided at all costs. We will take care of this matter, I assure you. But your faith must be brought to bear and overrule your anger."

My faith? My faith went out the window when I learned that some bastard had molested my son. I wanted to slap that sanctimonious son-of-a-bitch right there, and then start in on his greasy lawyer. But Jake took my arm and made me sit back down.

But, we settled. Just like the others. The agreement that was made was that this was under "the seal of confession," a fancy way of saying that we were under a gag order. Breaking it would be not just a legal offense, but also a mortal sin. What a load of shit.

I also remember the bishop calling this a "horrifying anomaly." It wasn't three years later that the newspaper carried the story of another "horrifying anomaly" involving another priest in a parish near Hillsboro. Then, in the nineties, all hell broke loose. All over the country.

But we settled.

A week later we had a new pastor at Holy Trinity. Not that I was there to see him. Some—most of the others—went back. They all praised the new, young man who had come straight out of seminary. I wanted nothing to do with him, or Holy Trinity.

So Corrigan disappeared to God-knows-where, we moved to a place in the country near Grafton, the Church was safe from the scandal it dreaded so much, and we were left to clean up the mess that a monster had made of our son.

What a mess it was. Vergil got into high school and proceeded to flunk just about every class. He got mixed up with a bad crowd, was suspended twice for fighting—he couldn't control his temper at school or at home. And to make matters worse, Jake died when Vergil was a sophomore. Heart attack. He was always overweight and never went to a doctor. I can't help but think that the thing with Vergil worked on him too. In a way, Jake was another victim of Corrigan's. I wasn't about to die on Vergil. He was my son. I would go to the gates of hell for him. Besides that, I was fueled by hate. Hate for Corrigan and for a system that allowed him to prey on my child get off scot-free.

I never knew what happened to the bastard. Didn't want to. Believe me, I scoured the *Western Catholic* every week for his name. They kept sending it even after I quit going to church, along with the envelopes from Holy Trinity. I never saw the name Corrigan there.

I guess I figured he was history.

After Vergil finally went to bed that night, I went to my room and opened the dresser drawer. There, under some nightclothes, was the pistol Jake always kept for protection. I actually thought about taking it, hopping in the Jeep and driving over to Saint Alban's and shooting the son-of-a-bitch. But I realized that I could never take another life, no matter how bad the person was. More importantly, that would leave Vergil in limbo.

Who would be there for him?

He was my son. I love him more than I hate Seamus Corrigan.

That's a pretty powerful love if you ask me.

MARGARET CHOSE TO SIT WITH the congregation during Sunday mass. She normally sat in the sanctuary when Father Jim presided, but she had a feeling that Father Corrigan would prefer that she not. Frankly, she was quite pleased to just be in attendance for a change.

Billie Frechette and Alice Greathouse were the altar servers. Margaret was looking for signs from Father Corrigan that he might have been put out by having two girls on the altar. There wasn't a thing he could do about that, however, since the diocese had been permitting this for quite some time. Margaret secretly hoped that Father Corrigan was irritated. Anything she could do to make his day was worth it!

She asked God's forgiveness for being petty. But she felt, somehow, that God would understand.

After the readings, Corrigan delivered his first homily for the people of St. Alban's. He started by flashing his smile.

"I'm Father Corrigan, and I will be stepping in as your parish moderator since Father Kennelly's health has taken a turn for the worse. Let me say, first of all, how much I enjoy this part of the diocese. It is truly a beautiful place. I will be coming here for the next several weeks, and then I will come less frequently. However, I want to take the time to get to know the parish and as many of you as I can. Please feel free to let your administrator know if you would like to visit with me when I am here and she can make the necessary arrangements."

'Your administrator?' Had he forgotten her name?

"The reading today, from the Gospel of Matthew, reminds us the lengths that people will go to punish those who speak a higher truth. Herodias was a woman who would brook no opposition. King Herod and his wife, Herodias, were apparently about the business of redefining 'family.' As it turned out, Herodias was Herod's niece. She had left her first husband, Philip, for Herod. It seems that Philip was Herod's brother. She married two of her uncles. But such details did not affect this woman and she was very influential because now her husband was the tetrarch of Gallilee. It's good to be the king. Most people just went their way and pretended nothing was wrong. But not John the Baptist. This inconvenient prophet had publicly spoken out about the lustful and incestuous carryings on behind the palace walls and called Herodias a few unkind things. That was the beginning of the end for John, who was the cousin of our Lord.

"Herodias conned her daughter, Salome, to entice Herod. Herodias was not above pimping out her own daughter to gain whatever she wanted. Herodias danced for Herod, and then, when Herod promised her anything she wanted, what did Salome ask of him? Exactly what mommy wanted—the head of John the Baptist. Herod was anxious because John was popular but his lust had led him to swear an oath. So he presented John's head to Herodias on a platter.

"The reading ends with John's disciples collecting his body, and says, 'then they went and told Jesus.'

"What can we take away from such a strange story? For one thing, the world does not reward the truth. It punishes it. The world rewards those who give themselves over to power and to lust. Lust is at the heart of this story. Power is its tool.

"The question we must ask ourselves in this life is, should we live according to the rules that the world gives us and thus live quietly and be left alone? Or do we dare to stand up for truth?

"Whatever we do, rest assured, when we make the choice, we will need to be ready to tell Jesus."

Well, at least he didn't talk for an hour, Margaret thought. Actually, it wasn't a bad homily. She wondered whether there might be hope for Father Corrigan after all.

But she couldn't get Vergil out of her mind.

AT FIRST SHE DIDN'T NOTICE Eli leaning up against his Ford pickup after mass. Margaret was standing off to the side while the parishioners shook hands and exchanged niceties with Father Corrigan. She was pleased to see Alice and her two boys at church, and visited with them for about five minutes. Then she turned and looked down to the drive where the cars were parked. Eli was imposing, as always, as he stood there with his arms folded. He wore sunglasses and wore only a short-sleeved blue shirt, jeans and his work boots. He seemed to be staring at the door of the church. She walked down the hill to where he was standing.

"Eli? I have been dying to get you to church! Now, what do I have to do to get you inside?" She smiled. Eli didn't.

"Yeah, Sister. Been a while. Not today." He turned and opened the door to his truck.

"Eli?"

He stopped.

"Is there something I can do for you?"

"No, ma'am. Not a thing."

Then he got in and drove away. Margaret looked up at the doorway to the church. Father Corrigan was still shaking hands and charming all of the people who stopped to chat with him.

When Corrigan flashed that smile, Margaret couldn't help thinking of the expression on the Piasa bird.

OMINOUS, BLACK CLOUDS ROLLED IN on Monday morning, causing Margaret to cut short her run. Then a thunderstorm shook the town and it rained more than two inches. People in Grafton respected the weather, feared it, and remembered. In the history of this place, floods were always a concern. The last one, in 1993, was the worst in Grafton's history. Before then, there were businesses and even houses along the river. They were no more. The resident population went from more than 900 to around 600, roughly about the size of Elsah, the village to the south. The inundation—and the posttraumatic stress--drove many further inland, leaving the town's economy in tatters. Sixteen years later things had improved, but the population had yet to return to its antediluvian level.

The rain continued Tuesday and didn't stop until late that night. Because of it, Vergil did not come into town. Margaret dreaded having to tell him and his mother that Father Corrigan had ordered her to fire him. She took advantage of the weather and put off this most unpleasant task. But on Wednesday, the sun came out again and she could not avoid it any longer.

The Atkins place was a mile east of Grafton on a county road. It was a one-story ranch with a metal shed that served as a garage for their two cars, and as a workshop. Jake Atkins had been gone for many years, so now the shed was where Vergil kept his gardening tools and other supplies. Margaret pulled into the drive around ten in the morning and saw Rachel's Jeep and the old Ford Taurus parked in the shed. She could see Vergil tinkering around inside.

Rachel came to the door dressed in a loose-fitting flannel shirt, old jeans, and wearing an apron.

"Morning, Sister."

"Good morning, Rachel. I'm sorry to bother you, but there is something I must talk with you about."

"Come in. "I'm just waiting on a cake to come out of the oven. Sit. Coffee?"

"That would be nice, thanks."

Rachel poured coffee into a white mug and placed it on a coaster and then poured coffee into her own cup.

"What's up?" Rachel was always one to cut to the chase. Out of respect, Margaret chose not to beat around the bush.

"I'm afraid I am going to have to terminate the arrangement we have with Vergil."

Rachel didn't say anything for about a minute. She took a sip of her coffee and then sat the cup down.

"Probably just as well," Rachel said.

Margaret was surprised by Rachel's response.

"That it?" Rachel said.

"Rachel, I have never had the chance to talk with you. I mean, to really talk with you. I want you to know how sorry I am about this."

"Sorry don't change things. If it's any help, I can guess why this is happening. But that don't matter either. I will find something else for him to do."

"Could you help me with something, Rachel?"

"What's that?"

"Do you have any idea why Vergil got sick the other day?"

"Touch of something," Rachel said, lifting the cup to her lips.

Margaret was being stonewalled. Rachel had always been laconic and now when Margaret needed to break through the barrier, she found herself totally disarmed. How do you converse with someone who won't open up any avenues?

"It's probably my fault," Margaret said.

"I know this isn't your fault."

"No. I mean the fact that you don't feel comfortable talking with me. I have been trying to organize everything, and so I haven't taken the opportunities I might have to get to know you better. To make you feel more comfortable with me. But Rachel, I care very much for Vergil and I would like to be able to care for you."

"Look, Sister. You're a good woman. I can tell that. But I don't need caring for. As for Vergil, he's got me. There's nothing you can really do for us and if there ever is I will be the first to let you know. More coffee?"

Margaret smiled and then drank the last of the coffee from the mug. She rose from the table, and so did Rachel.

"Thanks for the coffee, Rachel."

"No problem. Thanks for coming out."

As she stepped out on the stoop, she turned back.

"You used to go to Holy Trinity, didn't you? In Jerseyville?"

"Yeah. Before we moved here. Been a while."

"So you probably knew Father Corrigan."

"I know him."

Margaret nodded and smiled, and then walked back to her car. Rachel was still standing at the door as Margaret drove away.

In Grafton, she stopped at the fudge shop. The old house had antiques and knick-knacks on both levels and delicious fudge for sale behind the counter. It was busy today in spite of the weather. She bought a pound of dark and another pound of white fudge. She thought of her slightly expanded waistline, but quickly let the thought depart. Some things were just too good to pass up.

She went across the street to Maybelle's for lunch. A girl she didn't recognize was waiting tables. Her nametag read, 'Gladys.'

Margaret inquired after Alice. Gladys said that Alice had called in sick.

Margaret ordered the special—fried chicken, mashed potatoes, corn, and a dinner roll.

Her waistline was going to take a real beating today.

Eli

IT RAINED ON MONDAY, SO there wasn't much to do except piddle around the shed and try to straighten up the house. I guess being in the military made me self-conscious about keeping the house straight, although I am not sure why. I seldom have anyone drop by except Teri. And Teri could not care less what the place looks like.

I had to see what he looked like. He was bigger than I thought he would be. Was this the "Father C" that Melvin was writing about? I think it must be, because he said the name "Seamus" toward the end of his journal.

I can't explain how it felt to see him. I have been carrying so much anger around for so long, I thought I might want to go up and start wailing on him. But for some reason, I felt pity for the man. Go figure that. Then, I saw it all over again. The carnage in the garage and the deep-fried remnants of my brother and the smell that sometimes comes again to me in my dreams. The reason I would never char a burger or go anywhere there was a bonfire.

After lunch, I popped a beer and pulled out Melvin's journal and picked up where I had left off. I knew what was ahead. I was dreading it, even though I knew what was coming.

My God, what must life have been like for Catherine? She was so nice. Melvin met her at the school where he taught. She was a secretary. She was divorced and had two kids. Melvin was ten years younger, but you would never have guessed she was older by looking at her. She was quiet, thoughtful, loving, and very good-looking. Her older son was away at college and Teri, who was about 15 at the time, lived with her father in Jerseyville. She had lived with her mom for a while but after her mom married Melvin she couldn't take his moods for long stretches of time. She was always sweet to me and I liked her. Still do. Can't blame her for needing to get away. It may have saved her life.

Catherine had fallen for a Melvin who was calm, cool, quiet and caring. He was a fully functioning manic-depressive. He said that to me once when we were fishing. Sometimes he could laugh. I liked it when he did. I always figured show me a person who can't laugh and I will show you a person who is going to go nuts. Thank God I can still laugh at myself and at life. Don't get much of a chance to socialize but I still have a sense of humor. Can't work with dead people all the time and not have one of those. Melvin smoked a pipe, wore tweed in the fall and winter, and seemed to be the kindliest of teachers. It wasn't until after they got married that she saw the darkness, the highs that were euphoric and the lows that took him to the edge of self-annihilation. She had put up with it for three years. It was no wonder she had to get away. I only wish she had made it, even though I knew it would spell the end of Melvin. Better just him than the both of them. But she didn't make it.

The asphalt on the road was bubbling and crackling under the tires of my truck as I raced down the country road toward Melvin's farm. It had been our place until mom moved out and into town. She let Melvin move in after he and Catherine married. Melvin didn't farm, of course, but Jed Miller and his boys farmed it and my mom made a decent income from their labors. Melvin did keep two horses. He and Catherine liked to ride. The horses were the first things I noticed as I turned off the road and onto the long gravel drive leading to the house. They were standing near the fence. Had I looked closer, I might have noticed that they seemed spooked. But hell, what did I know about horses?

The smell hit me as I pulled up into the gravel driveway next to the house. Were they cooking out? Was that why they hadn't answered the phone? Then I realized what it was that I was smelling.

After I graduated, a bunch of us went to a pizza parlor in Jerseyville. We were drinking—nobody carded us in there since my buddy's sister was waitressing and was on duty by herself—and I went to light a cigarette with my butane lighter. It wouldn't ignite. So, genius that I was, I held the butane lighter up to my ear to see if I could hear a hissing. Instead of just pushing down on the butane button, I flicked it. Well, the lighter worked this time and ignited part of my shoulder-length hair. Everyone at the table laughed out loud. It didn't really catch, but it burned enough to raise a stink.

Burnt hair. That was what I smelled. Mixed with a cooked pork kind of smell. When I stepped out of the car at Melvin's, I noticed that the odor became worse. Sickening sweet. I couldn't tell where it came from.

Then I looked at the Impala. The driver's side door was open. It took me a couple seconds to realize what I was seeing. Something was lying in a heap near the rear bumper. I looked closer and saw that it was—human. Black stuff was spattered all around and the thing was lying in a huge puddle of it. My mouth fell open.

Catherine.

She was in her robe and it had come open and her eyes were looking at me. But her head was almost separated from the rest of her and it had gashes that were caked in clotted blood. Her hand was missing, and gobs of black blood covered her body and had soaked into the terry cloth.

A blackened, gnarled hunk of something lay at her feet near the passenger door of the Chevy.

Her hand.

I had to steady myself and backed up to lean against the truck.

"Melvin?" I said out loud. Then I screamed.

"Melvin! Where are you?"

I ran up to the house and noticed that the screen door was hanging from one hinge. I walked up the steps and went in.

Melvin! Where the hell are you? Jesus Christ! What happened?

"MELVIN!"

From Melvin Barstow's Notebook

Dec 1, 1967

I told him the story. The doctor listened as I blubbered, and then raged, and almost became physically ill. He tells me I need to put it down. All of it. So, here goes.

I was maybe 10 when we got a new priest. I had signed up at school to serve mass and the first time I saw Father C. he was wearing his black cassock. He was a nice looking guy, with a quick smile, and he seemed to care very much about "his boys", as he called us. I will never forget the Latin prayers. I spent hours memorizing, and then presenting in front of the other boys at the altar boy meetings. I had it down pat by the time I served my first mass.

Introibo ad altare Dei.

Ad Deum qui laetificat juventutem meam.

I proudly went unto the altar of God for my first mass. It was 6:30 in the morning. Somehow Billy Roberts and I pulled 6:30 that week for our first assignment. I was able to walk there, thank God, because sometimes mom couldn't get up. Sometimes she was hurting too much to get up, although she had to be hurting pretty bad to miss church. Church was all that kept her going sometimes.

Being an altar boy was the thing that made me the proudest. I wonder if years from now people will realize what it means to be Catholic the way we were. It wasn't just a religion; it was a subculture. The priest was more than a minister; he was the glue that held the community together. He symbolized our best; he was the pattern against which we judged ourselves, and our lives. Needless to say, his pattern was not reflected in my life. Except in my mother's heart. That is one thing I know for certain.

I wasn't into scouting; if I had been, I might have seen a lot more of Father C. He worked with the scouts and worked with a lot of other youth activities. As it was, I saw him a lot at school and at altar boy picnics. I remember when the school got broken into and a bunch of athletic equipment got stolen, we didn't have any baseball bats. We were in PE class one afternoon, out in a field behind the school, when Father C. walked up to the coach with a box.

He had bought bats, balls, and helmets, the whole works. We all crowded around him that day. He actually put his arm around me.

That same night my dad got drunk and damned near killed me, He would have if I hadn't run and hid in the neighbor's tool shed. At least I got his attention away from mom long enough for him to pass out. Not before he clipped me good on the side of my head though. It stung, but it didn't bleed. Not that time.

Father C., his arm around me, and my own father threatening to kill me – all in the same 24-hour period. Ups and downs? Manic-depressive disorder? My whole life was like that it seems.

I was changing. I had no idea what was going on at first. I began to feel things differently. In the springtime I seemed to breathe more deeply and to experience a strange yearning that came from somewhere I knew not. It was as though something was swelling up inside of me. It was swelling up outside of me too. I would wake up in the mornings almost in pain because of the swelling. Then I would roll over and push on the mattress and that made it feel better. Things that I had once overlooked now became a source of temptation for me. My mother subscribed to Life Magazine and I always loved looking though that magazine at the great pictures, pictures from all over the world. I had noticed women on the cover before, but now it seemed that each new edition carried a picture of a beautiful woman on the cover. One, in particular, carried a picture of a woman in a swimsuit, and the pictures inside showed other women in one-piece swimsuits. The Sears catalog, which I always perused with interest as Christmas came around, now tempted me with pictures of women in bras and girdles. A memory from my childhood, a memory of Grace, Grace with the ruby red lipstick and the sweet-smelling perfume, would present itself to me in my sleep. Even the encyclopedia was a source of temptation. I would find articles on ancient Greece, and there I would find reaching across the ages photographs of tombstones called *kouroi*, naked men standing face front, one leg in motion toward front, arms drawn tightly down alongside them, their privates pointing straight out. I even found these sorely tempting.

I was in the bathroom, lying on the floor naked after a bath looking at one of the *kouroi* when I rolled over onto my stomach and was overcome with a sensation I had never dreamed possible. I jumped up in terror because I had squirted something milky onto the shag rug in front of the mirror. I threw the encyclopedia in the corner, wiped up the mess, and went to my bed—which at the time was in the room next to my mother and dad's—and prayed for God's forgiveness.

Was this what Father C. was talking about when he put on his vestments before mass? I had read and memorized the prayers that the priest said before he put on each of his vestments. First there was the amice, a square, white piece of cloth with two narrow strings attached, that the priest would tie over his collar and around his shoulders. Then I would hold forth the long, white alb and he would reach his arms in and pull it over his head. Then, I would hold forth the long, white, woven cord. The cincture.

Gird me, O Lord, with the cincture of purity, and quench in my heart the fire of concupiscence, that the virtue of continence and chastity may remain in me.

Concupiscence.

I never really understood this strange, foreign-sounding word. Had I fallen victim to this awful thing, this thing that the priest prayed to protect himself from? Father C. had preached how important purity was ever since he started teaching the altar boys, but I never got it. Now I had fallen victim to it, a sin that had its roots in my own soul.

I just knew that I would burn in hell forever. I couldn't mention this to my mother. Never. Dad? That was a laugh. No way. He would probably beat me if he ever found out what concupiscence meant. The only way out of this damnation was confession. I never really had anything bad to say in confession before. Now, I prayed that I would have the courage to tell all and obtain the Lord's forgiveness.

Would Father C. understand? He was my only hope. He was the one man I could turn to. He was my priest. Of course he would understand. Besides, what choice did I have? My soul was in dire jeopardy.

I am tired. I will pick up on this later. I don't really want to write any more. My tremors are getting worse. I think I need to stop the Lithium again. The taste in my mouth is getting worse. What can it hurt?

Maybe I can write more later.

Dec 25, 1967

Christmas day. The light will come back. Will it? It gets worse about November. Some days I don't even want to get out of bed. I could just lie there forever. I drag myself out of bed and go through a routine. Catherine finds me especially hard to take in winter. I can't blame her, I guess. I just want to die.

Confession. There was something about confession that made me feel strange. The old confessional was carved out of oak and was dark from old varnish and years of candle wax and incense. Dark red curtains hung from the side doors where penitents go, and from the larger door in the center behind which the priest sat, waiting to dispense God's forgiveness.

I waited in line that Saturday afternoon for about twenty minutes, standing a decent distance from the box so as not to overhear anything that might be said. Voices seldom carried, but you still were taught not to get too close. The light went off above the box on my side, and I walked through the curtain and knelt in the darkness. I could hear Father C. mumbling to the person on the other side for a while, and then suddenly the door between him and me slid open and he said a prayer in Latin. When he finished, it was my turn.

"Bless me, Father, for I have sinned. It has been one week since my last confession."

So far, so good.

"I disobeyed my parents, and yelled at my brother."

"Yes," he said. "Is there anything else."

"Something happened to me, Father."

"Yes?"

"I have been having impure thoughts."

"What occasioned these?"

"I don't know, Father. I have been having them a lot lately."

"What did you do about them?"

"I was looking at pictures, and ...something happened?"

"Did you ejaculate?"

I was horrified. I wasn't sure what "ejaculate" meant, but I had a notion that it had something to do with that white, milky stuff and the way it made me feel coming out."

"I guess so, I think so."

He must have sensed my confusion. "Did fluid come out of your body?"

He knew. He knew. It was all I could do to keep from crying. Then I didn't try any more. I began to sob. "Yes, Father."

For a while, he just sat there.

"Did it feel good?"

I had to be honest. "Yes," I said.

"That's the devil's way. He gives pleasure in exchange for submitting to his temptations. Why did you look at those pictures?"

"I don't know, Father."

"Yes, you do! You wanted it to happen, didn't you?"

I swallowed hard, still sobbing. "I guess."

"How am I supposed to give you absolution, Melvin?"

Oh God! He knew who I was!

"You are probably going to go back and dig out those pictures again, because it feels so good. How can I, in good conscience, absolve you from a sin you are going to knowingly commit again and again?"

I was scared now. I had to be absolved.

"No, Father. I don't want to. I want to be good."

"You want to be pure?"

"Yes."

Do you know what concupiscence is, Melvin?"

"I'm not sure, but I don't think it's good."

"It's the greatest threat to your soul. It is what makes you want to look at dirty pictures and to make yourself feel good. Of course, the problem is, it comes with growing up. You are growing hair on your legs, right?"

"Yes." I was rather proud of the fact that I was starting to look like a man.

"And you are getting hair down there, too. Right?"

This embarrassed me a bit, but then I fessed up. He already knew everything anyway.

"You must fight it, Melvin! If it makes you feel any better, you must know you are not alone. Now that you are growing up, you will find that it bothers you more and more and it will until you are much, much older. It is something even I have to fight."

Father C. has to fight it too? For some strange reason that made me feel a little better.

"I can help you, Melvin. Who knows? You might even be able to help me. This is a battle that must be won."

I had no idea what he meant about helping him. I was just praying that this whole, horrid experience would soon be over and that I would be absolved and safe from the fires of hell.

"Is there anything else, Melvin?"

"No, Father."

He gave me three Our Fathers and three Hail Marys for my penance and told me to kiss the feet of the Virgin's statue on the side altar whenever I went to church and to beg her forgiveness. I thanked him and left the confessional. I will never forget how much lighter I felt inside, how much more easily I breathed. I felt as if I were floating out of the church.

Three days later, I made myself feel good when I woke up one morning and then cried because I knew I was doomed to hell.

Catherine is calling. I will come back to this.

ALICE WHITAKER PICKED UP HER boys after school and drove them to her mother's in Jerseyville. She was still in a great deal of pain. She had tried her best to cover the bruises on her face with makeup but she knew she would have to move fast to keep her mother from noticing. The boys did not say anything. They had heard everything the night before, and they were still terrified. She wondered how they could sit through school, but she had to take them. They had to have some normalcy in their lives.

She wondered now whether it was too late for Adam, her 12-year old. He sat in the car next to her now without saying a word. He was staring down at the floor, his fists clenched, his jaw set. At one point he opened the window allowing the hot air to rush in even though Alice was running the air conditioner.

"Adam, close that window."

He didn't even look at her. "Fine," he said, and then slowly rolled the window back up. Then he returned to his stone-faced perusal of the floor mat beneath his feet.

"Mommy?" Erik, her 6-year old, was sitting in the back. His voice was still raw from crying.

"Mommy. Why do we have to go to grandmas? Can't we stay with you?"

"It's just for a while, honey. Not long. Mommy has to take care of some things."

"Is Tommy going to hit you again? Please stay with us Mommy?"

Alice's heart almost split and a tear rolled down her cheek. What had she done to these kids? Tommy wasn't the father of either of the boys. Why had she chosen to risk not only her own safety but the safety and sanity of these two boys? Why?

Was it better to do that than to have to feel alone? At one time she had adopted the attitude that kids can bounce back from anything. Now she knew that her approach was very self-centered. It wasn't them, but herself that she was looking out for. Now she had not only scars and bruises on herself, but also in the hearts of her children.

"Honey, you know I love you, don't you?"

"Would that make you feel better?" Adam finally said something.

It started the way it always did. Tommy came home late. He came in drunk. Alice should have known better, but she started in on him. She was fed up with working while he collected unemployment. He lost his last job at the gas station because of his temper. And to make things worse he spent his free time drinking with his friends. He hit her in the stomach so hard that she threw up, and then he hit her in the face. He stopped that, took off his belt, and then let her have it across the back several times. He preferred hitting her where it didn't show too much. Then he went to bed and left her sobbing on the floor.

She was crazy to go back. Something inside told her that, but she was going anyway. But first she had to get the kids someplace safe. She didn't want them seeing that.

Erik, her youngest, hugged her tightly and begged her not to go back. But she kissed him and assured him that she would be back to get him tomorrow morning and not to worry. She had told her mother that she and Tommy had plans for the night, that they had just come up, and begged her to keep the boys. Her mother—a small framed woman in her forties whose face showed lines and creases stemming from a life of questionable choices and behaviors—invited her in, but Alice just waved and told her she would pick the boys up early for school.

Alice was sixteen when she got pregnant with Adam. Her mom was supportive of her—in fact her mom had been a sophomore at Jerseyville High School when she had Alice. Her mom understood. She was furious, but she understood.

The boy that knocked her up was older and had been out of school for several years. He was married to someone else, although the marriage was one in name only. He left Jerseyville shortly after Adam was born and Alice hadn't heard anything from him since. She dropped out of school leaving the dream of a diploma behind. Lately, she had come to regret that but not before she had Erik.

Erik's sperm donor had departed soon after she announced her condition, and the last she heard he was in Pontiac Correctional for armed robbery.

Tommy Harrison seemed different. She met him in Grafton one night at the Wharf, a riverside restaurant and watering hole popular with tourists and locals alike. He didn't look at her breasts when he talked to her the way most guys did, and he treated her very nice. True, he drank a bit more than he should, but all in all he seemed a great improvement over what she had known. He even seemed to get on with her boys.

After 2 weeks, she and the boys moved into his trailer in Grafton.

Things went okay until he got fired from the station. It had been going rapidly downhill ever since. Still, she remembered the boy he had been at first and felt that she could somehow help him work out his rough spots. Something about him appealed to her maternal instincts. He had suffered through a painful childhood, after all. A lot of it wasn't his fault. More and more, however, she was finding this relationship to be a painful proposition.

It was all her fault he told her repeatedly. She was by now so beaten down that she started to believe it. That's why she had to go back. After all, last night it had been she who started in on him. She made him do it. She didn't want it to end. They had had good times and she thought they could again.

It was almost 6 o'clock when she parked under the carport at the trailer.

Tommy was sitting on the deck drinking a beer.

LAW & ORDER **HAD BEEN ON** television almost as long as *Gunsmoke*. Margaret couldn't help noticing that the show had lost something lately. Like many endeavors that are fresh and vital at first, but in time lack the passion and retain only the formula, it just didn't grab her the way it used to. For one thing, she found it hard to like Linus Roach as the Assistant District Attorney as well as Sam Waterston. He was intense and good-looking—in fact he reminded her in some ways of Bill Templeton—but he lacked the hidden depths of the Jack McCoy character. She found herself watching more out of habit than anything, but she still turned it on every Wednesday if she had time.

She had just poured her fourth glass of Merlot when she saw car lights flash through the front windows and heard a car door slam. By the time she stood up, she heard someone knocking at the door.

Margaret opened the door and saw Alice clutching her stomach. There was blood around her mouth.

"My God, Alice! What happened?" Margaret took her arm and led her into the living room to the couch.

"I'm sorry, Sister. I didn't know where else to go?"

"You might consider the hospital. Although I am glad you didn't try to drive that far in your condition. Let me grab my keys. I will drive you myself."

"NO! I will be fine. Just let me sit a while."

"Let me look at you," Margaret said. She felt Alice's side. Alice cried out in pain.

"You have to see a doctor, Alice. If I have to drag you there myself. Who did this to you?"

Margaret had a suspicion. She remembered seeing the bruise on the girl's arm the other day in the restaurant.

"What's your boyfriend's name?"

"Tommy."

"He did this, didn't he?"

"He didn't mean to."

"Bullshit, Alice. You need to call the police, but you have to go to the doctor first."

"I won't call the police."

"Fine, then what in hell do you want from me? Did you come here just to rest up before the next round? Because believe me, I am not much for aiding and abetting criminal behavior."

"I'm sorry. I shouldn't have bothered you."

"Quit being sorry unless you get sorry over the right things. Okay. Forget the police for now. But you are going to the hospital. Come on."

Alice didn't argue this time. Margaret had her keys, and she lifted Alice up and walked to the front door.

The two women had just made it to the garage where Margaret's Elantra was parked when they saw car lights turn off of Main Street making a beeline toward the church. An old, red Chevy Impala came to a grinding halt in the gravel and Tommy Harrison jumped out.

"You get your fucking ass back home, bitch," he said, ignoring Margaret.

"Tommy, you get the hell out of here," Margaret screamed. "You've done enough for one evening."

Tommy laughed. He was quite drunk. "Hey, mind your own fucking business, *Sister*. I'm not Catholic. I don't have to listen to your hocus pocus. Now get out of my way." He grabbed Margaret's arm to push her aside.

That was his biggest mistake of the evening.

The next thing Tommy felt was his head being slammed against his car's roof. He saw stars for about thirty seconds and when he faded back into consciousness he found himself face-down on the gravel driveway, Margaret astride him, his right arm bent up against his back.

Margaret had her cell phone in the other hand and quickly pressed 9-1-1.

"SHERIFF COLLINS WAS TELLING ME about you, Sister."

Grafton Chief of Police Bob Burton had just shoved Tommy Harrison into the back of the police car.

"Didn't know she used to be a sheriff's deputy, did you Tommy? That'll teach you some respect."

Margaret was tending to Alice, who was sitting on the back seat of Margaret's Elantra with her legs outside of the car.

"Are you going to file charges against this idiot, Alice?"

Alice didn't say anything. Margaret turned to Burton.

"Very well, Bob. Then I am filing charges. Assault. Then I will work on talking some sense into Alice."

"You say one fucking thing Alice and I will kill you, goddamn it!" Tommy screamed from the cruiser.

"I'm going to get this piece of trash to the jail. Sign this, Sister."

Margaret signed the report and thanked Burton for coming.

"Always a pleasure, Sister. I'm a Methodist myself. If my wife weren't in the ladies' auxiliary, I wouldn't mind coming out here to see if your sermons are as persuasive as your left hook."

"I don't give sermons, Bob."

"Now I know I would like this church! Good night."

A LITTLE PAST MIDNIGHT, MARGARET sat in a very uncomfortable chair next to an examination table at Alton Memorial Hospital's emergency room. Alice had three broken ribs, several hairline fractures, a concussion and a nose three-times its normal size. At first, the doctor was concerned that her spleen had been ruptured. Fortunately, that was not the case.

When Alice awakened she was surprised to see Margaret sitting there.

"Thanks," she said.

"Don't thank me. He could have killed you. You need to do the right thing."

"I'm afraid. At first, I thought it was because I loved him. But I know now that it's because I am afraid."

"And that's the very thing he is counting on. You being afraid."

"I don't even know what to do. How to do it," Alice said. She winced in pain and grabbed her head with both hands.

"I will help you. I have filed charges and now you have to. We will get an order of protection. Can you move in with your mother for a while?"

"God, no. Oh, I could. But in a lot of ways that would be worse than living with Tommy. He just beats me."

Margaret decided not to ask.

"Okay. Then, it's settled."

"What is?"

"You and the boys will move in with me."

"You're kidding."

"Do I look like I'm kidding?"

Margaret knew she could convince Alice of the rightness of this course of action. Father Corrigan, however, would be a harder sell.

Margaret would have to figure something out.

MARGARET DROVE ERIK AND HIS older brother Adam to their first day of school the next morning. Erik talked the whole way there. She could sense his relief in having a safe haven, and he seemed to want to get back to being a kid. She marveled at the resilience of his young spirit. Adam was another story. He was sullen. Twelve year olds tended to be that way anyway, she had heard, but his demeanor was troubled. He wore his hair long and he had his mother's eyes. But if he said two words on the way to school

Margaret must have missed them. Margaret pondered what Jesus must have meant when he said that the only unforgiveable sin was a sin against the spirit. She prayed that Adam's spirit had not been sinned against irrevocably. Erik thanked her when she dropped them off, but Adam just got out and walked into the school. His shoulders were drooping and he walked very slowly. Margaret's heart ached for him. He was clearly suffering.

It wasn't until the afternoon that Alice felt like moving much. Margaret had placed a call to an attorney in Jerseyville in the morning, and after picking the boys up from school she drove Alice over to the courthouse to file an order of protection. The boys waited patiently in the hallway. Afterward they had an early supper downtown and then drove back to the trailer outside of Grafton to collect some of the boy's clothes. Before returning, Margaret drove to Wal-Mart and walked slowly—walking fast wasn't in the cards given Alice's condition—through the store picking out some new outfits for the boys. She also bought a nice dress for Alice. Alice was protesting the whole way but Margaret assured her that she—Alice—could pay her back when it was convenient.

By Friday evening, after looking after two boys, cooking for them, and making sure their rooms were habitable, Margaret was dog-tired.

It occurred to her, however, that she wasn't doing one thing that she had been doing regularly since she arrived in Grafton. She hadn't had one glass of wine.

She had figured out a way around Father Corrigan. Avoidance. At least for now.

Alice said that it wouldn't be a problem if she took the boys to her mother's Saturday and came back Sunday afternoon. Alice said she could ignore her mother for that long.

On Saturday afternoon, Margaret spent hours cleaning in order to ensure that there was no sign that someone else was staying in the rectory. She was just finishing up when the doorbell rang.

She looked outside and saw a police car in front. Bob Burton was standing on the porch. She opened the door.

"Sorry to bother you, Sister. But do you know where Alice is? She isn't at the trailer."

"Yes. She's in Jerseyville with her mother. She will be back tomorrow."

"She is staying with you?"

"Yes, but for tonight. Is there something wrong?"

"Can I come in?"

"Certainly."

"I have some bad news. I just heard about it this morning. I was off yesterday. Seems our friend Tommy Harrison was arraigned yesterday."

"Yes."

"He's out."

"You can't be serious."

"Dead serious. Apparently, Tommy has a lot of family in Jerseyville. One of his shirttail cousins is an attorney, a small-time lawyer who does divorces. This cousin is friendly with the judge and must have whined about what a good kid Tommy was and got bail down low enough so he could spring him. The trial will be in two weeks, but he's out running around somewhere."

"My God. She's in danger."

"Now don't panic. I can't imagine he would be so stupid as to go after her. But I'll call Chief Smothers in Jerseyville and Sheriff Collins and have them watch the house. You know what her mother's name is?"

"No. but have a phone number. You want to call from here?"

"No, just give me the number. I will call her and then contact the powers that be over there."

Margaret walked over and copied the phone number onto a sticky note and handed it to him.

"I will make a point of keeping a watch here too, after she gets back. She's coming back tomorrow?"

"Yes. Thank you. That would be wonderful."

"Sorry to ruin your afternoon, Sister. But don't worry too much."

"That's easy to say, Bob. I will worry if you don't mind."

"Yes, I expect you will. Talk with you later."

After Burton left, Margaret stood in the hallway for a moment. She realized she was biting her cuticles again. She pulled her hand away and ran up to her room.

She pulled open the top dresser drawer and reached beneath some underclothes and pulled out a Sigarms nine-millimeter semi-automatic pistol. What had possessed her to purchase this after she moved here was something she didn't completely understand.

Occasionally she would go into the countryside and practice her marksmanship skills. She wasn't a cop any more, but somehow part of her would always be. She felt for the box of bullets in the bottom of the drawer and then slid the pistol back underneath the clothes.

She prayed she would never have to resort to using a weapon on another human being. In all the years she spent as a deputy sheriff, she had never had to. She prayed that Tommy Harrison wouldn't bring it to that now.

Before closing the drawer, she picked up a small Bible that was on top of the dresser and set it on top of the clothes, right over the pistol. Perhaps God would keep her safe. But if for some reason He chose to test her, she knew how to use that gun.

MARGARET WAS PUTTING THE FINISHING touches on the Sunday bulletin when she heard a car pull up in front. She didn't get up, and shortly the door opened and Father Corrigan walked in and dropped his overnight bag on the floor.

"Does it ever cool off down here?" he asked.

"Good afternoon, Father. And no."

"Humph. Well, I'll go drop my things in the bedroom and freshen up."

"Make yourself at home. I am just finishing up some things." She wasn't about to leave her position at the desk.

Margaret had a roast in the crock-pot. Somehow she knew she would be having a few glasses of wine before she went to bed.

MARGARET PAID LITTLE ATTENTION TO the comings and goings outside. She busied herself setting the table and readying things for supper. At one point she walked into the office, wiping her hands with a dishtowel, and looked outside. A car with an elderly couple in it was pulling away. She didn't recognize them and realized that they were probably tourists who had stopped for confession. Then she noticed something else.

A red Jeep Cherokee was parked in front.

Margaret had to look twice to make sure that she was seeing clearly.

It belonged to Rachel Atkins.

MARGARET WAS WASHING HER HANDS when she heard

the front door slam. She walked out and saw Father Corrigan standing behind her desk going through the drawers.

"Can I help you, Father?"

"I am looking for your list of parishioners."

"That's all computerized. Is there anyone in particular you are looking for?"

Father Corrigan's face was bright red. "Computerized. Whatever happened to Rolodexes?"

Margaret walked over to the desk.

"Excuse me," she said, and sat down and pulled out the keyboard. "What is it you are looking for?"

"Atkins."

Margaret opened up the Excel spreadsheet that she had created to keep track of the members. Given the small number she had to keep track of, Excel was more than adequate. She had programmed a lookup screen and soon called up Rachel Atkins' information. She hit print and handed it to Father Corrigan.

As he looked it over, Margaret noticed two cars pulling up in front. Confessions were supposed to last until five and it was now only quarter till.

"Father, there are some people going into the church."

"Confessions are over. You'll have to tell them."

"But, Father …."

"Route 5? That's right off the highway east of town, isn't it?" He was looking at the address. "And who's Vergil?"

"That would be the boy you had me fire last week."

"The retard?"

Margaret wanted to slap him. She said nothing.

"If there's nothing else, I had better go and inform those people that confessions are over."

"You do that."

"Supper is almost ready, Father."

"Keep it warm. I am going for a drive."

With that, he took the paper and walked out the front door, got into his Crown Vic, and drove toward Main Street. She was not surprised to see that Rachel's Jeep was gone.

Apparently, Rachel had made Father Corrigan's day. Margaret didn't know whether to be concerned or elated.

IT WAS AFTER SEVEN WHEN Father Corrigan returned. Margaret served supper and it was obvious that Corrigan was still in a foul mood. They ate silently for fifteen minutes.

"Would you like some wine, Father?"

"I don't drink. Never have."

"Admirable." Margaret popped the cork off of the bottle of Merlot and poured a tumbler full.

"You're going to sleep well tonight," Corrigan said.

"I've had a hell of a week."

Corrigan reached into his pants pocket and pulled out a toy car. It was a Lightning McQueen from the Pixar movie *Cars*. He tossed it onto the table.

"You didn't mention that you had children staying here," he said.

Margaret took a slug from the glass.

"No," Corrigan continued. "I filled up in town and the guy behind the counter was real talkative. Talked about how I had a gutsy nun working at the church. He told me the whole story. About how you knocked some guy senseless who was beating his wife. And how you had asked the girl and her two boys to come live at the rectory."

She was caught red-handed. "They have no one and nowhere else to go."

"And you were going to tell me about this ...when?"

"You're right. I was trying to think about how to approach it."

"Two boys? How old?"

"Six and 12."

Corrigan ate a couple more bites of his food. The clock in the front hall was ticking, ticking, ticking. Finally, he folded up his napkin and took a drink from his water glass.

"Well, just to show you that I am not the beast you seem to think I am, I would like to congratulate you on your Christian charity."

Margaret said nothing.

"It would be nice to have some life around this place no doubt. It might keep you from tippling quite so much."

Margaret self-consciously pushed the tumbler away from her.

"Perhaps I will stay a little longer tomorrow. Perhaps I can meet my new houseguests before I leave," Corrigan said as he rose to go to his room.

"Thank you, Father," Margaret said.

But something about this situation sent a chill up her spine.

Seamus

HE THREW UP THE FIRST time. I remember him now. They lived in Jerseyville at the time and he was a nice-looking boy who always smiled. I took him fishing one day. We had been working up to it slowly—he was more reticent than some of the others. But that afternoon in my car, after we had caught some catfish down by the river, we had a little talk about how your body changes and then when I offered myself to him he threw up. All over me and all over the front seat of the car. I remember he cried. I comforted him after I wiped myself and the car seat up with some towels I had in the trunk. After that, he was a good boy. He was always there when I needed him. Until he got older. Like most kids, they get sullen, distant, and hard to reach. After a while he quit serving mass and quit coming to church. I never knew what happened to him. I don't know what it was that made him like he is now. I know it wasn't me. I never hurt him. He needed someone as badly as I did

Things have changed so much. Those people who made so much of this years back were pointing the finger at me for hurting those boys. They were the ones who had been hurting those boys. They needed someone like me, someone they could look up to, and someone who wouldn't always put them down. I needed them too, and nothing I did ever hurt them. There is a long tradition, going back to the ancient Greeks, of young boys having a long-term relationship with an older man. It was part of their education. It helped make them grow into well-developed young men. The Gospel of Mark talked about "the disciple whom Jesus loved." It wasn't Mary Magdalene, in spite of what Dan Brown thinks. It was John.

I knew there was something different about me from the first. When I started changing the way all boys do at a certain age, I just knew that I would never be like others. I can still remember how I stayed over at a friend's house on weekends. We slept in the same bed. He would wear only his briefs to sleep in and I would wake up in the morning and just stare at his bare back, his well-developed arms and shoulders, and I would be overcome with a want that inflamed me. I was seventeen the first time I had it off with a boy. He was younger, and I was his scout leader. He seemed to enjoy it as much as I did.

Oh, I fought it. I fought it for years. I entered the seminary because I knew I would never marry and I knew that the priesthood would give me a place to keep my private yearnings under wraps, a place that was safe from those who would speculate about my single state. My family practices the Catholic faith unfailingly, and I was raised to do the same. I truly wanted to be a good person, to sacrifice myself for God and serve his people. I fought it until I couldn't fight it any more.

It was in seminary where I learned that I wasn't that different. Several of my teachers took an interest in me. They told me of their suffering, and I helped them with it. They helped me too. There was a true brotherhood there. I knew I had found a home. I knew that it was all right. It afforded us relief from the burning desires and made it possible for us to serve God in relative peace. That wasn't wrong. It was the only way.

I didn't hurt those boys. God knows. It wasn't me. I just helped them and they helped me.

I asked to be re-activated during Viet Nam and spent several years there as chaplain near the DMZ. The horrors I saw there. Young boys with limbs torn off, some so badly burned that they died in agony. I held some of them while they died and prayed with them.

I had a boy there for quite some time. He was an NCO from Nebraska. I truly cared for him. Right up until the time he was felled by a mortar shell. That was the lowest moment in my life I think.

They sent me to a monastery in New Mexico after the diocese quieted all those parents from Jerseyville. That was unfortunate, but the past is the past. In the desert of New

Mexico the monks prayed with me in an effort to help me overcome my weakness, and reminded me over and over again that my desires were disordered and that, if I wanted to truly serve God, I would have to strengthen my faith and pray for the grace of God to help overcome my weakness. But the only thing that could help me overcome my weakness was helping others, young people, who suffered the same weakness. And they all suffer that weakness. It was a mutual thing. Always was. Had it not been for those kids that God sent to help I might not have been able to maintain my vocation.

I didn't hurt those boys. God knows. It wasn't me. They trusted me. They knew I wouldn't hurt them.

The urges aren't quite as strong, even though they haven't disappeared. The flesh is weak. I may actually be overcoming my greatest weakness, by the grace of God, with and coming of old age. The Church is my home. It is where I belong. I have served her well.

Like everyone else, I just want to die peacefully. The past is the past. That is why I became so enraged at that woman who inserted herself into the confession booth. She raged at me. Atkins. The boy who threw up. Those things happened over thirty years ago and she seems to hold me responsible for everything that has happened since. She infuriated me. People have no respect any more.

After Sister gave me her information, I got in the car and drove out on the highway and turned down the road to where she lived. I am not sure what I intended to do. Confront her again? As I neared her place and saw the outbuilding with her Jeep parked there, I slowed but then drove past. To what purpose? I cooled off. Apparently, the woman doesn't come to church anymore. I will just leave it be.

And pray that she will do the same.

I gassed up at the BP and learned a lot about what is going on in the parish. I made a mental note to discuss it with Sister Margaret. She is a cocky one. Give a woman an inch and she will take a mile. She is probably one of those wacky women who believe that a woman should be allowed to be a priest, something that clearly is disordered in God's plan. Still, she needs handling carefully.

Before returning, I turned down an access road that led to a quiet place along the river and got out of the car. I sat on a picnic table and watched the water rush by. I still remember my first-year philosophy teacher, Father Athanasius, talking about the philosopher Heraclitus. Heraclitus believed that change was the only reality. To illustrate, Heraclitus taught that a person couldn't put a foot into the same river twice. In fact, a person can't do it even once because, between the times the toe goes in and the heel goes in, the water flowing around the foot has changed. This river is ancient and has many spirits hovering over it. I sense them about me now. Spirits of the unbaptized as well as the baptized. Spirits that are wrestling with their pain. Spirits that are calling to me now. I feel one standing beside me now.

One like my own.

Thus is it willed where there is power for that which is willed. Ask no more. Isn't that what the ferryman said?

After an hour I left. It is comforting to know that the river will go on without me, after I am ferried across it, as it has since before humans ever lived on its shores.

Rachel

I TOOK THAT PISTOL OUT back of the shed and shot at tin cans the other day. I am actually not a bad shot. I must have used up a whole box of bullets out there. At first it scared Vergil, but then he seemed fascinated at what I was doing. He wanted to do it too so I showed him how. He fired at the cans and missed of course. Then after a while, he could hit them too. Not consistently, but every now and then.

That helped get rid of some of the rage. But not all of it.

Saturday afternoon, I watched the clock. Then I left around four and drove to the church.

I stood in line behind an older woman and by the time I

climbed into the booth there was no one else in the church. The door slid open.

"Bless me, Father, for I have sinned. It has probably been more than a quarter century since my last confession."

"That's a long time," the bastard said in his soothing voice.

"I am overcome by a desire to commit murder."

"My. You must be very angry. Who is it you want to murder?"

"You."

There wasn't a sound in the church for maybe fifteen seconds.

"Me? Why would you want to murder me?"

"You know, when we took the blood money from the diocese all those years ago, we were put under the seal of the confessional. Okay. I'm in the confessional. So I can tell you, in here, exactly what I think.

"How dare you? How dare you come back into our lives and dredge it all up again? I would have thought they would have sent you to some far off island somewhere to rot. But no. You have no business here."

"Excuse me, but you are making a sacrilege of this sacrament!" He was outraged.

"It is you who are doing that! It is you who make a sacrilege of everything holy you dish out, you who commits sacrilege by showing up in our lives and walking around as though you have every right to parade your sanctimony in front of God and everyone who goes here. Did you actually think people wouldn't remember?" I was not making any attempt to keep my voice down now.

"That is quite enough," he said. "Get out of here now." The window slid shut and I heard him stand and open the door. I was right behind him.

Suddenly, I saw myself face to face with the man who had defiled my son. I wanted to claw his eyes out, but all I could do was holler at him.

"You go and crawl back under whatever rock you disappeared under all those years ago and leave us in peace, you bastard!"

Then I turned and walked away. I was shaking. I was on

the verge of tears, but I'll be damned if I was going to let him see me cry. I ran to my Jeep and pulled away from the church just as he opened the side door and walked quickly toward the rectory.

I thanked God that I hadn't brought the pistol.

"FORGIVENESS. THAT IS AT THE heart of Christ's message."

There were about fifty people in the congregation this morning. The air conditioner was working overtime but it was still very warm inside the church. Father Corrigan took a swallow from a tumbler of water that sat underneath the pulpit.

"You remember when Our Lord encountered the woman who had sinned? What did she do? She cried tears and they dripped onto his feet, and then wiped his feet clean with her hair. The others were outraged. This was a woman of the streets they told him. But what did he do? He admonished *them*. He had come and taken his seat and none of them had offered to wipe his feet, which was customarily an act of hospitality, but this woman was doing it with her tears. He looked kindly at her and sent her on her way to live her life in peace.

"It is easy for us to judge others, unless we have walked in their shoes. The people who sat at the table with Our Lord did just that. It was they, not the woman who had lived a life in sin, whom he condemned.

"Let us remember that. As you forgive, so are you forgiven."

IT WAS ABOUT THREE IN the afternoon when Alice pulled in front of the church. She saw a black Crown Vic parked in front. She didn't think anything about it.

"Grab your things, boys."

Adam got out of the back seat and picked up his gym bag. He was obviously not thrilled about his new arrangements. Erik, on the other hand, bounded out and ran up the steps to ring the doorbell.

Alice stopped when the door opened and there stood, not Sister Margaret, but a big priest with a wide smile on his face.

"Well, well," the priest said. "And what is your name?"

"Erik." Erik wasn't a bit shy. Then Corrigan looked over his shoulder at the older boy who had just stepped up on the porch.

"And yours?"

At first Adam didn't say anything. Then his mother walked up next to him.

"His name is Adam. I'm Alice."

"Well, come in. By all means."

They walked into the rectory. Margaret was standing near the doorway to the office. She widened her eyes in an attempt to convey to Alice that it was okay. Alice looked confused so Margaret decided to speak up.

"Father Corrigan knows about our temporary arrangement, Alice. We discussed it and he is fine with you staying here."

"Oh."

"Yes. I think it is wonderful that you have such a friend in Sister Margaret. I wanted to welcome you personally." He turned again to Adam. "How old are you son?"

Adam looked at his mother before answering. She nodded her head.

"Thirteen."

"Well, I hope you are comfortable here, Adam. Perhaps when I come down next weekend we can spend some time getting to know one another."

"Boys, go on up to the rooms and put your stuff away," Alice said. She was clearly nervous. "If you don't mind, Father, I will too."

"By all means," Corrigan said. "I'm heading back and I will see you next weekend. Needless to say, you won't have to clear out next time before I get here."

"Thanks, Father," Alice said before turning and going up the stairs.

"Nice looking kids," Corrigan said. "I'll be off now. I'm fine with this, but please try not to bring in any more strays between now and next week," he said flashing a smile.

"I'll try to remember that, Father."

"Yes. You do that. Have a good week."

"Same to you."

Margaret closed the door behind her and stood with her back to the door and let out a long breath.

"**I ALMOST WET MY PANTS** when he opened the front door." Alice was putting dishes in the dishwasher. Her hair was tied into a ponytail and she wore a tank top and shorts. "I thought you weren't going to tell him."

"That's the beauty of living in a town the size of Grafton. He stopped at the gas station and Charley Robson was working. Charley makes everything his business and he spilled the beans. I hadn't anticipated that."

"But he was okay with it. Are you surprised?"

"No. Shocked." She was anxious too but she didn't want to bring that up.

"I mentioned to mom that he was the new priest down here. She was surprised because they sent another priest to Jerseyville after Father Kennelly left."

"Oh?"

Alice turned around and leaned against the countertop. "I don't know whether I should mention this or not."

"Okay."

"It's probably idle gossip. But mom grew up in Jerseyville. When she was a kid something happened there but she wasn't sure what it was."

"Happened? I'm not sure what you mean."

"When Father Corrigan was there. It was a lot of years ago. There were rumors but she didn't pay much attention to them."

"About Father Corrigan."

"Yeah."

Margaret's face flushed and her stomach turned a bit. The chili sauce that she had covered her hot dogs with started to do flip-flops.

"What kind of rumors?"

"Well, some of the kids were talking about him and some of the altar boys. But it wasn't so much the rumors that she remembered as it was what her uncle told her mother once when he was at the house."

"Her uncle?"

"Yeah. Uncle Pete was the police chief then. He said that he drove to Springfield and met with someone at the diocese. He told them that either they pull Corrigan out of the parish or he would arrest him."

"Did she know why?"

"No, but it doesn't take much imagination."

"What happened?"

"I guess shortly after that Corrigan left the parish. I was thinking about that when he was talking with Adam. I wanted to throw up. You don't suppose …."

"Well, I don't want to suppose anything but for the time being we will just have to make sure that Father Corrigan isn't around the boys."

"If you don't mind, I will probably go back to mom's next Saturday. The lesser of two evils. Surely the diocese wouldn't do that. They wouldn't send a priest to a parish who had problems like that."

Margaret was biting her cuticles again.

"I would like to think not. But don't worry. As long as I am here you are all safe."

"Sister, I so much appreciate your help. But I don't know how much longer I can take advantage of this. You know Tommy's out?"

"Yes. Bob Burton came by. But right now this is the safest place for you. The police are watching the rectory."

"I feel so bad taking advantage of you."

"You aren't taking advantage of me. I asked you, remember. Besides, I really enjoy the company. You are doing me a favor."

"But I can't mooch off of you."

"I don't expect you to. You cooked supper tonight, didn't you?"

"Hot dogs and potato chips? Yeah, I'm a real gourmet cook."

Margaret's stomach did another tumble. "Well, *I* didn't have to cook. So you can cook every now and then. You can even pick up some groceries. Who knows, I might even ask you to help around the office."

"I will be happy to."

"Then when things quiet down we can work on getting you a better place to stay. Someplace where the boys will be comfortable. A trailer doesn't quite cut it—no offense."

"None taken. But it will be a while before I am able to do something like that."

"Whatever it takes. I'm in no hurry. Meanwhile, you have a roof over your head, the boys have their own rooms, and we have a television. And maybe now that you haven't as far to go and as many complications you can start attending church more regularly."

"I knew there was a catch!"

"You better believe it." Margaret reached over and patted Alice's good arm.

"Oh, there's one other thing."

Alice looked suspiciously at her. "And that would be?"

"I exercise in the mornings. That means you do too."

"Exercise?"

"Yes. You know. Get up. Move around."

"Uh, you *jog*. Do I look like I can jog?"

"You can walk. So can I."

Alice looked down at her stomach. "Well, I don't suppose it would hurt any."

"Actually, it will help immensely."

"You're not saying I'm fat, are you?" She laughed.

"I'm saying we can both use it!"

They were interrupted by some commotion from upstairs.

"Well, you will find out what it is like raising two boys, that's for sure," Alice said as she walked through the office and up the stairs. "What in God's name is going on up there?" She screamed.

Margaret smiled. She glanced over at the half-empty bottle of Yellowtail. She decided she didn't need it tonight.

At one in the morning she awoke. It had been a mistake not to have that glass of wine. So she went downstairs.

From Melvin Barstow's Notebook

April 15, 1968

Doctor Engfresch is pleased with my writing. But it makes me nauseous. I didn't want to go on. I had a bad spell a week ago and Catherine was terrified of me. I wonder if the medicine is working as well. I almost struck her. She ran out of the house.

I have been okay since. I will try to pick up where I left off.

A week or so after confession, my dad came home drunk again. Mom was feeding baby Eli, and he threw a bowl at her. It struck Eli a glancing blow and Eli started screaming. My dad told mom to shut him the fuck up. I had had enough. I picked up a vase of flowers off the table, dumped the water, and threw it at him. It struck him right between the eyes. My mom screamed because she knew what was going to happen next. He staggered and felt the blood running down his face. He looked at me and said, "I'm going to kill you, little spawn of Satan!" Then he lunged for me and caught me by the shirt. It ripped and I struggled out of it but not before he clobbered me with the back of his other hand. I hit the leg of a chair and blacked out. When I woke up, he was gone and mom was holding me. I went to my room and shut the door. That night I got out the Life magazine. Afterward, I cried.

I was serving mass that week. I got there about ten after six and when Father C. walked in he noticed the lump on the back of my head. He asked if I was okay and I started to cry. Then he opened his arms and reached out to me. I put my head on his stomach. I remember that it was soft, like a pillow, and it rose and fell as he breathed. I can't smell Old Spice any more without remembering Father C.

After Mass Billy Meyerscough—the kid who had been assigned early mass with me—left and Father C. told me to stay. He told me he understood that I was struggling with many things and asked what he could do. I didn't say anything.

"You're still doing it, aren't you?"

I knew what he was talking about. I shook my head.

"We must fight it, Melvin. I can help you and you can help me. You want to do that don't you? You don't want to spend eternity in the darkness of hell, do you?" I assured him I did not.

He walked over and closed the door that led to the altar, and put the latch on the door that went outside. He took the cincture from the vestment closet and told me to kneel down. Then he put my hands behind me and tied them together with the cincture. "This will help us fight the devil, Melvin. Trust me." I guess I did. Even when he unbuttoned his cassock and unzipped his trousers. My heart began to beat so fast I thought it would explode, and when his thing popped out it was huge.

"You must take it into your mouth, Melvin. It is the only way." I protested, but then he took my head in his hands and directed my face onto the large, purple thing that stood out of his pants. I did it. I did it until he moaned and the white, milky stuff squirted all over my face and down on my cassock. Then, he undid the cincture, and brought me to my feet and hugged me again. I honestly don't remember what I was feeling. I guess I believed that I was helping him, but somehow I felt like I was doing something wrong. But I couldn't be, could I? Father needed my help.

In the months that followed I helped Father again and again. Several times in the rectory he helped me.

I'm sorry. I can't do this anymore. What he did was wrong. So very wrong. I never wanted to admit this because somehow I felt that he did it because I wanted him to. Was I to blame? For years, I thought so. It all started because I looked at dirty pictures. Or worse. They weren't that dirty. I made them dirty. The white radiance of my eternity would be stained for all time.

Catherine tempted me. I failed at seminary and settled for teaching in Alton at St. Justin's. I kept the faith. I continued to fight temptation. I put Father C. out of my mind. I had managed to protect my little brother. After dad died, I knew he would be okay. He and I are very close. He never goes to church any more and mom doesn't seem to try too hard to make him. I love him.

Catherine wore dark red lipstick. Like Grace. She was nice to me. I asked her to dinner and then we were going out a lot. To movies, dinner. Then one night, I was overcome by temptation once more and fell into sin. We married shortly thereafter. What else could we do? We had sinned.

I am feeling better for the most part. But sometimes I still fall into temptation. When I get like that, I have Catherine kneel with me and pray. But she doesn't' seem to mind temptation.

She actually lay down and begged me to do it to her.

She doesn't understand. She will suffer for all eternity.

I must go and take care of the horses.

It is a beautiful day today. I shouldn't worry. God will take care of me.

Father Seamus left and went to Vietnam. He had helped me. He was a good priest. He was my priest. He loved me. I just didn't understand that.

Catherine is yelling for me to come eat. I am not hungry. I don't want to look at her.

I must go and take care of the horses.

I'm not going to do this anymore. I don't feel I need to. I will pray instead.

God will help me through this. I just need to pray. I don't want to burn in hell but that may be what I deserve. God help me. God help us all.

Eli

THE REAR ENTRANCE OF MELVIN'S house led into the kitchen. The room was in a shambles. Dishes were broken. Two of the kitchen chairs were turned over and a cabinet door was hanging by one hinge. A storm had passed through, or so it seemed. But Melvin wasn't anywhere to be seen.

I was breathing so fast and my heart was racing. I was afraid I would pass out. I went into the living room and fell onto the sofa. Then I reached over and picked up a phone and started to call the operator. Then I noticed something. Something outside.

I got up and walked over to the front window. There was an expanse of lawn and on the other side of it was the paddock. There was a metal horse trough under a tree in one corner.

Why would smoke be coming from a horse trough?

I set the phone down and walked out through the front door. I opened the gate to the paddock and walked over to the trough. I saw four large gas cans lying around, apparently empty. The smell I had smelled earlier got worse and was starting to gag me.

Then I saw the axe. It was black with blood and hair was matted on the blade. I then noticed a hole near the bottom of the trough that looked like it had been made with an axe. It took some real rage to chop through that. The water had emptied out and the ground I was standing on was still saturated. It squished beneath my boots. The trough had been drained and a towel stuffed into the hole.

Then I went close and saw what was in the trough.

The smell alone made me turn and lose whatever was in my stomach. I walked away and threw up some more. I remember the two horses looking at me. They were skittish. They sensed that this was human business they had best keep their distance from.

I finally got the courage to look again. I couldn't tell for sure what I was seeing at first. It looked like a burnt mannequin sitting there. It was black, charred, burnt beyond recognition. It was small, shrunken. But there was a head, black and brittle though it was. The thing appeared to have arms that were held out straight but there were no hands at the ends of them. Nor were any feet visible at the ends of the stubs that looked like legs that were holding the ghoulish thing in a sitting position. The thing was still smoldering. It had gone through an inferno.

I backed away and fell to my knees and onto the saturated ground. I knew what I was looking at. What I would be seeing in dreams from that day to this.

The two horses that had given silent witness to the burnt offering of Melvin Barstow were the only ones who heard my scream.

'OH GOD! MELVIN!"

"YOU'RE KILLING ME," ALICE SAID.

"We're only on Main Street, for heaven's sake."

"You gotta understand. My idea of exercise is to walk from the TV to the fridge."

"And that, Alice, is precisely the problem. You need endorphins."

"Endorphins. Aren't they illegal?"

"Endorphins. The hypothalamus and the pancreas naturally produce them during strenuous activity. They call it a runner's high. It stimulates your brain."

"Isn't there another way to get them?"

"Well, orgasms produce them," Margaret said. "But that's an option not currently available to me."

Alice had to stop because she was laughing. "Truth is, it hasn't been available to me either. Most guys just grunt and go."

Margaret didn't say anything. A fleeting memory of the night she spent with Bill Templeton in the back of his cruiser several years back passed through her head.

"Well," Margaret said, "I always suspected that celibacy was like marriage—after the honeymoon phase."

"I think I am going to quit trying. It always ends up bad."

"I've read that you only find something when you aren't looking. Maybe that's true of love."

"Love? Funny, but when you are younger I don't know whether you think about love. You just think about having someone so you aren't alone. But then, it seems, you're lonelier than ever with someone there."

"Yeah. We started lowering our standards about lots of stuff some time back. Doesn't have to be that way though. Hopefully, it won't always be."

"My mom had lots of boyfriends. None of them was very nice."

"And your dad?"

"He left when I was about five. I kind of remember him. He came back once to see me. He was married again and living in Kansas. Don't know why he bothered. He was a truck driver and he had a stopover in Illinois. Actually, though, he was kind of nice. I think I would actually have liked having him around. But mom was not easy to live with."

"Works both ways, Alice. Don't be too hard on your mom."

"What about you? Your mom and dad."

"Mom died when I was too little to remember. Car accident. My dad was sheriff up in Morgan County. I spent the first twelve years of my life living in an apartment attached to the County Jail. He was a great dad though. He never married again. Being sheriff and raising a headstrong daughter was all he cared about. I guess I was lucky, although I sometimes wished he had someone to love. When I got a little older, anyway. I thought he sacrificed everything for me."

"I heard Chief Burton say you used to be a deputy sheriff. I gotta stop. Really." Alice walked over and leaned up against an old oak tree to catch her breath.

"I was a deputy in Sangamon County for quite a few years before going into the convent."

"That explains how you took Tommy down. Good stuff to know."

"Haven't done anything like that in a while. Guess it kind of stays with you. You ready? We can just head back. Baby steps."

"Just drop me off at the clinic."

"Nearest one is in Alton. That's the other way."

"In that case, just shoot me. Shoot me now."

ON **MONDAY, AFTER ALICE TOOK** the boys to school and went to work at Maybelle's, Margaret called the chancery.

"Ann, this is Sister Margaret in Grafton."

"Good morning, Sister. How can I help you?" For some reason Margaret always envisioned Ann, whom she had never met, as having a tight bun on top of her head that squeezed so hard it sucked out her humor and her humanity.

"I need to speak with the Bishop, or perhaps the chancellor."

"The Bishop isn't in town this week, and the chancellor is quite busy. Perhaps I can be of assistance."

"Could you have the chancellor call me back, Ann? I am becoming quite concerned about some recent incidents here in the parish."

"What kind of incidents?"

Margaret was biting her cuticles. She didn't want to go too deeply into this with Ann Fisher, but the woman blocked access to the power structure as efficiently as Cerberus, the three-headed dog of Hades, kept souls from escaping across the River Styx.

"Well, Ann, I don't know how to characterize them. But they seem to stem from several peoples' reactions to Father Corrigan. I don't know why."

"People take a while to adjust to a new priest."

"Do they normally throw up?"

Ann didn't say anything. Margaret had her attention.

"I'm sure it's nothing," she said finally. "I will mention this to Father Corredato."

"Please do that. And I would appreciate a call back as soon as possible."

"He's very busy but I am sure he will get back with you as soon as he can."

"Well, that's good because I may have a situation here and I want to have some idea what I am up against. I don't think that's unreasonable."

"Of course, Sister."

Ann Fisher didn't have many social skills but being patronizing was one she had perfected.

"Good. I'll look for his call."

Margaret hung up the phone. Hard.

"Bitch!"

Then she blessed herself.

LIFE AT THE RECTORY SOON worked its way into a routine. Now that school had started, Alice took the boys before going to work and picked them up after school. Alice bought groceries once a week, and she and Margaret worked out a cooking schedule. Alice was to cook on Mondays and Wednesdays, Margaret on Tuesdays and Thursdays. On Fridays, Alice planned to take the boys somewhere to eat and Margaret would stay home, eat leftovers and put the finishing touches on the Sunday liturgy and bulletin.

The boys had settled in and seemed content, at last, in their new surroundings. Adam, however, was still quiet around Margaret. She discussed her fears about depression with Alice, but since Alice did not have insurance she believed her hands were tied. Margaret offered to call Stephen Rundix, a doctor in Grafton who was a Christmas and Easter member of the parish, to see if he might see Adam as a favor to her. Alice was reluctant at first but finally agreed. Margaret wrote it down on her task list and told Alice she would make the call.

She telephoned the diocese twice more, only have a clearly aggravated Ann tell her in a very polite and officious manner that Father was unavailable, that he had been apprised of her concern, and that he would call her as soon as he possibly could. The subtext was clear: *Don't call us, we'll call you.*

As of Thursday—almost a week after she had first called—Father Corredato had not called her back.

SANTINO "SONNY" CORREDATO WAS a cool customer. Rarely did he get flustered, even in a heated confrontation. This made him perfect for the role of chancellor of the diocese, particularly in parish meetings where the subject of parish consolidation was being discussed. People can get ugly when their parish churches are threatened with closure.

But over lunch at Saputo's Italian Restaurant with John Calhoun, one of the attorneys for the diocese, he found his cool hard to maintain. He had ignored the persistent calls from that nun in

Grafton, and happened to mention this annoyance in passing over a glass of Scotch. Calhoun became quiet for a minute, then asked what it was concerning. Sonny mentioned Father Corrigan and noted that he had little patience with parish administrators, particularly nuns, complaining about their priests. "It's not like we have a bunch to choose from," he said. "She should be glad she's got one at all. He's quirky as hell, but he's a priest!"

Calhoun wiped his face, set his napkin on the table, and scooted his chair back.

Then he told Sonny something that chilled, but which upon reflection should not have surprised him about Seamus Corrigan.

Sonny listened carefully and became increasingly whey faced. When Calhoun finished, Sonny downed what was left of his Cutty on the rocks.

"So how in hell is it that nobody bothered to mention this to the chancellor of the diocese?"

"It was an oversight," Calhoun said. "The records are sealed, and it was thirty years ago. I only happened upon it myself when I was going through some papers in preparation for the audits. When you mentioned the name Corrigan...."

"*Dammit, John.* We talked about it eight months ago when Seamus asked to come back here from Texas to be near his sister. Van Dyke was sitting there in the meeting."

"To be fair, Sonny, Van Dyke probably had no idea either."

"You mean, this whole thing had been buried so deep you couldn't even find it?"

"For thirty years, I'm afraid. Once sealed, it was forgotten."

Sonny processed this for a minute or two.

"So, John, how many more are there like this one?"

Calhoun looked at him and then shrugged his shoulders.

"Find out," he said.

Sonny stood up and threw two twenty-dollar bills on the table.

"This is just fucking perfect," he said. Then he turned and walked out of the restaurant.

SONNY CORREDATO WAS CONSIDERED a *wunderkind* when he was a student at Saint Dominic's High School. There he excelled in academics and athletics. He was a running back on the football team that made it to the state for the first time in the school's history. Tall, broad shouldered, with a thick mane of black hair and Hollywood good looks, he shocked all of his classmates by announcing at the end of his senior year that he was entering the seminary. There he continued to excel in his studies and, after he graduated from Mundelein, the diocese sent him to the American College in Rome. He spent four years there and was awarded a Doctorate in Sacred Theology. When he returned to Springfield, a prominent place in the chancery awaited him.

He had been chancellor for ten years and in that time had served three bishops.

The first, Bishop Erik Kjellander, had stepped down in the wake of allegations that he cruised the streets of Springfield picking men—some allegedly underage—up off the streets. Kjellander staunchly denied the allegations. In time, as public concern—fueled by an aggressive publicity campaign by local victims rights advocates—began to grow, the church decided that it had had enough. The scandal wrought by the abuse of young people by priests was rocking the church worldwide and the bishop's activities—even if unproven—were not making the problem any easier to manage. So, Kjellander "retired."

Corredato knew the truth about Kjellander. The older man's activities were sometimes overheard in the residence at night. He also suspected that Kjellander had encounters in his office. His suspicions were confirmed when he went to his office early one morning before the building was open. There he encountered the bishop coming down the stairwell wearing a sleeveless A-shirt, black trousers, his belt loosened, and loafers with no socks. Then Sonny heard footsteps start down the stairs from above, only to reverse when whoever it was sensed someone else in the stairwell and go back up, closing the steel door behind. Kjellander had clearly not been expecting to encounter anyone, judging by the look on his face. Corredato simply said "Good morning, Bishop," and went on up to his office.

Most of the men in high positions were placed there because Kjellander could trust them—and for very good reasons. Sonny preceded Kjellander, but he was thought to be trustworthy and so retained his position. But he was relieved when Kjellander was sent into retirement. He had his own peccadilloes, albeit he was more discreet, and he did not savor the possibility of having a spotlight shining on the chancery.

A younger man who had formerly served as chancellor to the diocese of Cincinnati, Robert Van Dyke, replaced Kjellander. Van Dyke was a scholar and had a good reputation as a fundraiser and disciplinarian. He adopted a new openness regarding priest-pedophiles, openly settled a number of cases to the tune of six million dollars, and formed a committee to "investigate" activities in the diocese. This amounted to little more than a public relations ploy and terminated with a report that shone a light on the activities of the former bishop (no surprise there), and one or two other priests whose activities were already publicly known and for which the diocese had paid dearly. And then, as though nothing had ever occurred, the problem seemed to go away. Collections were picking up and the faithful, it seemed, were placated. The quiet and affable bishop had pulled the diocese out of the doldrums and things were once again on an even keel.

The current bishop, who was appointed after Van Dyke resigned for health reasons, was a very different sort. Bishop Greg Patterson, formerly adjutant Bishop of Minneapolis, Minnesota, was a former lawyer who joined the priesthood late in life after the death of his wife and daughter in an automobile accident. Whereas Kjellander was portly and jocular, and Van Dyke serious and somewhat effeminate, Patterson was a tall, well-formed man whom women found attractive for his thick mane of salt-and-pepper hair and his bright blue eyes. He was in his sixties, but from the look of him he could easily knock another man down. This was no accident: Patterson used his own money to install a workout room in the chancery. The bishop's attention to fitness did not affect his chain-smoking, however, and Sonny sometimes found himself discussing important matters out in the quad (summer or winter) while the bishop finished an unfiltered Camel. Physical strength aside, Sonny soon learned that the bishop could be most devastating with a few well-chosen and imminently logical words. Patterson's years as an attorney had served him well.

Most of the men who had been appointed by Kjellander still held their positions in the chancery office. Corredato was not surprised that Van Dyke had kept them on, since many of them had been Van Dyke's students at Mundelein. It was somewhat surprising, however, that Patterson had kept them on board. But he had only been in office for a few months, and now there were rumors that he was thinking about making changes. The new bishop was biding his time and marking the territory.

Corredato didn't want to be among those changes. He gloried in his position of power and authority and had worked far too long to obtain and maintain his preeminence. His indiscretions had never been widely known and he was careful to keep them private. He chose his partners carefully and they, like him, were men who had a lot to lose. His current love interest had been with him for several years now. So far he had managed to stay on the right side of the new bishop and planned to keep it that way.

But Sonny Corredato was about to learn that his private life wasn't as well cloaked as he thought.

ON THURSDAY EVENING, CORREDATO WALKED down the hall of the Cathedral residence and knocked on Father Corrigan's door. He knew what he had to do. It wasn't going to be easy.

"Just a minute," Corrigan said. Corredato heard the older priest moving around and shuffling across the floor. When the door opened, Corrigan was in his stocking feet but still dressed in black. His top shirt button was open and his white mini tab stuck straight out from the left side of his collar. He smelled faintly of alcohol, disguised quickly and inadequately with mouthwash.

"Can I have a minute, Seamus?"

"Sure, Sonny. Come in. Have a seat."

Corredato sat on a love seat opposite the recliner where Corrigan sat. A lamp on the end table dimly lighted the room and the blinds were drawn so that late summer sun made no inroads. A large Spanish crucifix with dried palm fronds stuck under the legs of the corpus was the only adornment on any of the walls. A large bookshelf containing hundreds of tomes stood on one side of the room, and a large LG flat screen TV hung on another.

"I wanted to mention something to you about Grafton."

"Yes. Lovely little town. I am going back Saturday."

Seamus, your services are not going to be needed in Grafton any more. I'm sorry. I should never have offered it to you and that I regret. Now, however, I must recall you.

That was what he was going to say. But he couldn't. Just yet. He became suddenly, haltingly conscious of the long-standing bond that existed between him and the older man.

"That's what I wanted to talk with you about, Seamus. You know, a parish moderator doesn't have to be there every weekend. The position is canonically necessary, but your presence is not. Other priests who are closer can cover it for you. Even when Father Kennelly was moderator, as close as he was he only went there infrequently."

"It's no problem, Sonny. It's a beautiful drive, and it gets me out and about. It's a good feeling being a part of a parish again. It isn't hurting me at all. I'm as healthy as ever. Besides, I have nothing but time on my hands. It ...helps."

Corredato could see the bottom of a Jack Daniels bottle half hidden by a tablecloth covering the end table next to Corrigan's chair. The glass from which Corrigan had been drinking was under the table as well but was not hidden at all. He sat silently for about a minute. Corrigan suddenly became anxious and pushed the recliner up straight.

"It...*isn't* a problem, is it, Sonny?"

"I don't know, Seamus. I received a call from the nun there. She wanted to talk with me about some people down there. She seems to think that they might be upset ... well, that they may have had an unpleasant experience and that your presence there may be bringing some of it back."

Ann Fisher's description of the problem had been perfunctory, as indeed had Sister Margaret's. But, after what Calhoun briefed him over lunch, Corredato realized what a horrible mistake he had made.

"Sonny, what are you saying?" Corrigan's eyes welled up, and his face was turning red. For a moment, Corredato thought the old priest was going to burst into tears.

"All I am saying, Seamus, is that...there may be a problem. There was, after all, that unfortunate situation in Jerseyville years ago. We don't want to dredge that up again."

Corrigan's expression went from sadness to anger.

"That happened when you were a snot-nosed kid, Sonny. You weren't there. You don't know what went on. Those kids were lying and their parents were out to get whatever they could. It was a witch-hunt. It's a fine thing when a few disgruntled parishioners can drive a priest out of a parish with innuendo."

Corrigan sat back in his chair, his anger somewhat abated.

"Sonny, come on. I remember having you in class in the junior seminary. We ...*helped each other*. Remember? Help me now."

Corredato remembered. Turmoil began to boil up in his stomach as he remembered the "counseling" sessions conducted by Corrigan in a student room at the junior seminary, sessions in which Corrigan eventually "helped" him with his weakness. It had been his baptism into Corrigan's "mutual relief" society. It had clarified his sexual orientation and cast a shadow over his vocation that still hovered. For an instant he wanted to throw up. Instead, he stood up.

He was about to bring down the hammer when Corrigan's tone went from angry to conspiratorial.

"How's your...friend...over in...Decatur, isn't it?"

Sonny's face turned beet red. *Go ahead, Seamus was saying. Cast the first stone.* A paralyzing dread filled him and he found himself near tears. *After all, he had had sex with this man.*

"Seamus, I am helping you. I have given you a mission. Now, I must ask that you conduct that mission more circumspectly. Let there be spaces in your togetherness with the people in Grafton. That is all you need do. You don't have to go every week."

Sonny was horrified about the way his resolve had melted so quickly in the face of his old mentor.

Corrigan stood up.

"Okay, Sonny. I am gong Saturday, but I will have the nun make other arrangements after that and then make occasional visits. As you say."

Corredato suddenly felt the old man's pain and a prophetic vision of himself facing a like and lonely future filled with regret flashed before his eyes. He reached over and touched the old man's arm.

"Thanks, Seamus. That's all I am asking."

Corredato walked out of the door, but turned before he walked away.

"And Seamus? I am helping you. I always have."

"I know, Sonny. You're a good boy. You always were."

IT WAS AROUND FOUR AND Rachel Atkins was working in the garden. Vergil hadn't been weeding lately. He just wandered around the place, sometimes piddling with his tools in the shed, sometimes just sitting down by the mailbox waiting for the postman. That was where he was when she started. When she stood up half an hour later, she looked down and saw that Vergil wasn't at the mailbox any more. She knew the mail hadn't come. She picked up the basket of weeds and began walking around the house. She heard the side door of the house slam, and then…heard the Taurus start up. She dropped the basket and ran around in time to see Vergil backing the car out of the shed and then watched as he turned it and drove out onto the road.

She screamed, "Vergil! *No!*" She ran into the house to grab the keys, and then to the shed where she jumped into the Jeep. She backed out and turned quickly toward the road. He had gone north on the blacktop. She had to catch him. He hadn't driven in years. If she lost him, she might never see him alive again.

She saw him get on the highway, her heart pounding. She turned onto the highway and was about a tenth of a mile behind him. He was doing sixty-five. She sped up to stay with him.

"Oh God, Vergil! Oh God!" This could be bad. She needed help. She grabbed her cell phone and rang the first person she could think of, almost losing control of the wheel in the process.

"THIS IS SISTER MARGARET."

"Sister, this is Rachel. Vergil got in the car and is headed toward town. He may be coming to the rectory." Her voice reflected the panic in her heart.

"I'm in the car now just leaving the rectory," Margaret said. "Where is he?"

"He is coming up on Main Street."

"I'm going in that direction. Stay with him." She pushed a speed dial button that was connected to the police station. A man answered.

"This is Sister Margaret from St. Alban's. We have a situation. Vergil Atkins apparently took his mother's car and is heading for town on the highway."

"Verge? Jesus. Didn't know he could drive."

"Well, he can. The problem is we don't know where he will go or why. I am going to try to head him off, and his mom is following him. You might want to send a car to help us. I pray we won't need you, but you need to have a head's up."

"This is Jim Jenkins, Sister. I'll call it in."

"Thanks, Jim."

Margaret was approaching the highway when she saw the Taurus at the stop sign. The car, with Vergil driving, turned west and sped up. She passed the intersection just as Rachel arrived at the stop sign. Rachel turned onto the highway and followed. Margaret hit the speed dial.

"Jim? He just turned west onto Main Street from the highway. I am right behind him and Rachel is behind me."

"Gotcha!"

About a mile past the Fin Inn, she saw Vergil's car turn off the highway onto an access road that went to the river.

"Oh, Mother of God!" Margaret was afraid that he would drive right into the river. She hit the accelerator and, coming up on the access road, swung hard in behind Vergil.

As she neared the river she saw the car. It was stopped. She slowed and pulled up behind it. When she got out, she saw Vergil standing by the riverbank.

Then, she saw what Vergil had in his hands.

He was holding a pistol.

Rachel pulled up behind her, got out and started to run toward Vergil. Margaret grabbed her arm.

"Rachel, he's holding a gun. Where did he get a gun?"

Rachel put her hand to her mouth. "Oh God! No! He must have taken it from the dresser drawer."

"Okay. Just settle down. Let's go, quietly and carefully. Just stay with me and don't excite him." Margaret could see that Rachel was in a bad way. She didn't need two problems.

They walked slowly toward the bank and stopped about ten feet from Vergil. He was looking across the river.

"Vergil?" Margaret spoke softly.

Vergil turned slowly and looked at her.

"Hi, Sister. You still mad at me?"

"Vergil, I'm not mad at you. I'm here to help you."

"You know there are no cucumbers. Cucumbers. It's my fault. I was bad."

"You're not bad Vergil."

Vergil looked at her and his eyes began to fill up. A large tear eventually slid down his face. Then he looked at his mother.

"Mom? I'm sorry. I was bad."

"It's okay, Vergil. It's okay."

"Vergil, can I have the gun?" Margaret held out her hand. Vergil looked at her, and then looked at the gun. He whirled and fired six shots into the river just as the patrol car pulled in behind Rachel's car. The young cop, a woman named Clair Peterson, jumped out and pulled her service revolver. Margaret turned to her.

"Wait! Please. The gun's empty now."

"Sister, back off!" The officer had adopted a firing position.

Then Vergil turned around slowly and handed the pistol to Sister Margaret. He started to cry like a small child who had been caught doing something he shouldn't. Rachel ran up, threw her arms around him, and rocked him slightly back and forth. Then she began to bawl in relief.

"I had to fix it, Mom."

"Thank God. Thank God. I love you, Vergil. I love you."

The officer holstered her pistol and held her hand out. Margaret gave her the gun. She popped the cylinder and ejected the six empty cartridges.

"What in hell is going on?" the officer asked.

"If you'll let them go home, I will explain what happened. You can talk with Rachel later."

"Okay by me. He broke the law though, discharging that weapon."

"Not to mention driving without a license. He has...problems. But he isn't a problem. Bob Burton knows him."

"Okay, Sister. I'll take your word for it. Whose gun?"

"It belongs to Rachel. He must have taken it."

"Damned dangerous leaving guns around with someone like him in the house." She turned to Rachel who was walking Vergil back to the car. "You got a FOID card, ma'am?"

"Yeah."

"I'll bring this out later and check that card," the officer said. "I'll have someone drive the car back too."

"Thank you," Rachel said as she put Vergil in the passenger side of the Jeep. Then she looked at Margaret.

"And thank you, Sister. Thank you for helping my son."

MARGARET WAS DESPERATE NOW AND tired of being ignored by the chancery.

"Ann, I am still waiting on Father Corredato—or somebody—to call me back. It's Friday and I called Monday."

"Sister, I will tell Father you called. I am certain...."

"I am certain he will call me back when he gets damned good and ready, but I need to talk with him now. I don't think he wants this problem to bite him in the ass, and if he keeps avoiding me...."

"Sister, foul language isn't going to help you one bit. Remember your place. I will tell him you called."

"My place is parish life coordinator for this parish. I am doing that job but I am badly in need of some assistance from the diocese that gladly accepts whatever donations it can get from these people!"

The line went dead. Margaret slammed the phone down. She didn't know whether to scream or cry. Why? Why couldn't she talk to someone? Anyone. Maybe she overstepped her bounds, but she didn't know what else to do.

It took another hour, but finally a call came in on the bat phone.

"St. Alban's, this is Sister Margaret."

"Sister Margaret, this is Father Corredato. I am so sorry that I didn't get back with you sooner. Ann Fisher said some things that have been going on in the parish upset you. How can I be of assistance?"

Upset me? Margaret sat down.

"Father, I simply need to know if there is anything about Father Corrigan's past that I should be aware of. I have had several...situations that lead me to believe that certain of our parishioners remember him—and not favorably. These people may have known him from Jerseyville some years ago. I am not trying to dig up dirt, Father, but if I have to work with these people I need to understand what I am up against."

"Well, Sister, I gathered it might be something like that when I read the message, so I went through all our records here and I can assure you that there is not one iota of information in any of our records concerning any un-priestly conduct on the part of Seamus Corrigan. I do know, however, that Seamus can rub people the wrong way at times and has a tendency to say what he thinks. He's considered the diocese's archconservative. I think he was even a member of the John Birch Society at one time. Perhaps some of the people who reacted to his views were among those who didn't care for him. But if you are worried about anything...well anything such as I think you are worried about, I certainly cannot substantiate anything like that based on what we have here. I'm sorry."

"Well, I simply needed to know and I thank you for calling back." A lot of questions were going through her mind, but she didn't know what exactly to ask or how to follow up. But she had only a few minutes of a window here, given the difficulty of obtaining an audience with anyone in Springfield, so she took a shot.

"Father, could there be anything—anything *not* in the records at the diocese?"

Sonny took an audibly deep breath.

"I am not sure what you mean...or how I would know that since I am here at the diocese. You see?"

"Yes, I know. I take it you are not aware of anything like that."

This woman was starting to get under Sonny's skin. He almost said, *"Asked and answered."* Yes, he was aware of something. The courts, however, sealed it at the request of the diocese. So he was justified in stonewalling her. *He was just doing his duty.*

"Sister, I'm really sorry. I just don't have any information that can help you. But, given the bishop's insistence on transparency with regard to the kinds of things I think you are alluding to, I don't believe that a situation like this could come about. Again, I am sorry."

It struck Margaret that everything that Corredato just said constituted anything but an answer to her question. The bishop's insistence on "transparency," laudable as it was, was of recent origin and thus bringing it up was not responsive to her question. The only thing she got from what Corredato said was that she was getting all she was going to get out of this conversation.

SONNY CORREDATO HUNG UP THE phone. His stomach had been doing flip-flops ever since he picked up the phone to call her back. He rubbed his hand over the back of his neck and looked out his office window. He prayed that, after his talk with Seamus, things would settle down.

The last thing the diocese needed was another scandal.

The "past is the past" approach may have worked quite well at one time, but many of the claims that had been settled by the church in recent years stemmed from incidents twenty, thirty years ago. The problems with Seamus—about which he had been honestly unaware when he became chancellor and later recommended the older priest for the position of moderator at St. Alban's—had been settled, it is true. But what if others were to remember? How would this reflect on the diocese that had done so much recently to assure the faithful that they were doing everything on the up and up?

How would it reflect on him?

It should have come as no surprise to learn that there were many, many others whose lives had been touched by Seamus Corrigan in the same way that his had been when he was a very young man.

Sonny left his office and went into the empty Cathedral and knelt before the statue of the Virgin. He knelt and prayed for guidance, and prayed that nothing bad would come from his mistakes in judgment. From his inability to do what was expected of him in his office as chancellor.

"Mother of God," he prayed. *"Help me do what I haven't the strength, or the heart, to do."*

RACHEL HAD SLEPT UNTIL SEVEN. She spent much of the night crying. Before going to bed, she sat on the porch in the swing with her arm around Vergil.

"When you were a little boy," she told him, "you used to love to play baseball. You would throw the ball up in the air and try to catch it, but you didn't know that the ball didn't just fall in your glove. You had to follow the ball to catch it. Sometimes the ball would drop and hit you, and you would cry."

"Did you hold me?"

"Yes, I held you. Then I got you a softer ball. After that it was okay."

Vergil laughed. For a few minutes it was as though he didn't suffer from chronic brain damage, like he was her little boy again. He was a forty-year-old little boy, but her little boy nonetheless.

Rachel was encouraged by friends to put Vergil in a home where other severe traumatic brain injury persons lived, or at least to find one part-time. But the nearest place was too far away from her. For a mother who loved her son the way she did, a block away would have been a block too far. She never regretted taking care of Vergil at home. Yes, he was unpredictable. She never knew when she would have to endure one of his rants, catch him exposing himself by the road, or masturbating in the garden. After every such behavior, he would cry. The agonies of dealing with his condition were heartbreaking, but the moments when he hugged her and responded to tenderness were what kept her alive.

Some said that Vergil was lucky to be alive. She sometimes wondered, as painful as it was to admit. He had fallen into a bad crowd, drank and did drugs. The night of the accident he was riding with three other boys who were playing chicken across a busy road. The collision killed a family in a passing car and killed all of the boys except Vergil. And Vergil, in a sense, died that night too.

No one could know the horrors she endured after the accident. After he had been released from ICU, Vergil experienced episodes of "storming." They explained the physiology to her, but all she could remember were the horribly chaotic scenes in which Vergil had to be literally tied or held down on the bed to keep him from causing more damage to himself. She screamed during one of these fits, unable to endure it herself. It was like something from *The Exorcist*. At one point she prayed that he would die, because she couldn't stand to see him suffer like that. Her son was never going to be the same.

She knew that his choice, his terrible, irrevocable choice, was what led up to it. It was what had taken him away from her. But she never felt the same way about God after that.

She had long ago given up on the church. God was the last to go for her.

When it was time to go to bed, Vergil hugged her and said, "I love you mom."

Sometimes she just wanted to die, but Vergil was keeping her alive. Nights like that made it all worthwhile. Still, nothing she could do could change the past or make the present any better. She felt so helpless. So worthless.

When she awoke the next morning, Vergil wasn't in his bed. Not unusual. She went down and made coffee and started on some eggs and bacon. When breakfast was finished, she hollered out the side door for Vergil, but he didn't answer.

She poured another cup of coffee and looked outside. She walked out of the side door and over to the shed, where she punched the code into the keypad. The large aluminum door slowly slid up.

When it did, she saw Vergil hanging from a rafter with clothesline around his neck.

There was no doubt.

Vergil Atkins was dead.

Vergil

SOMETIMES I REMEMBER AND CAN think about things. I remember my dad and how mad he was at me. He said he wasn't later, but I think he was. I remember doing things I shouldn't, and doing H. And I remember the night they all died. Yes, I do remember that now. Father C was right about me, I guess. He said I couldn't be good without his help. This is all because of me. Concupiscence. That's what he was always talking about. I used to call it cucumbers because he looked like that when he would pull it out. A pink cucumber. Sister must know because I can't go back and work in the garden. I don't work in the garden here anymore. I don't do much of anything. Mom let me shoot at cans and I liked it. I guessed that if I could fire that off into the river where he took me I would stop the bad stuff that Father C warned me about. He liked me. I guess I wasn't good enough for him because after a while he stopped asking me to go with him places. Like Sister. I must have done something wrong. But I fixed it today. Mom won't have to suffer any more. I will fix that too.

I love you mom. I'm sorry I wasn't a better son. Now I have changed. I have truly changed. Like those seeds I put into the pots.

I love you mom.

TERESA NUÑEZ SAT ON THE porch of the Atkins home with Rachel for half an hour while the coroner did his work, and until they zipped up the body bag containing the corpse of Vergil Atkins. She hated this. Rachel sat motionless in the swing, staring out across the property, not crying. Teresa was very concerned about this woman staying by herself and tried, unsuccessfully, to convince her to stay with a neighbor or a relative. Rachel said there were no relatives. Several of the near neighbors—Tom and Marge O'Brien, Claire Fogarty, Angie Frechette—had been there since Teresa arrived. Marge was sitting in a chair on the porch near the swing. Claire Fogarty was straightening things in the kitchen.

God, how she hated this.

Teresa was in her mid-fifties, and for more than twenty years had been a deputy for the Jersey County sheriff. Now Chief Deputy, she was responsible for supervising the other deputies and conducting investigations of more serious crimes. She had been here long enough to convince herself that there was no crime, but it certainly was a tragic scene. Her heart ached for Rachel Atkins. Seldom had she felt like crying in the face of a situation, but it wouldn't have taken much to set her off today.

Too much about this hit close to home.

She and her husband, Joaquin, met and fell in love in San Diego, where she worked with NCIS and he was a pharmacist on the naval base. They married after leaving the Navy and had a daughter, Maria Teresa. Maria Teresa was always troubled, and eventually—when she was fifteen—she was diagnosed as having bipolar disorder. One night they came home from having dinner with friends to find Maria Teresa had hanged herself from the branch of an oak tree in their back yard. She never got over that, and being here today was terribly difficult for her. Her husband worked now at the Wal-Mart in Jerseyville where he had worked since the pharmacy downtown closed. That was only fair, since it had been Wal-Mart that was chiefly to blame for the downtown store's demise.

When Maria died, their marriage died too. But they were still together.

Terry Smart, the coroner, walked up to the porch and signaled for Teresa to come down. She excused herself and followed him over to his car.

"We will autopsy, but I don't think there will be any surprises here," he said.

"Thanks, Terry."

"God, this makes me sick."

"Me too." She patted his arm and walked back to the house.

"Rachel, where do you want them to take...Vergil?"

Rachel looked up at Teresa and just stared. For a moment, Teresa wondered whether she had even heard the question.

"Rachel?"

"What do you mean? *Take him?*"

"After the autopsy, which funeral home would you like them to turn him over to?"

"Brenner's, in Jerseyville," Rachel said. "I will bury him next to mom and dad and Jake. They can handle the details."

"Yes, ma'am. Is there anything else I can do?" She looked over at Marge, who was still sitting in the chair at the end of the porch. Rachel was just staring out over the property again.

"I am so sorry, Rachel."

"Thank you for being so kind," Marge said.

Teresa walked to her car and left the scene of the second most horrifying sight her eyes had ever beheld.

MARGARET CLEANED THE SANCTUARY IN the early afternoon. When she returned to the office, she saw the message light blinking on the phone. Claire Fogarty had left a message asking her to call back. Margaret fixed herself a glass of tea, sat at the desk and dialed Claire's number. Claire answered on the second ring.

For ten minutes after Margaret hung up, she sat staring out the front window. She remembered seeing Vergil tinkering in the yard, carrying his basket of vegetables, or just standing there awaiting specific instructions that he was going to have to follow for the day. Tears slid down her cheeks and she wiped them away with her sleeve.

She went back to the church and knelt in the front pew. She prayed for the soul of Vergil Atkins. He was such a sweet man. Troubled, yes, although she still was not privy to the nature of his sufferings. She knew the story of his injury, and the role his own decisions had played in the whole affair, but there was so much she didn't know. Not a week earlier, she had gone to his home and removed one of the joys from his life by telling his mother not to bring him back. Now she chastised herself for not standing up to Father Corrigan, for not telling him to back off and let her make the decisions that needed to be made around here. She felt like a coward. Worse.

She was still not sure the extent to which the incident with Father Corrigan, when Vergil reacted so violently upon seeing him, might have influenced Vergil to take such an extreme action. She remembered the look in his eyes at the river before he emptied the gun into the water.

"God, forgive me," she said aloud. She was still uneasy over the incident, the reaction of Vergil, and the reactions of both Rachel and Eli to Father Corrigan. Something wasn't adding up.

She vowed to spend whatever time was necessary to do the math herself.

ALICE TOOK THE BOYS TO Jerseyville early Saturday because she wanted to pick them out some clothes at Wal-Mart before going to her mother's. Margaret mowed the yard and perspired through her shorts and her tank top before she was through. Then she weeded the garden—Vergil's garden. She knew he would be watching and he would be quite upset to see the mess it was in.

By ten o'clock, she guessed Rachel Atkins would be up, so Margaret showered, changed into her white blouse and navy skirt, and drove out to the Atkins' place. She noticed that the garage door on the shed was open and that Rachel's Jeep was gone. She surmised that she had stayed somewhere else and decided that she would have to come back some other time.

She drove to Alton to pick up some groceries for supper. She was planning on fixing a chicken casserole with potatoes and vegetables. Nothing fancy, but the cupboard was almost bare. She picked up some things for meals later in the week—cereal for the boys' breakfasts, pop tarts, eggs, bacon, hamburger, hamburger helper, and assorted other things—before driving home. It was almost four when she pulled into the garage. She noticed that there were three cars parked in front of the church. It was almost time for confessions to start.

There was, however, no sign of Father Corrigan's Crown Vic.

She took in the groceries and put them away and looked at the clock.

Ten after four.

She looked out the front window. Still no Crown Vic.

Then, as she turned to go back to the kitchen, she saw the car pull up in front of the church. Father Corrigan got out and walked quickly to the church putting his stole over his head as he walked.

"Nothing like being punctual," she said to herself as she returned to the kitchen.

"I GOT STOPPED OUTSIDE OF town by the local constabulary," Corrigan said between bites. "That's why I was late. There was a time when, as soon as a policeman saw the collar, they waved you on. But those days are over."

Margaret was moving her food around on her plate, sipping Merlot from her tumbler, and was only half-heartedly listening to what Corrigan was saying.

"Why'd you get stopped?"

"Said I was speeding. I probably was," he said, flashing his million-dollar Irish smile. "Anyway, she took her sweet time before finally letting me go."

Margaret decided she just couldn't find anything to like about the man who was sitting across the table from her. She loathed the way he ate. He chewed loudly and sat with his elbows on the table. She knew he knew better because he hadn't done that at first. Surely his seminary training had left him with a modicum of proper etiquette. But it seemed that, the more relaxed he became, the more his true character displayed itself.

"There was a death this week in the parish," Margaret said finally.

"Oh. Anyone noteworthy?"

Margaret felt herself torn between wanting to cry and wanting to throw the wine from her glass into the face of Father Corrigan.

"Not really. It was only Vergil. *The retard.*"

Corrigan stopped eating. "My, my. That was sudden."

"Suicide usually is."

Margaret thought she detected, even if only for an instant, a change in the demeanor of Father Seamus Corrigan. It was like the sensation you perceive on a sunny day when a wisp of cloud passes briefly between earth and sun, casting an ephemeral shadow that is forgotten as soon as it is gone.

"When is the funeral?" he asked as he resumed eating his dinner.

"Don't know yet. It isn't going to be here."

Corrigan looked up at her. "I thought they were members of the parish."

"Rachel Atkins doesn't come to church. She is Catholic, but I surmise that something happened to cause her to lose her faith. She came here from Jerseyville some years back. Did you know her?" Now she felt like a cat toying with a cornered mouse. She was enjoying herself.

Corrigan wiped his mouth with the napkin and took a drink of water.

"The name is somewhat familiar. They were probably at Holy Trinity when I was there. It's a shame. You know, people claim to lose their faith for so many reasons. Perhaps if she hadn't lost hers, that boy would be alive today."

"Sins against the spirit."

"What?"

"Our Lord said that the only unforgiveable sin was the sin against the spirit. I wonder who sinned against Vergil's spirit. And, of course, I added to that when I told his mother he couldn't work here anymore."

"Oh, that's what this is about. Well, you can ease you conscience on that score, Sister. I made that decision and I stand by it."

Margaret finished the wine from her glass. Corrigan stood up, thanked her for supper, and announced that he was going for a drive. It was a lovely evening and he loved the river. Margaret cleared the table, but left the dishes stacked up on the sink.

She opened another bottle of Merlot and went into the living room. As Father Corrigan's Crown Vic pulled away from the church, she poured another tumbler full of Yellowtail.

She set her iPod on her Bose player and touched the 'Play' icon. Alison Krause began singing "Down to the River to Pray." Not many knew that Krause was a Decatur, Illinois girl. Great song. She hoped Father Corrigan did some serious praying down at the river.

"Have a nice evening, Father," she said aloud as Alison Krause's number ended and as Elvis started singing "Tender Feeling."

By eight-thirty, the bottle was almost empty and Margaret was sleeping soundly in her chair as the music played on softly. It had been beckoning for some time, and she had finally surrendered herself to the blessed numbness found in decent wine.

Seamus

ARE MY TEARS FROZEN? I sometimes feel, even though I am still here, that my soul has crossed over. Is it the Jack I am drinking from a bottle inside this paper sack? Or is it a premonition?

It is quiet here as the sun drops behind the trees on the other side of the river. It is hot, and yet I find that I am shivering. The old yearnings have not completely died away. Oh, they are not of sufficient power to cause me to seek out assistance, but they are there. I remember how they overshadowed every other objective in my life for so long. Nowadays, there is not the stigma attached to people of my persuasion—unless, of course, you are a person pledged to celibacy. "You will not touch a woman, and so your vows are rock solid," my mentor in seminary once told me as we took care of one another's needs. He went on to be a bishop. I often remembered those quiet nights in his apartment when he was the rector. He was the first to recognize my special needs and to tell me that I was not alone.

I have been a good priest. The smell of candle wax and incense is in my blood and has been since I was a child. My mother died happy knowing that she had given a son to do God's work. I have not disappointed her. I have grown old in His service, and that is the sum of my life.

God's grace is a gift. No works can achieve it, nor destroy it. It is a gift from God. My eternal disposition is a *fait accompli*.

The river runs by and the sun slips slowly behind the trees. The light speckles and glows from the water like a vision from Renoir and the stars begin to make their appearance against the purple sky. I look up at one point and see the giant bird. They still nest near here, the huge eagles whose talons so awed and terrified the ancient red men who once peopled these shores. The talons that probably gave rise to the Piasa legend.

I watch as the giant bird soars and then comes down, down as though to snatch me up and carry me away to where the river runs no more.

Where is that place? Will I ever know? Will the good that I have done here be remembered?

THE WHARF WAS CROWDED, BUT it usually was on Saturday nights. A Missouri band called The Ozark Celebration was playing to an appreciative, if highly inebriated crowd of late summer revelers along the river.

Mark Grayson was standing next to the bar with his father, Bobby, and a friend named Jack Greider. They were among some forty bikers who had stopped in Grafton for the night on their way back to St. Louis from the bike races in Springfield. Grafton was a popular stopover for them and they had decided to spend the night before returning home, even though home was only a few more miles away.

Mark was tall and muscular in his sleeveless tank top. His right arm bore a tattoo of an eagle with arrows in its talons, and his left bore a heart with a cross and lilies emblazoned across it. His hair wasn't quite shoulder length, but it was neatly combed. He was a nice looking guy with thick eyebrows and regular features. His father, somewhat shorter and with less hair, shared Mark's facial features and musculature and a stomach that spilled over his jeans. Jack Greider was short, plump and had scars on his face and a scowl that belied his general affability.

Greider walked away at one point to talk with a woman who had attracted his attention over by the bar. She had long, blonde hair and a figure that was still attractive in spite of the fact that she was probably a good ten years older than a lot of the guys in the place. They struck up a conversation and after a while disappeared into the parking lot.

Mark was content to shoot the shit with his old man and some of the other guys who wandered over during the evening. He wasn't looking for any action. He was tired. He had to be back on the construction site Monday. His dad owned the company, and they were finishing up a project they had been working on for several months. Another project was waiting for that one to finish up. His dad had a good reputation, and they were among the few crews in the St. Louis area who weren't hurting for work in spite of the lousy economy. A good reputation goes a long way. Grayson Builders had a good reputation.

Two years after 9/11 Mark graduated high school and—swept up in the wave of patriotism that hadn't yet ebbed following the attack on the World Trade Center—enlisted in the National Guard. He did a one-year tour in Iraq where he manned an M-2 Browning .50 caliber machine gun above an armored Humvee for dozens of round trips from base camp to Baghdad. On three occasions, insurgents had fired on his convoy and Mark returned fire killing several of them. Miraculously, he returned home without a scratch. Several of his friends weren't so lucky. One of his buddies, Tom McLaury—with whom Mark had graduated high school--was killed when an IED tore through the passenger side of the Humvee directly in front of Mark's. Mark had seen enough violence in Iraq to make him appreciate his country and wish for a quiet life near family and friends. He knew he was lucky to be alive.

Mark had worked for his dad since coming out of the service. His dad was tough, but fair. Bob Grayson hadn't always been. When he was younger he had been a member of the Rough Ryders, an outlaw motorcycle gang that was familiar to many in Missouri and Illinois. Mark had heard that you had to have committed a murder in order to become a full-fledged member. Mark never asked, and his dad never said, but Mark knew his dad had done time at Menard Correctional in Chester. But something happened to Bobby that turned him around. He had been a good father who made no excuses for being rough on Mark to ensure that he didn't follow in his footsteps.

On the back of Bobby's sleeveless leather shirt was a distinctive insignia: a ring of flames with a sword in the center. The sword of truth. The gang that Bobby—and Mark and Jack (though Jack was still a work in progress)—belonged to now was Bikers for Christ.

It was coming up on midnight and Mark was getting more and

more tired.

"Hey, pops," he hollered at his dad. "Let's bug out of here. I'm beat."

"What's the matter boy," Bobby said. "Can't you keep up with the old man?"

Mark set his empty beer bottle down on the bar.

"Not even going to try, old man!"

"Okay, okay, sonny boy. Where the hell is Greider?"

"He's somewhere with his latest fling."

"Well, he won't be long! Give him a few minutes!"

Mark laughed and ordered another beer.

TOMMY HARRISON WAS SHIT-FACED on the patio and was taking a beating from a few of his buddies over his recent troubles. A guy they all called Cracker was really getting on his nerves now.

"Boy, Harrison, that's really something. I hear a nun roughed you up!"

"Fuck off."

Cracker didn't let up.

"I've heard those nuns can be tough! What'd she do, hit you with her ruler?"

The other guys at the table laughed. Harrison was seething, but he wasn't sure he could see well enough to do anything about it.

"Hey, baby," Cracker hollered at one of the bar girls. "Bring us another round. Only give Tommy boy there a glass of Blue Nun."

That did it. Tommy leaped across the table and pounced on Cracker. The two hit the floor and began rolling around. Tommy was too drunk to get in too many punches, but Cracker popped Tommy good on the side of the head. He felt blood start to run down his face.

By that time, he was in the clutches of one of the bouncers, a guy named Eddie Brown who weighed 240 pounds and had arms like ham hocks. The other bouncer, a big black guy wearing a gold chain, held the others at bay by the table.

The bouncer quickly moved Tommy away from the table and across the main bar area to the front door where he unceremoniously threw him out into the parking lot.

"Have a nice night," Brown said, slapping his hands together as a symbolic brush off. Then he stood there with his arms folded and watched Tommy struggle to stand. Tommy finally managed to stumble to his car.

Once inside, he slid down on the seat and slipped into unconsciousness. It only took a few minutes, however, for him to wake up with a new sense of purpose fueled by alcohol and a sense of injured merit.

"Fucking nun," he said as he started his car.

MARK, BOBBY AND JACK GREIDER walked out to get on their bikes and head back to the Reubel Hotel.

"Well, Jack, I'm proud of you," Bobby said. "You lasted longer than I thought you would with that chick!"

"Hey, fuck off Bobby! At least I got some."

"Hope she didn't give you the gift that keeps on giving."

"I practice safe sex."

"Yeah. You usually do it with Sally Palmer and her five friends! Can't get much safer than that!"

"You're not funny, Bobby," Jack said.

"I thought it was funny," Mark said. He really had. He hadn't heard that expression before and it took him a minute to get it.

"Well, the apple doesn't fall far from the tree, Mark!"

"Where the hell are our bikes?" Bobby said. There had been ten bikes parked outside when they got there. Now, their bikes were somewhere amid about fifty others.

Inside, the music had stopped and the revelers were starting to filter out. Most were walking just fine, but a few had to be held up by their friends.

Finally, Bobby found the bikes, and he, Mark and Jack soon had the engines roaring as they headed toward Main Street.

MARGARET AWOKE FROM A DREAMLESS sleep. There was a noise outside of the house. She listened, and then heard it again. It was coming from the porch.

The iPod was still shuffling through songs. The Doors were playing "People are Strange." Her mouth was dry and her head felt as though it would explode any minute.

Then she heard it again.

She thought about going upstairs. The gun was in the drawer. She hadn't given Tommy Harrison a thought for a few days. There had been no further contact with him. She picked up her cell phone and noted the time. It was twelve thirty. If he hadn't surfaced by now, chances are he wouldn't.

She had fallen asleep with the light on in the living room. She walked over and flipped it off. The house was completely dark.

For a moment, she thought about calling the police department, but then decided that she was a big girl. It was probably just a raccoon.

She walked into the hallway. The grandfather clock was ticking away.

She looked through the glass in the front door. There was nothing there. She almost turned to go upstairs to bed, but then she decided to look a bit closer.

She opened the door and stepped out onto the porch. There was a slight breeze and she could see the moon high in the sky surrounded by stars. As hot as it had been, it was almost chilly. She hugged herself and walked down off of the porch.

"Bitch!"

She turned in time to see a figure moving toward her. Too late. The man hit her and sent her sprawling onto the grass. She tried to sit up, but was hit again squarely in the jaw by a closed fist. She blacked out for a moment, and then came to only to see Tommy Harrison astride her.

"I'll teach you to fuck with me!" he said, hitting her again. She was not quite unconscious as she felt her blouse being ripped open. She couldn't move.

"HOLD UP!"

Jack Greider swung his motorbike off of Main Street and turned down Maple, the street that St. Alban's Church was on. Mark and Bobby followed him and came to a halt.

"What's the problem?" Bobby said.

Jack was going through his pockets.

"Jesus Christ! That bitch got my wallet!"

Bobby and Mark started to laugh. Mark was almost in tears.

"This isn't funny, you assholes!"

"Bet you thought she loved you for your charm and good looks!"

Bobby said.

"Hey! What's that?" Mark was looking over the top of his bike at the Church. "Somebody's going at in the yard down there?" He revved his engine and took off. Bobby followed.

Mark swung up to the rectory to see a man on his knees with a woman kicking at him. The woman's blouse had been torn open and the man was trying to pull her panties down.

"Hey, asshole!" Mark yelled. "Get off her!" Mark got off the bike.

"Mind your own fucking business," Tommy said.

Mark ran over and grabbed Tommy by the shoulders and lifted him off the struggling woman. Tommy punched Mark in the jaw, but the blow wasn't hard enough to stun him. Mark responded with a blow to the side of Tommy's head that knocked him down for good. Tommy lay in the yard groaning.

"Throw me my jacket from the bike," Mark said. Bobby got it out of the pouch and tossed it to Mark just as a police car swung into the drive with its lights flashing. Mark covered the woman and helped her sit up.

"Hands where I can see them!" It was Bob Burton.

Mark raised his hands and stood. Bobby and Jack raised theirs too.

"You okay, Sister?" Burton said.

"Sister?" Mark said.

"Shut up, boy!" Burton said.

"Bob! It's not them. They were helping me."

Burton looked at the three bikers.

"It's true, man," said Bobby. We just happened along and saw this guy trying to—"

"They are okay, Bob. It's Tommy Harrison."

Burton heard a groan from the grass behind Margaret, and then saw Harrison trying to sit up.

"He attacked me, Bob. He would have raped me if these guys hadn't come along."

Burton holstered his weapon and walked over to Harrison. He cuffed him and stood him up.

"Did he—"

"No. They got here first. But he slugged me good before they got here. I want him put away this time."

"I'll go to the courthouse myself this time with the sonofabitch." Another patrol car had pulled up and Burton put Harrison in the back seat. Harrison's head hit the frame of the door. "Sorry," Burton said. He wasn't.

"Sister, you better see a doctor. We need to get photos."

"Can't you take them, Bob? In the house? I really don't want to go to the hospital. My jaw hurts, but they won't be able to do anything about that."

"No, but I will call Steve Rundix. We can go to his office. He'll get up for something like this. You can ride with me. You boys mind coming along and giving me statements?"

"No, sir," said Bobby. "Man shouldn't treat a woman like that."

"Sure. Let's go." Burton helped Margaret into the car. Then he turned to Bobby.

"You Bobby Grayson?"

"That'd be me."

"It's been a while."

"That's good, chief."

"Yes, it is. See you at the doctor's office. Just follow me."

"Sure will."

"YOU'RE ONE LUCKY WOMAN," BURTON said to Margaret as they drove to the doctor's office.

"I broke all the rules," Margaret said. "I had a little too much wine last night, and I wasn't paying attention. I wasn't scoping my surroundings as well. He caught me off guard."

"Well, he's done it now. Attempted rape, assault with intent, violating parole…we do this right and he won't be bothering anyone for a while."

You know that biker?" Margaret said.

"Sure do. I arrested him several times years ago. He was one bad dude. He was a suspect in several murders and did time for a vicious attack on another biker."

"You're kidding?"

"No. Bobby Grayson. Something changed him. Not sure what it was, but ever since he got out of prison he has been a model citizen. Has a couple of kids. I think one of those guys was his boy. Has his own business in the St. Louis area. Does construction. Now he's into some Biker's for Christ thing. Solid citizen."

"Well, they sure came through for me."

"Yes, they did. Like I said, you're one lucky woman."

"Think providence might have anything to do with it?"

"Sure. Maybe. Here we are."

Margaret got out of the car as the three motorcycles pulled up alongside. Bobby Grayson dismounted and took Margaret's arm to walk her to the door.

Burton had called Dr. Rundix and his wife, Vebeka—who also doubled as the doctor's nurse. Stephen Rundix was a second-generation Lithuanian who was able to attend SIU-School of Medicine because the community of Grafton paid his bills in exchange for his pledge to remain in the community for five years. He had practiced in Grafton for ten years now and was showing no signs of wanting to leave. His wife, a long-legged blonde beauty and former beauty queen from Denmark, met Stephen in Springfield where she worked as a nurse. They were a model couple in every sense of the word; and even though they had no children, they seemed happy together and had been very good to and for the community. The two were more than glad to help out the Chief and Sister Margaret.

The shock of almost having been raped hadn't set in, but Margaret was cop enough to make certain that every available piece of evidence was documented. Steve Rundix was thorough in his examination, but Margaret assured him that there had been no penetration. Vebeka gave her an ice pack for her face and then took all the necessary pictures for the chief in order to document the file. She made certain that every scratch was photographed. It was humiliating, but Margaret gladly subjected herself to it because she knew it meant putting Tommy Harrison away long enough for Alice to get her life back.

It was after three when Chief Burton returned Margaret to the rectory. The bikers followed Burton and waited nearby while the Chief walked Margaret to the house. She turned to them before she went in.

"I can't thank you guys enough. Really."

"No problem, ma'am," said Bobby. "Anytime you need anything, you call. Here's my card."

She was slightly surprised that a biker carried a card until she looked closely at it. It read, "Grayson Construction – Robert

Grayson – University City, Missouri." Bobby's cell number was printed at the bottom. He even had a website.

"Thank you. Oh! I almost forgot. I still have your jacket!"

"Well, you don't want to be taking it off now," Mark said. "Hang onto it. We won't be leaving until tomorrow. I will swing by for it."

"Thanks again!" Margaret said.

"Sister?" It was Jack.

"Yes?"

"I hope you don't mind my saying this, but you are the prettiest nun I ever saw."

Margaret smiled, and then winced in pain. "I take that as a compliment, Jack."

"My God, Jack," Bobby whispered. "Leave it to you to hit on a nun!"

"What?" Jack said. "I was—*I was just being nice.*"

"Let's just go."

The three bikers backed their Harleys up and took off down Maple Street.

It wasn't until then she realized that Father Corrigan's car wasn't parked in front. She hadn't given him a thought before. She assumed he had come in while she was sleeping in the living room. But his car was nowhere to be seen.

Her head was hurting too much to worry about that now. She went up and fell on the bed, not bothering to undress or even to take off the jacket with the Bikers for Christ emblem on the back.

She slept soundly until after eight the next morning. It was Alice who woke her up.

"SISTER? SISTER, WAKE UP."

Margaret opened one eye. The left eye was swollen shut and her jaw hurt like hell.

"My God, Sister," Alice said. "This is all my fault."

Margaret sat up and put her head in her hands.

"You didn't hit me."

"No, but Tommy did. And it's all because of me."

"I'm the one in pain, Alice. Quit trying to steal the spotlight."

"Sorry. Can I—get you anything?"

"My pistol is in the top drawer. Shoot me. What are you doing here?"

"Chief Burton called early this morning to tell me that Tommy is in jail again. Then he told me what happened. I brought the boys back early because I thought you might need me."

"Early. It's Sunday!" Margaret jumped up and looked out her bedroom window.

"Did you by chance see Father Corrigan anywhere?"

"No."

"He left last evening after dinner. Said he was going for a ride. His car wasn't there when I got back this morning, and I must have forgotten. What time is it?"

"A quarter past eight."

"Mass is supposed to be at nine." She reached into the jacket pocket.

"Nice, uh, jacket. Didn't know you were into motorcycles, Sister."

"It's a long story. Hey, run down and see if my cell phone is on the table in the living room."

Alice walked to the stairs and hollered down.

"Adam! See if there is a cell phone on the table in the living room."

"Yeah, there is."

"Bring it up, please."

Adam walked up the stairs and came into Margaret's room.

"Jesus! What happened to you?"

"Adam, watch your language!"

"It's okay," Margaret said. "Everyone else is going to be saying the same thing. Thanks, Adam."

Margaret flipped through the list of numbers on her phone looking for the Cathedral residence. No one would be in the chancery today. She found it and dialed.

The phone rang about five times and Margaret was afraid the answering machine would pick up. Finally, a woman answered the phone. It must have been the cook or the housekeeper.

"Cathedral rectory."

"Hello? This is Sister Margaret at St. Alban's in Grafton."

"Good morning, Sister. This is Angela. I picked up in the

kitchen."

"Angela, is someone there? I mean one of the priests?"

"No. I am afraid they are all at the Cathedral. Can I help you?"

"I don't know. I am calling about Father Corrigan. He was supposed to be here this morning. He was here last evening, but now he isn't. I need to know where he is."

"Well, I haven't seen him dear. He didn't come down for breakfast this morning, but then I wasn't expecting him."

"Can you check?"

"Sister, it wouldn't be seemly for me to go upstairs."

"Can you check the garage, maybe? He drives a black Crown Victoria."

"I could do that, yes. Is there a problem?"

"Well, I am concerned. Mass is supposed to be at nine o'clock and he isn't here."

"Maybe he's running late, dear."

Margaret didn't want to go into it now. "Can you just check the garage and tell me if his car is there?"

"Certainly. Give me your number and I will call you back in a few minutes."

Margaret gave her the telephone number and hung up.

"Alice, we have a problem. If we don't have a priest, we are going to have to have a prayer service with communion."

"Yes?"

"Look at me. I need to do some major makeup, and I am going to need help. Can you help me?"

"Help you—how?"

"I will lead most of it, but I will need you on the altar as well. If for no other reason than to make sure I don't fall on my face. I am still dizzy from the Vicodin Dr. Rundix gave me."

"I get nervous in front of people, Sister."

"You'll have to get over it. You can read, can't you?"

"Of course I can read."

"You will have to read a few prayers. I will take care of the rest of it. Now, help me into the bathroom and see if we can do something about this face."

"Perhaps you ought to lose the Bikers for Christ jacket. You're progressive, but that might just be a bit outside of the box."

"Oh, yeah." Margaret took it off. Her side hurt when she bent her arm back. "Thanks."

NINE O'CLOCK CAME BUT FATHER Corrigan didn't. Margaret managed to conduct the service with Alice's assistance. Alice actually got into it after an initial bout of nerves. The two boys sat in the front pew and snickered a few times, but a look from Alice settled them down. It was a full house. She had never seen so many regular parishioners in church at one time, and even the husbands were there. Word travels fast in a small community, and by now everyone was talking about Sister Margaret's battle with Tommy Harrison. The men had had a hard time adjusting to a nun running the show, but now many of them looked on with admiration. It took getting the hell beat out of her to make them accept her. But, Margaret decided, if that's what it took, then so be it. God can bring good from evil. It was a blessing to see such a full house.

Even Stephen and Vebeka Rundix were there, in the front pew. It wasn't Christmas or Easter, but there they sat.

Angela hadn't called back before the service, and Margaret felt her cell phone vibrating during communion but couldn't answer it.

After the service, people crowded around to visit with Margaret and to offer their assistance. Marge O'Brien and Claire Fogarty were visiting with Alice. Claire invited her and the boys to dinner. "I can't seem to get Sister to come anymore," she said, "so maybe you can drag her along with you." She turned and ruffled Adam's hair. He winced, and then smiled at her.

"You're quite a gal," Jim Fogarty said to Margaret as he shook her hand. "I'm honored to have you here."

Jim Fogarty seldom said anything. Coming from him that meant a lot.

"Thank you, Jim," Margaret said.

"Nice shiner, Sister," he said, smiling.

"Other duties as assigned," Margaret said. When she smiled, it hurt.

When the crowd thinned down, Margaret walked back into the church and called back the number that had rung during the service.

"Father Corredato."

"Father, this is Margaret Donovan."

"Yes, Sister. I tried to call you."

"Sorry, but we were in the middle of service."

"Yes. Angela told me about your call. She apparently went to the garage and thought Father Corrigan's car was there, but it was a Cadillac. We have a visiting priest here and she really doesn't know one car from another. Before she called back, I came back in and she told me why you called."

"Father Corrigan?"

"He isn't here. I thought he was there."

Margaret couldn't say anything at first. She was thinking.

"He was here for confessions. After dinner, he said he was going for a drive. After that—well, we had some trouble here and I didn't notice that he hadn't returned until this morning."

"That's not like him. What do you think?"

"I think, Father, that I had better notify the police."

CLAIR PETERSON, THE OFFICER WHO had responded to the incident with Vergil at the river, came and took the report. She asked all the right questions. When was Father Corrigan last seen? Had Margaret checked his residence in Springfield? The only one Margaret didn't know how to answer was the one about whether anyone might have a reason to harm Father Corrigan. She fudged: "Not that I am aware of." Then Clair asked if any of his things were there. Margaret hadn't thought about that.

She and Clair went up to the large guest room—which doubled as Adam's room—to see if Father had left his travel bag. It wasn't there. They asked Adam about it when they came downstairs, but he said nothing was in the room when he got there.

"Of course," Margaret said. "He arrived late and went straight to the church. He didn't bring it in as he usually does. He must not have brought it in for dinner." Clair thanked her and said she would be in touch.

Margaret sat in the living room for several hours and eventually dozed off. Alice picked up around the house, fixed a nice lunch for the boys and put Margaret's in the refrigerator. Then she sat on the front porch with lemonade while Margaret snoozed.

At two o'clock Alice woke Margaret up.

"Sister, Chief Burton is here."

Margaret looked up to see Bob Burton, hat in hand, standing in the living room. She sat up and started to stand.

"Stay there, Sister," Bob said. "I gotta tell you, this was mostly a quiet town before you showed up."

"Part of my charm," Margaret said, wincing at the pain in her arm as she adjusted herself in the chair. She remembered how Bill Templeton always said that. A lot of Bill had rubbed off on her. "Have you found Father Corrigan?"

"Not Father Corrigan. But we found his car."

"Where?"

"Down by the river, west of town about a mile. Technically, it's in the county."

"But he's not there?"

"Not a sign."

"Can I go with you and look?"

"Can you walk?"

"Of course I can walk. I'm not an invalid. Just a little battered."

MARGARET KNEW THE MINUTE BOB Burton turned off the highway where they were going. It was the same spot Vergil had driven to the evening she and Rachel followed him. Bob pulled up behind Clair's patrol car. There was a county car there as well. The cars were parked outside of a length of crime scene tape, behind which Clair was standing and talking with a female deputy Sheriff.

Bob and Margaret got out and walked over to the two policewomen.

"Hello again, Sister," Clair said. "This is Teresa Nuñez, chief deputy from Jersey County.

"Pleased to meet you, Sister." Teresa reached across the tape and took Margaret's hand. Nuñez' was tall and her handshake was firm. She had the shape of a pear and Margaret took her for a woman in her fifties. She had a new perm and wore fashionable wire-rimmed glasses. She was in uniform. "Bob talks about you a lot. Understand you used to be a cop."

Margaret was distracted. "Yes. For a while." She looked the scene over. The car was parked about twenty feet from the edge of the river and a picnic table stood about thirty yards away. She saw Father Corrigan's overnight bag on the table. "Any chance I can check things out?"

"Sure, Sister," Nuñez said. We've checked things over pretty well and there doesn't seem to be much evidence to disturb."

Margaret ducked under the tape (*God it hurt!*) and walked over to the table. Next to the overnight bag was a paper sack laying on its side with a bottle of Jack Daniels in it. The whisky had spilled onto the table and had dripped onto the ground. The smell of alcohol was pungent from where she stood. She brushed mosquitoes away as she looked around her. Teresa Nuñez walked up behind her.

"We're going to have that bottle dusted, of course."

Margaret nodded and then walked over to look inside the car. Nothing was out of the ordinary and she noticed that the keys were still in it.

"Sister," Teresa said, "come over here."

Margaret turned and followed Teresa down closer to the river. Teresa pointed to a brushy area. There, plainly visible, was a black penny loafer.

"Does that look like his shoe?"

Margaret thought back to the first day she met Corrigan. He did wear penny loafers.

"It looks like it."

"Sister, is there any reason why Father Corrigan might have—"

"Walked into the river?"

"Well—yes."

Margaret looked at Teresa and then looked back at the shoe. She didn't answer.

"Clair told me about the incident out here a little while back, with the Atkins boy. You think it is a coincidence?"

"No, deputy. That's too much of a coincidence for me."

"Well, if he went into the river with the water this high we will play hell finding him. But we will bring in a diver. This is county jurisdiction, and fortunately we have some hobbyists who have done this sort of thing."

"Yeah. That'd be good. No sign of a struggle anywhere, or blood?"

"Nope. Looks like an abandoned picnic—with Jack as an appetizer. You know anything about this priest that might help us?"

"Actually, deputy, it's what I don't know that bothers me. That and the reason that I don't know it. I suspect, however, that we will be learning a lot about Father Corrigan."

"I see. Well, I have the feeling we will be seeing a lot of each other," Teresa said. Then she turned and walked back up to where the others were standing.

Margaret looked up to see a hawk circling overhead. She wondered if he had seen where the spirit of Seamus Corrigan had gone.

MARK GRAYSON TURNED ONTO MAPLE Street and swung his Harley in front of the rectory. Two young boys were in the front yard. They looked at him strangely as he dismounted and walked up to the porch.

"Hi, fellas," Mark said. The boys just looked at him.

He rang the doorbell.

Alice was fixing supper. She had her hair tied in a ponytail and was wearing shorts and a tank top which showed a lot of cleavage. The exercise program had been working and she not only felt better but she had shed a few pounds in strategic places. She wiped her hands on her apron and walked over to open the door. When she did she had to take a breath. Standing at the door was one of the best-looking guys she had ever seen.

"Uh, hi," she said.

"Oh, hi. I was—looking for Sister Margaret." Mark was a bit surprised to see a nice-looking young woman at the door.

"Well, she is out at the moment, but she should be back soon."

"Oh, she's feeling better then?"

"Yes. Oh! You must be—"

"Yeah. I'm Mark. Mark Grayson. She has my jacket." Mark held out his hand, and then became awkwardly aware that the screen door was still shut. Alice opened it and took his hand.

"Hi. I'm Alice."

"You, uh, work here?"

"Well, actually, I am kind of temporarily living here."

"Your boys?"

"Yes. They didn't bother you did they?"

Mark laughed. "No. But I think they are trying to figure out who I am."

"Wait here," Alice said. She disappeared into the house and then reappeared with the jacket.

"Thanks," Mark said.

"I should thank you. You really helped Sister Margaret. I don't know what would have happened if you hadn't been nearby."

"Well, I hope they put the asshole away for a long time."

"You and me both. Say, would you like some lemonade?"

Mark turned around and saw the boys looking closely at his Harley.

"Well, that sounds nice. Besides, the boys seem to be interested in my bike. Maybe I could tell them a few things about it."

"Sounds great!" Alice said.

WHEN BOB BURTON DROPPED MARGARET off she saw the Harley in front in front of the rectory. After she went in, she learned that they were having a guest for dinner.

"It's a way to say thank you," Alice said as they ate. But Margaret suspected from the way the two looked at one another that it was a bit more than that.

Margaret hadn't been feeling that well, but the atmosphere around the dining room table was life-giving. Even Adam was laughing. Mark was very entertaining and Margaret couldn't help warming to him.

"Oh, my God!" Alice said suddenly, dropping her fork and putting her hand to her mouth. All four sat staring at her.

"Oh, Sister. I am so sorry. I forgot. You had a call while you were out."

"That happens. Nothing to have a stroke over."

Alice winced. "It was the bishop."

"The bishop? THE bishop?"

"*Sorry*. But he said to call him back whenever you could. *He has a cell phone!*"

SONNY CORREDATO WAS PACKING. HIS vacation was starting and he and his long-time friend, Jeremy, were heading south to the Mississippi Gulf Coast. Jeremy was an attorney from Decatur. Thanks to Sonny, some diocesan business had been sent his way through the years. It was the least he could do. His relationship with Jeremy had lasted for more than five years.

The disappearance of Seamus had unnerved him. There was still no news as of this morning, but the sheriff was speculating that Seamus might have walked into the river. He remembered the last conversation he had with the old priest and how agitated he, Corrigan, had become. Had that set him off? Or was it something worse.

Sonny needed some time off. The timing couldn't have been more perfect.

Around ten in the morning the phone in his room rang, just as he was about to take his bags to the garage.

It was Ann Fisher. The bishop wanted to see him. Now. He looked at his watch, took the bags to his car, and then went up to the office.

WHEN SONNY WALKED INTO THE office, Ann was on the phone. She was a slim woman with hair cut shoulder-length who dressed nicely. Her nose was sloped and pointed and her eyes were dark brown, enhanced by a pair of glasses of the style made popular by Sarah Palin. They looked a whole lot better on Sarah Palin, Sonny thought. She was on the phone, but she pointed to the bishop's office as a signal for him to go in. He walked over and knocked.

"Entrée," came a loud voice from behind the door. Sonny opened it and walked in. Bishop Patterson sat with his feet up on the desk looking out the window. He wore his clerical suit with a collar and the soles of his size eleven wingtips were the first things that Sonny noticed.

"Sit down, Sonny. Sorry to delay your vacation, but I want to talk to you about something."

"No problem." Sonny sat in the large leather chair across from the oak desk that had originally belonged to Bishop Griffin, the first bishop of the diocese.

"Well good, Sonny, because I have a problem. What I want to know is what in hell is going on with Seamus down in Grafton?"

Sonny felt his face go flush.

"I have a priest that has disappeared, and apparently there has been some conversation between you and the administrator down there—let's see, Sister Margaret?"

"Uh, yes," Sonny said. He was starting to sweat.

"When, pray tell, were you going to let me know about it?"

"Well, I didn't take it that seriously. After all, you were in Rome. I didn't see the need—"

"Judgment call. I see. Well, in this case, it turned out to be a piss poor one. I have been back since Friday, incidentally, because we have breakfasted together every day since. On a hunch, I checked Father Corrigan's files. When nothing turned up there, I made a call to the attorney. Seems this priest was the subject of some settlements quite a few years back. That never made the papers and he went off the radar for a while. To another state. Now he's back, and we send him into a parish?"

"He is only serving as moderator."

"He shouldn't have been serving as janitor."

"I didn't know about those incidents when I recommended him for Grafton," Sonny said.

"But you do now, don't you? You knew last week because Calhoun mentioned that you had lunch. Anything else I should know, Father?"

"No. I am very upset about Seamus' disappearance. I have known him for years."

"Well, we can hear all about that this afternoon. I lied. I am not delaying your vacation, I am canceling it. At least for today and possibly longer. Seems a deputy sheriff from Jersey County is coming in to talk with me about Father Seamus. I'm not going to suffer through this alone. Three o'clock, my office. You will be there. Along with Calhoun."

"Surely, you're not going to tell them about—the earlier problems."

"It's under seal. I know. But I am bishop, and if it will help clear up this mess you are damned right I will tell them about it. If it won't, no. But that's my call."

"Yes, bishop."

Patterson swung his legs down off the desk and sat up straight.

"You like Jack Lemmon?"

"The actor?"

"Yes. The actor."

"Well, I'm not much of a movie buff, but I liked him in—what was it?—*Grumpier Old Men*, or something like that."

"With Walter Matthau. Loved it. Anyway, in the eighties Lemmon played a priest in a movie called—I think it was *Mass*

Appeal. It had been on stage before it was a movie. He did a great job, as always. It was about a priest who had a young assistant—a seminarian or a newly ordained priest, I don't recall—and there were questions raised about this young man's sexuality. Lemmon defended the young priest and delivered a line that I have never forgotten. He said, "Celibacy is celibacy, even if your thing is goats." Patterson sat back and laughed out loud. "That killed me. Even if your thing is goats."

"Pardon me, Excellency, but what does this have to do with Father Corrigan?"

"I'm not talking about Father Corrigan. I'm talking about you, Father. You see, I am a fairly liberal-minded person. I am tolerant of all sorts of things. I had a friend in the service who was gay, and I was the only one in the platoon who knew it. I didn't care. I loved the guy. Had been with him in college and we served together in the jungle. It was before don't ask don't tell, and he would have been drummed out if anyone knew. Hell, he was the platoon leader. He didn't hurt anybody, he had no ill effects on the platoon, and he was my closest friend. He was my closest friend right up until he died from AIDS. I firmly believe that a person's sexual preferences are, at least in part, pre-programmed. That isn't their fault. But when a man is a priest there is a real difference. His nature doesn't change, but his behavior has to. He has taken a vow of celibacy. And, as Jack Lemmon said, "Celibacy is celibacy, even if your thing is goats."

The bishop stood up and walked around the desk.

"Have you been keeping your vows, Father Corredato?"

Sonny's face began to twitch uncontrollably. His characteristic resolve, battered by the recent turn of events, started to melt. He realized that he had for quite some time freely walked down a path that had led him to this moment, a moment of decision. He looked at Patterson, who stood staring at him now without anger but rather concern, and started to shake. Then he burst into tears, hiding his face in his hands. The bishop regarded the distraught man for a few seconds and then returned to the other side of his desk where he stared out the window.

"Three o'clock Father. We'll talk more about this later. Just be on time this afternoon."

BOB BURTON DROVE WEST OUT of town and turned down a gravel road leading to the river. He pulled up behind a county car and two black vans. He waved at Teresa Nuñez. She walked over to his car. He could see, down in the water, three boats trolling along the river.

"Any luck?" Bob asked.

"They just went in. With the water this high, and as fast as the current is going, we're just going through the motions here. If there is a body in here, it would have carried downriver to the Mississippi pretty quickly."

"Well, they float so surely it would come up somewhere."

"If it doesn't get caught in a boat propeller, or snagged along a shoreline, or caught on a log somewhere down the road, or snagged on a barge. But for that matter, it could even turn up in Louisiana."

"What's your gut tell you about this?"

"Haven't a clue. I am going to Springfield later today to meet with the bishop. As good a place to start as any, I guess."

"You're handling this yourself? Thought you were getting close to retirement." Bob smiled.

"Well, I figure I might as well get my hands dirty one last time."

"If you need anything, let me know."

"Sure will, Bob."

Teresa walked back down and sat on top of the picnic table and watched the boats circle and drop their draglines. There were dark clouds coming from the southwest, the wind was picking up, and the Illinois River ran high and relentless toward the Mississippi.

"*Great*," she said to herself. "Just what we need. More water along the River Road."

THE CENTRAL ILLINOIS DIOCESE DOES not manage catholic cemeteries, as is the case in some other jurisdictions. Each parish manages its own cemetery, sometimes utilizing a board set up for that purpose. At St. Alban's, management of the cemetery was left to the pastor; in other words, to Sister Margaret.

Tom Mattingly from Brenner's Funeral Parlor in Jerseyville phoned early Tuesday morning. He explained that Vergil was to have been buried in Rachel's family plot in Jerseyville, but that

Rachel had a change of heart and now wanted him buried in St. Alban's. He apologized for not calling sooner, but he had, quite frankly, forgotten; the autopsy wasn't completed until Monday. He asked Sister if it was too late to make arrangements. Burial would follow a service at Brenner's on Wednesday. Margaret said she would contact Eli. She didn't think he could be ready by tomorrow. They might have to put it off until Thursday.

She tried calling, but he didn't answer.

One of the formalities of burial in a Catholic cemetery is a baptismal certificate, so she placed a call to Holy Trinity in Jerseyville, hoping to save Rachel the trouble. The secretary located it and told Margaret she would fax a copy to her shortly and put an original in the mail.

Margaret wasn't in as much pain and her face no longer looked like she had stepped out of a prizefight. She could smile without crying at least. She grabbed her keys and purse and drove to the cemetery.

When she arrived, no one was at the house. She walked across the road and through the gate. She saw, over against the fence line separating the cemetery grounds from a cornfield, a mound of dirt. She walked over and looked down. Eli was digging a grave. It was already about six feet deep. When had he started?

"Morning, Eli," she said. He stopped digging and wiped his face.

"Morning, Sister."

"Somebody die?"

He looked at her strangely. "Vergil."

"Oh. That's why I am here. The funeral home called me this morning to see if we could be ready."

"They're a day late and a dollar short. Rachel...told me she was burying him here. I got started yesterday. I chose this plot. I will send the paperwork in later."

"Well, that's great. I was hoping it wouldn't be a problem."

"It's the least I can do, Sister."

"I agree. Thanks, Eli."

Margaret phoned Brenner's on the way back to the office. As she drove she reflected on her conversation with Eli. People down here were self-sufficient, so it didn't seem too out of the ordinary for Rachel to have called the cemetery on her own. She might have mentioned it to Brenner's, but that didn't matter. Rachel was probably doing good to get up of a morning, let alone worry about protocol. Vergil sometimes worked for Eli, after all. *"It's the least I can do,"* Still, something struck Margaret as strange.

When she walked back into the office, she sat down before noticing a sheet of paper in the fax machine. She reached over and pulled it out. It was the baptismal certificate from Holy Trinity.

Margaret looked it over, and started to reach into the drawer for a file folder to put it in. Then she stopped.

She picked up the baptismal certificate and read it again. The resolution wasn't the greatest on the faxed copy, so she read the names again to make sure she was seeing what she thought she was seeing.

"Mother of God," she said.

She grabbed her keys and headed back out the door.

MARGARET TURNED INTO RACHEL ATKINS' driveway. Seeing the Jeep in the shed, she knew Rachel was home. She walked up and knocked on the front door.

"Come in," Rachel said. Margaret opened the door and walked in. She saw Rachel sitting at the kitchen table drinking iced tea.

"Rachel? I thought I would drop by. I hope I am not disturbing you."

"Sit down, Sister. Iced tea?" Rachel's face was drawn, and she looked like she had lost weight. She looked exhausted. Grief will do that to you.

"No, thanks."

Rachel sat staring at her glass and saying nothing.

"Brenner's called. About the burial. It is all set. Eli...Eli is already digging the grave."

Rachel looked up at her for the first time since Margaret had walked in. "Good. I wasn't going to bury him out there, but...I decided he would be closer that way."

"Yes," Margaret said.

"That it?" Rachel said. Margaret decided to stick her neck out.

"No, Rachel. Not really."

"What, then?"

"Rachel, I never have gotten to know you well. I don't know whether that is my fault or not."

"Mostly mine," Rachel said. "I'm not a real friendly type.

Nothing personal."

"That's what I am talking about, Rachel, because I wonder if that's true. Or if there might not be…something else going on."

"Something else?"

"Father Corrigan. Did he abuse Vergil?"

Margaret saw Rachel's right eye twitch. *A tell.*

"The past is the past," Rachel said. "I got nothing to say about that."

"Rachel, do you hold the church…and by extension me…responsible?"

"I was under a court order not to talk about this, but Vergil's dead now so they can go to hell. Look, Sister, I don't hold you responsible for anything. You were always nice to Vergil. Do I hold the church responsible? You bet I do. They sent that bastard back here to rub our faces in it. That was a crime."

Margaret reached over and touched Rachel's hand. Rachel didn't pull away. Margaret thought she saw a tear in the woman's eye. Margaret's worst fears were realized now, and she wondered if perhaps she was sitting across from the woman responsible for Father Corrigan's disappearance.

"Does the Jersey County sheriff know about this?"

"Teresa Nuñez was here this morning. I guess the bishop must have come clean."

The bishop told them? She sensed something different about Bishop Patterson when she called him back. He listened. Was there a new climate in Springfield?

"Rachel, I got a copy of Vergil's baptismal certificate from Holy Trinity. I was surprised to see—"

"That Eli Barstow is his father?"

"Yes."

"Eli's name isn't on the birth certificate. But, being the good Catholic that I was, I didn't want Vergil to be fatherless on the baptismal certificate. So I listed Eli. Jake married me when Vergil was a year old. He gave Vergil his name and treated him like he was his own. He knew the whole story. He was a good man."

"It sounds like he was. How did Eli deal with it?"

"With what?"

"Having his son raised by another man?"

"Eli never knew. Eli wasn't serious about me. I was crazy about him, but I was just one of the girls he liked to run around with in high school and before he went overseas. I didn't find out I was pregnant until he went into basics. I never told him. I knew he wasn't serious, and I wasn't about to trap him. I should have known better. I trusted him to wear condoms. Sometimes he did, but at least once he didn't. Sorry...I don't mean to—"

"It's okay, Rachel. I know about that stuff."

"Oh, yeah. You're a pretty thing. Guess you weren't always in the convent, huh?"

"No. I wasn't." Margaret blushed.

"Anyway, Eli knows now."

Margaret's heart skipped a beat. *"You told him?"*

"The other night, after Vergil died. I had no one else so I went over there. Eli and I have that in common now: we have no one. I spilled the whole story...how Vergil was born after he went overseas, how I didn't know whether he was alive or dead in that prison camp, about how Jake raised Vergil and about how—that priest took advantage of him. You know that Eli spent two years as a prisoner in Viet Nam?"

"I had heard that," Margaret said. "How'd he take it?"

"I think he was in shock. I didn't mean to hurt him, but I had to tell him. He couldn't have any more kids, and he lives all alone and I wanted him to know that something of him did come into this world—for however short a time. That's why I decided to put Vergil out there. He would be where his father could be with him and care for him."

"Did you mention this to the sheriff...I mean to the deputy."

Rachel did not respond.

"If you had, she might have thought—"

"That there was another person who would be glad to see Seamus Corrigan dead? She would have been right. I never saw a man in such a rage as Eli was the other night. He was mad at me at first, I think, for never telling him. Then he ranted about that priest. At one point I was scared. He had been drinking before I got there. He has no one and living like that can work on a man's heart. He's got no one besides...." She hesitated. "He is living in isolation, and now he realizes that a part of his life that he never knew about is over and he hadn't even the smallest part in it."

"It's the least I can do." Eli's words came back to Margaret.

Now it made sense. It really was the least he could do. He was doing this for his son, neatly shaving the sides of the grave, creating a perfect rectangle to receive his flesh and blood.

"Sister?"

"Yes."

"I don't hold you responsible for any of this, even though you do represent a church I no longer respect. I haven't been very friendly, I realize that. But you seem a decent sort. The service is going to be held at Brenner's. I don't go to church any more, as you know, so there won't be a mass. But I don't feel right having one of the men from the funeral home lead a prayer service. Would you be able to lead us in prayer at the service, and see Vergil to rest at the cemetery?"

"I would be honored, Rachel," she said.

It was the least she could do.

It was raining by the time Margaret drove back. Thunder rumbled overhead and she saw several lightning strikes across the river. Rachel was right. She is going to be, at the very least, a "person of interest." Margaret wondered about the exchange that took place the night Rachel came to church during confession, and remembered how agitated Father Corrigan was afterward. She certainly had the motive. But Margaret couldn't see her doing it. Rachel had every reason to feel the way she felt about Seamus Corrigan, and she vented a righteous anger at him and at the institution that suffered him to continue serving the people of God.

Who could blame Rachel for wanting to hurt Father Corrigan? *But did she?* Margaret didn't think so.

Eli, on the other hand, was a man who could crush the life out of another person. Margaret didn't know him well at all. She wondered if anyone did. Rachel told him about Vergil, which gave him a motive.

But Margaret also remembered how Eli reacted to Father Corrigan from the first—*before he knew about Vergil.* There was something more going on.

Had Rachel Atkins unleashed hell by telling Eli Barstow that Vergil—his only son—had been molested by a monster whose sexual depredation may have been a contributing factor in the tragedy that was his life?

Or had Seamus Corrigan been overcome at last by the horrors he had sown and simply walked into the river?

"WHAT DO YOU THINK OF Mark?" Alice was running now. She had a sweatband on her head and a sexy running outfit she recently picked up in Alton. She was taking her figure seriously.

"He really seems like a nice person," Margaret said.

"For a biker?"

"He's more than a biker. Bikers are good people too. He works hard and he doesn't seem to do things he shouldn't. At least as far as I can tell."

"No, he doesn't. The kids are really crazy about him too. Adam especially."

"That's always good. Kids can really make a difference to some men."

"I really like him too."

"Let's see, I might have guessed that when I noticed you drooling the other evening at dinner."

"Very funny. He is coming Saturday to take the boys and me to the zoo. Then, Sunday, he wants to take me out to dinner. Uh...the boys—"

"Can stay in their rooms. I don't have a date Sunday night. Where are you going with this?"

"I don't know, but I think I would like it to go someplace."

They ran another quarter mile and then Alice held up her hand to stop for a minute. Cars flew by on the road as they stood looking down at the river.

"You know, now that Tommy's not around, I really need to start looking for a place."

Margaret looked at her. "You're not thinking about...moving in with Mark?"

"Well, it hasn't gone that far...but I have to admit—"

"You value my opinion, Alice?"

"Of course I do."

"Don't. Just yet. I mean, I am not in a hurry to have you and the boys go—just don't jump in like that right away with a guy you just met."

"Well…I don't know that I could do that just yet—I mean afford my own place."

"Is that what modern romance has evolved to? Any old port in a storm?"

"What do you mean?"

"I mean, girls today go from one situation to another and they tell themselves it's about love when it is really just about having a warm body nearby and a place to live on the cheap."

"Are you mad at me?"

"No. I am mad at the fact that, somehow, young people have their priorities all screwed up. You, yourself, should know what I am talking about. How long did it take you to move in with Tommy?"

"He seemed nice."

"But how much of it was convenience, and how long did you look the other way while he eroded your self-esteem and created an emotional nightmare for your kids?"

"You are sounding like my mother."

"Well, maybe you should listen to your mother more. Look. You're right. I don't mean to preach, but the bottom line is that I have come to like you very much. I truly do. I just want you to like yourself enough to set your own direction in life and not depend so much on having a man that you will jump on the next one that passes by."

"You don't like Mark? I thought you did."

"Not my point. For all I know, he could be the best thing that ever happened to you. All I am saying is let it come to you. Don't be in such a hurry. And don't jump in because you need him. Do it because you want him and make damned sure he wants you—and for the right reasons."

Margaret turned back and started running again. Alice followed.

"I can't keep taking advantage of you like this."

"We've had this conversation. You're not." Margaret stopped running. "You're…*family*. You're the only family I have right now."

Alice felt a surge of emotion and then she reached over and hugged Margaret. Margaret hugged her back tightly.

"Let's hit it," Margaret said. "I have a funeral today."

BRENNER'S WAS A LARGE, WHITE brick, one-story building with a well-manicured lawn. As Margaret pulled into the parking lot, a man in a black suit walked up to her car. When he recognized her, he waved her around to the front of the processional, put a flag on her car and asked her to leave her keys.

The interior of the parlor consisted of several small rooms. For a large service, folding chairs would be placed in each room and for those in the back two rooms the service was audible from speakers mounted on the walls. Only one room was needed today. Margaret signed in and walked up to the large TV that was mounted on the wall in the first room. A DVD was processing photographs of Vergil at various stages of his life to the tune of "You are the Wind Beneath My Wings." Margaret saw a baby in a bassinette, and then a young, good-looking boy in a baseball uniform. There were pictures of Vergil and (Margaret assumed) Jake with Vergil holding up a catfish that he had apparently caught. There were pictures of the three of them in front of their home in Jerseyville. Noticeably absent were any pictures of first communion or confirmation or any other memento of a religious occasion.

When Margaret walked into the main room, she saw Rachel standing near the coffin with a well-dressed man and a woman. She later learned that the man was Jake's brother. He was visibly upset. Margaret caught a glimpse of Eli Barstow sitting in the back row. He wore a blue shirt that was almost too tight with a striped tie. He wore blue jeans and work boots. She nodded to him as she passed and he nodded in return. She walked up to Rachel and took her hand. Rachel introduced her to Jake's brother and his wife, and then walked over to the casket.

"They did a nice job," she said. She was having a hard time keeping her composure and Margaret reached over and put her arm around her shoulders.

"He is with God, Rachel. Of that I am certain."

"That's the only thing I am certain of, Sister."

MARGARET READ FROM THE GOSPEL of John. She chose the story of Lazarus, of how Jesus had arrived too late, and of how—in one of most poignant phrases of scripture—John wrote, "Jesus wept."

"Jesus weeps today," Margaret began. "Just as all of you who loved Vergil weep. But Our Lord's tears today are tears of joy. He has brought Vergil home. Home from the trials of this life, home from the pain that he experienced in his life, home from the limitations of his body to a new vision of God and His heaven. We weep for ourselves because we miss him, but he is not weeping. Of that I am certain. When you find yourself weeping, let it happen but never forget the moments when you laughed with him, when you loved him, when you found in him the vitality of youth and the wisdom that even those who suffer as he suffered carry with them.

"I cannot tell you how many in the parish I serve have enjoyed the fruits of Vergil's labors. He tilled the garden, he planted the seeds—some from seedlings he grew at home and then transplanted later. He weeded the garden religiously. My greatest fear is that, when I arrive at the Day of Judgment, Vergil will be standing next to St. Peter complaining what a mess I made of the garden after he left us. But I plan to keep that garden going, even though it will never be the same, because it was important to Vergil to put things in the ground and watch them grow.

"In order for a seed to grow, it has to die. It has to stop being a seed in order to become a plant that provides us with sustenance. Vergil has died, and now he grows with God and is somewhere where he can help us, all of us, by watching over us and praying for us as we continue our journey here.

"Rachel? Rachel, I have come to know how much you loved this boy. He will never be far from you. You brought him into this world, you cared for him, and you gave him the best that you had. You got from him his love and that love lives on in your heart. Never doubt that he is with you or that you will be with him again. We have the promise of the Savior on that point, and it is a promise I expect Him to deliver upon when we find ourselves at death's door."

Margaret glanced up and found herself looking directly at Eli Barstow. Eli was several rows back, but he was looking back at her.

"For all of you who loved this man—this fine, decent man—be assured of the promise of eternal life. Your relationship with him will last through the ages. God bless you all."

"Let us pray...."

MARGARET LED THE PRAYERS AT the cemetery in near 100-degree heat. Eli stood to the side near the dirt pile, perspiring heavily as the sun beat down on him. The prayers were short, and then Margaret walked over and hugged Rachel and shook hands with her brother and sister-in-law.

As she walked toward her car she saw a Jersey county car parked on the road by the main gate. Teresa Nuñez was standing next to the front fender with her arms folded. Margaret stopped and waved, but Teresa must not have seen her. She just got into the cruiser and drove off trailing dust in her wake.

Margaret turned around to see Eli, still standing quietly as he had during the final prayers. The others had returned to their cars, but Eli's eyes were still fixed on the box that contained the flesh and blood of the only child he would ever have.

At that moment her heart ached for Eli Barstow.

THE FOLLOWING FRIDAY AFTER SCHOOL, Adam had his first appointment with Stephen Rundix. Rundix was a general practitioner and made no pretense of having specialized training in psychology, but he felt that he was capable of evaluating Adam and then he would see what he thought was needed from there. This was *pro bono*. This was for Sister Margaret. He would give it his best shot.

Adam wasn't crazy about going there. He didn't want his friends to think he was crazy. Margaret told him it wouldn't be a problem because Dr. Rundix wasn't a shrink, he was a doctor. "If anyone asks, tell them you have an infection of the gonads. That will shut them up."

"What's that," he asked.

"Don't ask," she said.

"Adam Whitaker?" The nurse called his name from the front desk. He put down the *Time* magazine he had been flipping through and followed her down the hall. She knocked on a door and then opened it for Adam.

"Adam's here."

A tall, blonde, nice looking gentleman stood from behind his desk and offered his hand.

"Welcome, Adam. I am Doctor Rundix. Please have a seat. Can I get you anything? A soda pop maybe?"

"No. Thanks."

"Do you know why your mother asked me to see you?"

"I guess. I mean, not really. She thinks I am messed up, maybe."

"Are you, Adam?"

"Messed up? I don't think so."

"Why do you think your mother thinks so?" Rundix sat back in his chair and tented his fingers.

"I think she feels guilty."

"Guilty? Why?"

"I don't know."

Adam stopped talking. Steve Rundix sat patiently for about two minutes.

"Does something about this make you nervous, Adam?"

"I don't know. Maybe."

"What is it?"

"You gonna tell my mom?"

"Tell your mom—what?"

"What I tell you."

Rundix laughed and put his hands flat on the table. "Oh. Your mother asked me to talk with you but let me assure you that whatever you say in here is between you and me. I will not share anything you tell me with her or with anyone else—unless you specifically tell me that you want me to. Now, there may be one exception. If, after we meet a few times, I determine that you may be suffering from depression—and we'll talk more about that over the next few weeks—then I might recommend that you begin taking a prescription. I'm not saying that I will, because I am not a big believer in giving medicine like that to kids. But if I do, I will need to tell your mother because she will have to pay for the medication. But as to anything that you share with me, it stays here. Does that help?"

Adam shifted in his chair. He was noticing a photograph in a black frame that hung on the wall behind the desk. He recognized Dr. Rundix, even though he wore sunglasses, and he also noticed the beautiful, blonde woman who sat behind him on a large motorcycle.

"Who's the babe?"

Rundix turned around and saw the picture that had grabbed Adam's attention. He laughed out loud again. Adam decided that he liked that laugh.

"Oh, Adam. The 'babe' you are referring to is my wife, Vebeka.

And yes, she is a babe. She would love you for pointing that out, I don't mind telling you. She works with me here. Maybe I will introduce you later. Mind you, however, she is very, very married and I'm a very jealous guy."

Adam laughed. He was starting to relax.

"You ride a motorcycle?"

"I sure do. So does Vebeka."

"A Harley?"

"Is there any other kind?"

"My friend Mark says Harleys are the best."

Rundix smiled. "I couldn't agree more. So, Adam, do you think you can trust me?'

"Sure. Can I have that Pepsi now?"

Rachel

Oh my God, I am hartly sorry
For having offended Thee
And I request all my sins because I dread the loss of
*   heben and the pains of hell.*
But most of all because they offend Thee, my God,
Who art good and deserving of all my love.
I firmly resolve with the help of my grace
To sin more and to avoid occasions of sin.

WE WORKED WITH HIM SO hard on this, and he had just about got it right before he had to make his first confession. We sometimes had to keep from laughing as he repeated the prayer. We kept reminding him that it wasn't his grace, but God's grace that would help him; that he was regretting his sins, not requesting them; and that he didn't want to "sin more," but to "sin no more."

We were nervous when he walked into that box; but of course we will never know how he did when the door slid open.

He was only six years old, for God's sake. What does a six year old know about sin? It took a priest to introduce him to that.

I had a dream about Vergil last night. He was a little boy again and I was holding him before he went to bed and reading to him from a Dr. Seuss book. He laughed and laughed and I laughed and then I hugged him tighter and then, finally, he went to sleep.

Then, in my dream, it was his First Holy Communion. The priest was passing out the hosts, and before my eyes the priest transformed. Instead of the chasuble, he now wore a white alb, red slippers, and a bright red cloak. A gust of wind caught the cloak, blowing it around him. His eyebrows were white, and there was a glint in his eye. I realized I was looking at the Pope. Then his face changed again and this time I screamed. It was the scream of a dream, one wherein no one hears you. Or no one cares. The face had changed into to that of Seamus Corrigan and suddenly, as Vergil walked up to get the host, the red cloak was thrown over him. When the priest-Pope-or whatever it was opened the cloak, my Vergil was gone.

MARGARET TELEPHONED THE JERSEY COUNTY sheriff's office a few days after Vergil's funeral to talk with Deputy Nuñez. A man answered the phone.

"Nuñez? Hang on." He put his hand over the phone, and Margaret could hear him talking to someone else in the office. "Anyone seen Teresa Jane?" Then he came back. "She's not in, Can I leave a message?"

"Yes. I have left a couple of messages, but please ask her to call Sister Margaret at St. Alban's."

The man wrote the number down.

"Got it." He said.

Life in the parish was speeding up with fall approaching. The ladies of the parish were getting ready for their annual Labor Day bake sale, an event that drew people from the whole county. Even

Alice was getting into this, helping spiff up the church hall and experimenting in the kitchen with different kinds of cakes.

Margaret led the Sunday service the week after Corrigan's disappearance. Father Jim was unavailable, although he assured Margaret he would be available the following week and pretty much after that.

Margaret was seeing more of Mark Grayson, as were Alice and the boys. The Saturday that Mark picked them up in the Grayson Builders crew cab, Margaret sat on the porch and watched them drive off. Even though there was only ten years separating her and Alice, she felt like a mother watching her kids go off on holiday. She had come to enjoy having children in the place and the banter that she engaged in with Alice. Alice was a decent, if somewhat misguided girl and Margaret was thrilled to see her engaging in life in a positive way. Mark was a very nice young man with a future, and she prayed every night that their relationship would be a positive one.

The kids didn't return until late in the evening. Margaret entertained herself with merlot and watched the lights down by the river. She dozed off in the chair by the window and Alice woke her when they got home. Alice noticed the empty bottle next to the chair, but didn't say anything at first. She had to help Margaret up the stairs.

"You're starting to worry me," Alice said as they reached Margaret's room.

"Go to bed, Alice," said Margaret. "I am fine."

Adam had changed since he started seeing Dr. Rundix. Margaret saw a difference in his bearing. He no longer slumped when he walked, and there was a spirit in his gait that she hadn't seen before. She ran into Rundix at Maybelle's one afternoon, and he thanked her for sending Adam his way. He said he really enjoyed visiting with him. "He's a good boy," Rundix said. "I don't think his mother has any worries."

Erik and Adam were even excited about learning how to tend Vergil's garden. Margaret worked with them a few times, and now they treated the garden as if it were their own.

"Well, Vergil," Margaret said aloud when she prayed in church one evening, "looks like you've found someone who cares as much about that garden as you did."

Margaret was a bit put out that Deputy Nuñez never returned her call. She had heard nothing about the investigation, and she wondered where it was going. She was also wondering if Nuñez had all the information that she, Margaret, possessed. Yes, Eli was a man capable of killing—but the more she thought about it, she wondered if he was a man capable of murder? There is a difference. "Thou shalt not kill" is the English translation; the Hebrew, she learned, is actually closer to "That shalt not do murder."

Margaret was no longer a cop. What she had learned from Rachel might have caused the cop to delve into Eli a bit more. Did he own a gun? Where was he the night Father Corrigan took his drive along the river? But she had learned it in the capacity of a spiritual advisor, not a cop. It isn't the same as confession, but for Margaret it carried a similar weight. It aroused her interest, but there was only a suspicion and not a clear threat. Still, she wondered where Nuñez was taking the investigation.

Apparently, the diocese was concerned too. Ann Fisher had called twice to see how things were going. They had telephoned Deputy Nuñez as well, with similar results. Margaret noticed something about Ann that was different. After Margaret had spoken with the bishop, Ann's attitude was no longer imperious and condescending. She spoke to Margaret as though Margaret had a brain in her head. Nice change.

IT WAS SATURDAY AFTERNOON AND confessions were set to start at 4:00. Margaret was alone in the office—Mark and Alice and the kids were in Jerseyville. The front door burst open, and Father Jim Clancy walked in carrying a 12-pack of Miller Light.

"Hey! You busy tonight?"

Margaret looked at the beer in his hand. "Why? Need a date?"

Clancy laughed. "Something like that! I thought you could use some company after confession. And we can celebrate my degree."

"Your degree?"

"Yes! I just got my Master's from the University of Phoenix."

"Master's? In what?"

"English Literature."

"You're kidding!"

"Would I kid about something like that?"

"University of Phoenix—that's online isn't it?"

"Isn't this the greatest age to be alive? Been doing it for a couple of years."

"Why?"

"A mind is a terrible thing to waste. I live in Calhoun County. I like to read. Or all of the above. So, want to help me celebrate?"

"I'll go you one better! I have some hamburger in the refrigerator. We'll grill out!"

"You supply the meat—I'll do the grilling. That's a man's job."

"Okay. I'll grab my burkha and grovel at your feet."

"Funny. Keep the beer cold."

IT WAS ALWAYS GOOD TO laugh, and Jim Clancy was on a roll after dinner. He was a little younger than Margaret, but the two of them had always hit it off. After burgers—which he burnt on the grill—they sat drinking Miller Lite and reliving Clancy's years at Illinois State University where he was a basketball player and party boy, at least to hear him tell it.

"Okay," Margaret said, after her third beer, "I'll ask the question."

"I'm committed to celibacy, sorry!"

"Different question."

"Oh. Sorry, it's just that I am so used to having women hit on me."

"Right. Well, that raises another question."

"I'm not gay."

"That wasn't the question. Will you let me ask the question?"

"If you get me another beer."

"Get it yourself." Margaret was starting to feel the effects of the Miller Lite. "The question: So, whatever possessed you to become a priest? Sounds like you were having a pretty fun time in college."

Jim swallowed the last of his beer and then stood up. "Oh, well, if we are going to get serious, then I need to go pee—and get another beer. You ready?"

"Sure, why not. I'm not going anywhere tonight." She handed him her empty.

"I'VE BEEN A CATHOLIC ALL my life, probably like you. My folks were good Catholics. I am one of seven kids, four brothers and two sisters. So, the church has always been there. As a result, I have a deeply ingrained religious sense, and even though I was never serious about much it was always there, just under the surface. But I wasn't ever thinking about the priesthood. I was thinking about girls, basketball, parties—you know, the usual stuff."

Margaret sipped her beer. "Okay?"

"I was diagnosed with leukemia my senior year. I was engaged to be married, looking forward to graduation, and then—BAM!—the rug gets pulled out from under me."

"I'm sorry; I shouldn't have put a damper on the conversation by asking you this."

"Oh, no. It doesn't bother me. I experienced a miracle. A complete and total remission. I went from a guy who was given six months to a guy with a bright future. Two years later, I entered the seminary."

"Just like that?"

"Of course not. After I found my new lease on life, the Catholic guilt kicked in. Not really. What I mean is that being on the brink of death makes you a little crazy, and when you are plucked out of death's clutches it makes you start thinking. Why? Was there a reason? Could it be that I was put in that situation in order to be forced to look at where my life was going?"

"The girl?"

"Actually, she kind of dropped off the radar after it looked like I wasn't long for this world."

"Nice."

"I don't blame her. She still writes me. She was scared. Hell, I was scared.

"And, the rest is history. Okay, your turn."

Margaret told Jim how she had graduated from Illinois College and then worked for several years as a sheriff's deputy. She told him that the death of a fellow-deputy and friend caused her to question her life's choices and led her eventually back to the church and to the convent. She didn't mention that the deputy, who was shot on the highway following a supposedly routine traffic stop, had been her lover and that he had been very, very married.

"Wow! A cop!" Jim said. "Speaking of which, what gives with

the Corrigan investigation?"

"Beats me. I can't get the sheriff to call me back."

"What do you think?"

Margaret bit her lip and took another swig from the bottle. "I really don't know. They were assuming, I think, that he might have walked into the river."

"Suicide?"

"Maybe. I'm not sure. You said you knew Corrigan? Didn't you?"

"No. I'd heard about him."

"What'd you hear?"

"Rumor and innuendo."

"Humor me."

"Well, I entered seminary with my degree, and of course I knew which side of the barn my cows came from—if you know what I mean. A lot of the guys had been in seminary since college. Some of them who came from places like Chicago may have been in a seminary since they were kids. Anyway, a priest I served with after I was ordained apparently had been in seminary since he left high school. He went to the old junior seminary out west of Springfield before they closed it for lack of students. He told me a story that made my skin crawl."

"Okay, I'm all ears."

"He said that the first night he arrived at the school, after the parents all went home, he was assigned to the kitchen crew and his job was to wash dishes. Everyone was in a good mood, they were getting to know one another, and everything seemed copacetic. Well, then an upper classman came back to the kitchen and told all the freshmen to line up. He had straws in his hand. All of the freshmen were told to draw a straw from his fist. My friend drew a short one. 'Okay,' he says, 'what do I win?' Come to find out, he 'won' a trip to a counseling session with—guess who? —Father Seamus Corrigan.

"Seems that the good Father Corrigan was a friend of the rector. He would visit the seminary once each week on a Tuesday or Wednesday night and spend the night, have dinner with the students, and then meet with one student to 'counsel' him. My buddy said that the drawing of straws was probably the rector's idea, because he didn't want his friend Seamus to feel like no one wanted to talk to him. And, get this; the 'counseling' didn't take place in an office or a classroom. My buddy had to go to an empty student room that Corrigan was given to spend the night. Get the picture?"

Margaret's stomach was starting to churn. She wondered, at first, if it might be the four beers.

"So, my friend goes, knocks on the door and Corrigan walks out with his black shirt and trousers, his collar open with his white collar sticking out. Big smile. Come on in. Lots of jokes and affability—you have seen it. Then my friend said things got weird. The conversation changed to how your body starts doing funny things when you are a teenager, and at one point he tells him to pull his pant leg up to make him see the hair, and how the hair is evidence of the changes. He even runs his hand along the hair on my buddy's leg at one point."

"My God," Margaret said.

"Fortunately, my buddy's cow had been out of the barn a few times in high school. He knew enough to know this was all wrong. He stood up and walked out. Said Corrigan gave him a 'C' in a 1-hour music class he taught—where most of the time was spent telling jokes apparently. Only 'C' he got in seminary.

"Okay, so let's do the math. My brother sold cars for a while, and he once told me that when you add up all the contacts you have as a salesman, and then add up all the sales, it comes out to be one out of three. On average, for every three people you talk to, you will sell a car to one of them. Now, in the history of the junior seminary, there were probably—what?—twenty kids in a class during its heyday, two classes, and forty kids. Take that times the number of years that Father Corrigan was teaching there and staying one night a week, that's how many guys who went through there—some of them ordained—who might have been 'ordained' into Corrigan's view of life. His friend, the rector, was letting him into the garden and he was going after the low-hanging fruit."

"You think the rector knew?"

"Maybe he was just too trusting, too naïve. Nah! I think he knew. Oh, and it gets better."

"Better or worse?"

"You tell me. When he was down in Jerseyville, I hear that Father Corrigan loved kids so much he spent a lot of time at the Alton orphanage."

Margaret put her head in her hands. She opened her mouth but she couldn't speak.

"Yeah," Clancy said. "Really sucks, doesn't it? So, let me get us another beer because you are no doubt asking why in the hell I still think that the church is worth it. It's simple. The Holy Spirit."

"You're going to need to help me out here."

"You read, right? Ever hear of a guy named Boccaccio, or his book, *The Decameron*?"

"Yeah, but I never read it. It's kind of like the Canterbury Tales, isn't it?"

"Yes, only Boccaccio finished all the stories he started. Okay, it's the Black Plague, and ten people are holed up for ten days in order, hopefully, to avoid contagion and they decide that each one of them will tell a story a day for the ten days to pass the time. And, some of those stories are pretty racy. But there's one that I never forgot. First day, second story.

"It's about a Jew whose Catholic friend convinces him to visit Rome, the seat of the Catholic kingdom, in hopes his Jewish friend will see the light. Well, the Jew goes to Rome and guess what he sees? Debauchery, chicanery, fraud, and simony—you name it, it is going on and perpetrated largely by those who are running the church, and I mean from the top down. It was the Renaissance, remember, when the popes raised kids in the Vatican. So, the Jew comes back home and, to the delight of his friend, he converts to Catholicism! His friend asks him what had done it for him. The guy replies that while he was in Rome he saw the carryings on, such carryings on he hadn't seen in his life, on the part of the people whose life was supposed to be dedicated to guiding and guarding the church. They were the ones bringing it down. But, he added, I also noticed that in spite of what goes on there, the faith of the common people grows and their devotion is unapproachable. He concluded that it wasn't the jerks who are in charge that were causing this, but the Holy Spirit itself. Therefore, the Jew said, this must be the one true church.

"End of story."

"That's some story," Margaret said.

"And that's why I will always be a Catholic. Politics might do some damage, and flawed individuals—sometimes very flawed individuals—may be in charge, but the Spirit rests on the Church. I have faith in that, and that, my dear girl, is why I am a priest and will be until I die."

"There's something different about this bishop, I think," Margaret said.

"Patterson? Haven't had the honor."

"I'm getting good vibes. We will have to see."

"Well, his predecessor is why I am here. He wanted to get us all gung ho about raising a few million for an expansion of the chancery, and I opened my mouth at a Deanery meeting and suggested that perhaps in a parish like mine, where a steel mill had recently closed, it might not be the best thing to start pushing them for more money. Three weeks later, I get my notice. That's how I ended up in mosquito-infested Calhoun County. Truth is, it was the best thing he could have done. I love the people there, and I am happy as a lark." He looked at the beer in his hand. "Well, perhaps I am getting a little too happy," he said. "Got any coffee?"

"MARGARET, DON'T GO THERE."

Her father was speaking to her. She was looking directly at his face. He couldn't have been more than a foot away from her.

"Where, daddy? Don't go where?"

Then, her father was gone. She now stood on the road by St. Alban's Cemetery facing the front gate. It was dark, so dark she couldn't see her hand in front of her face. It was raining. Lightning illuminated the tombstones behind the iron fence and thunder rolled ominously.

Margaret walked across the road and into the cemetery. Intermittent flashes of lightning lighted her way to a large pile of dirt near the fence line. She kept walking until she was standing at the edge of the hole.

A hand grabbed her ankle. She screamed. A body stood up in the grave and started to pull itself out, but its elbows couldn't gain traction in the mud.

Lightning lit up the sky again and she saw the white face of Seamus Corrigan. His clothing was covered with mud and his chest had a small round hole over the heart.

Then he was on top of her, ripping at her blouse. She

fought and scratched, but he pulled her underwear down and was penetrating her. It was cold as it entered and his eyes were red and when he closed them there was a scowl of ecstasy on his face....

MARGARET SCREAMED AND SAT UP. She was shaking and waving her hands in the air, clawing and scratching at—nothing. She had gone to sleep with the TV on, and there was a color remake of *Night of the Living Dead* on HBO. She rubbed her eyes, reached over to grab the remote and clicked the TV off. In a moment, she was asleep once again.

IT WAS 11:30 WHEN MARK pulled up in front of the rectory. The boys jumped out and said good night to Mark.

"Be quiet, fellas," said Alice. "Sister is probably sleeping."

The boys walked up and unlocked the front door and went inside. Alice and Mark stayed in the truck for ten more minutes.

When she walked up on the porch, she turned and waved good-bye. Mark waved, backed out, and then headed toward Main Street.

When Alice walked in, she saw Margaret sitting in the chair in the living room. She was sound asleep. Alice sighed, and then walked over to the chair and knelt next to her.

"This can't be good," she said to herself. She decided not to wake Margaret. She kissed her on the forehead and went upstairs to bed.

A WEEK AND A HALF LATER, Margaret had to be in Jerseyville for Tommy Harrison's trial. She arrived on time and waited about two hours on a bench outside of the courtroom until she was called to testify.

She answered the prosecutor's questions about what had happened on the night Tommy attacked her, and sat stoically while the photographs of her injuries and torn clothing were admitted into evidence and passed around to the jury. Afterward, the prosecutor asked her if the man who attacked her was in the courtroom.

"He's sitting right there," Margaret said, pointing at Tommy. "That's Tommy Harrison." Harrison just stared at her. He was dressed in a suit and wore a tie. He looked like someone on his way to Sunday school.

Aaron Brown, the court-appointed attorney for Tommy, stood and walked over to the witness stand.

"Sister Margaret, do you think it's possible that my client might have mistaken you for a burglar, that he might have thought that the woman he loved and her kids were in danger? It was, after all, very late. Are you usually up that late?"

"As I said, I was awakened by a noise outside. Alice and the kids weren't even home. But, I suppose if Tommy has a thing about wanting to rape burglars then that might be a possibility. But, barring that, I am afraid I would have to say no."

Several of the jury members chuckled.

Brown sat down. It was a weak attempt to create reasonable doubt. But then he was a court-appointed lawyer. He wasn't paid enough to try that hard. He was, however, smart enough to know that going after a nun on the witness stand was dangerous. Especially a nun who was a former cop.

"You may step down, Sister," the judge said. "And thank you."

She encountered Mark and Bobby in the hallway when she walked out of the courtroom.

"How'd it go," Bobby asked.

"I think it went fine."

"Well, we'll do our level best to send him away," Mark said.

MARGARET WAS WALKING BACK TO her car when a Jersey county car parked alongside her. Teresa Nuñez got out.

"Good afternoon, Teresa," Margaret said. Teresa turned and smiled at her.

"Hi, Sister."

"I have been trying to call you," Margaret said. *Don't you ever call people back?* "Have you learned anything?"

"I'm afraid the investigation is stalled. I have talked with everyone I can think of who might have had a reason to do bodily harm to Father Corrigan, but I am unable to find anything that links them to him on the night in question. Your bishop was very helpful, incidentally. The divers came up with nothing, but we are just waiting and hoping that his body turns up somewhere down the river. Sorry, but that's where it stands."

Margaret was torn. The cop in her wanted so badly to ask about the interview with Rachel and to mention what Rachel had told her about Eli. But she couldn't. She wasn't a cop any more, and the nun in her prevailed. It bothered her, however, to see that Teresa was hanging everything on the assumption that Corrigan had walked into the river. On the other hand, she had learned long ago to bend the theory to fit the facts, not the other way around. The facts were simple.

Fact: They found Seamus Corrigan's car by the river, together with a half-empty bottle of whisky. A shoe was found by the water's edge. The possible inferences: either he walked into the river, or someone took him away, alive or dead.

Any man with any character, knowing what he had done to Vergil and God-knows-how-many others through the years, might be overcome with guilt and grief and give up on life. *Was Seamus a man with a conscience after all?* Did Vergil's suicide rend his heart and drive him over the edge?

Fact: at least two people had a motive for harming Corrigan, Rachel—whose only son was just buried; and Eli, who just learned of Vergil's abuse by Corrigan and that Vergil was his only son. Plus there was something else about Eli that Margaret didn't know but saw quite clearly. Alice mentioned that his brother had committed suicide years ago. Could that be tied into this as well?

Margaret didn't believe that Rachel could do such a thing, but then she also learned long ago that anyone is capable of murder. Eli was a real dark horse. But without a way of linking either of those people to the crime scene—if in fact there was a crime scene—perhaps she would have to go along with the suicide scenario. That required waiting to see if a body turned up. And, given the might of the Illinois and Mississippi Rivers, that might never happen.

This was really eating at her. She knew she would do things differently, but she wasn't able to. She was letting it get her down. Her role now was to keep confidences, not report them to law enforcement—at least without knowing for certain.

"Okay. Will you keep me informed?"

"As soon as I hear anything, I will let you know. The diocese has been calling too, and I have been as lax about returning their calls as yours. I will try to give them a call, but if you talk with them you can pass the information on."

"I will," Margaret said.

"How'd the trial go? I heard you were supposed to testify today."

"Well, I think good. I hope so, anyway."

"So do I," Teresa said. "So do I." Then she smiled and walked into the courthouse.

Eli

I DUG VERGIL'S GRAVE SINGLE-HANDEDLY. It was a labor of love. It knocked me for a loop when Rachel told me that he had been my son all along. For forty years I have had a son and I have lived alone when I could have been a part of his life. I was so pissed at Rachel, until I got to thinking about it. She lost a lot too. More, in a way.

Melvin was only my brother.

I ordered a nice stone for Vergil. He would like it, I think. It will be here in a few days and I will be there when they set it. He is here now with me. I gave him a nice place to rest and I can take care of him now.

It's the least I can do.

I sat reading Melvin's journal again last night. Then I decided I never wanted to see it again and threw it in the trash. I will burn it all later, and that will be the last of it. It's all over now.

Those guys I buried in Nam were just practice. Did someone somewhere, up above, foresee that I would someday have to dig a grave for a child I never knew? What kind of God would do that, know that it was coming and just set me up like that? I wish sometimes I had died in the jungle, that I was one of those guys in a grave that no one ever found, instead of living to come back to a life with no one. Instead of learning after forty years, that I had a son all along. It killed me to see the pictures that were playing at Brenner's. It might have been me playing ball with him, it might have been me fishing with him. Maybe had I been there, I might have thought twice about trusting a strange man—even one wearing a collar—with my son. Especially knowing—or suspecting—what I knew about Melvin.

Seamus Corrigan deserves to spend eternity in the lowest part of hell.

It's funny, but I kind of pitied the bastard that day when I saw him shaking hands with people outside of the church. I really didn't want to kill him after all. One thing dad always said was "two wrongs don't make a right." That sunk in, even if everything else about the old man sucked. I never had to kill, even in Nam. Never got the chance. That mortar attack got me before I ever faced down a cong. As many times as I wanted to kill that gook wearing those boys' dog tags, I doubt I would have if given the chance. He had to live with himself for however much longer, and I figured living with yourself when you're a prick is punishment enough.

That's why when she showed up at the house telling me that Corrigan was dead and that he was in her trunk, I told her to get the hell off my property. She screamed and cried and reminded me of everything the bastard did. So I gave in.

I mowed the better part of the day, and then parked the tractor in the shed. When I pulled in, I noticed a black shoe lying in the dirt near the chest freezer. I picked it up, opened the freezer, and dropped it in. The priest's eyes were open, his eyebrows frosted over, and his skin white as a ghost's. Never in a million years would I have done anything like this. But Vergil was the son I never knew I had. The priest took away something from him. He killed his spirit. It was bad enough what he did to Melvin, but he took away my son before I ever got to know that he was mine. There might have been some time left with Vergil. No more. All of a sudden, I knew she had been right. I didn't feel bad about this anymore.

"Your time is coming, priest," I said. "Somebody is bound to die one of these days."

I closed the lid and went in the house to fix something to eat.

"SISTER, I AM WORRIED ABOUT you."

Alice was running well this morning, only stopping once for a breather. They had just turned into the village of Elsah.

"What are you talking about?"

"You realize that I have come home several times to find you passed out in the chair? The kids saw it too."

"I had a few drinks. Father Clancy stopped Saturday evening and we cooked out and drank a little too much. I'm sorry, but it's hardly the end of the world."

"I've been thinking about that. You know the night Tommy jumped you? I was surprised because I saw you handle him the night you took me to the hospital. Were you drinking that night too, because—?"

"Alice, come on. You're making something out of nothing."

"Am I?"

"Yes."

"I care about you too, you know."

Margaret stopped.

"I know you do. And I appreciate that. But don't worry. I'm fine."

They finished their run. Alice had a point that Margaret considered and then quickly put out of her mind.

MARGARET SPENT WEDNESDAY AFTERNOON IN Alton. It was her week to pick up groceries. She loaded up on things she knew the boys would eat, and tried to pick up some things that would be good for them too. It was tricky to get them to eat right, she was learning. They will gladly eat hamburgers, hot dogs, macaroni and cheese, but she also picked up fish and chicken for them and they would eat it because it was there. She also picked up Gatorade and powdered lemonade because Alice didn't like them drinking so much soda pop.

She passed the liquor section and almost walked out without picking up anything. But just before she checked out, she walked back and grabbed several bottles of Yellowtail merlot.

She had just finished putting things away when she saw a car pull up in front of the rectory. It was a small, dark blue Saturn. A priest got out and started walking up to the house. He was tall and slender with a full head of white hair. He finished a cigarette he was smoking and flicked the butt into the gravel.

Margaret met him at the door.

"Good afternoon, Father," she said. "What can I do for you?"

"Sister Margaret, I am Bishop Patterson."

Margaret really didn't know what to say. She just stood there.

"I am sorry to just drop in, but do you have a minute?"

"Certainly. Forgive me." She opened the door. "It's just that—"

"I know. You expected a retinue. Unfortunately, my valet was busy today."

Margaret laughed out loud. "You're different from I'm used to, that's all."

"I can only hope so, Sister."

"Please sit down. Can I get you something to drink?"

"A Manhattan, maybe?"

"Well, I was thinking more along the lines of a lemonade."

"That's fine. I was kidding, actually. I don't need anything."

He took one of the chairs in front of the desk. Margaret pulled the other chair up and sat facing him so as not to adopt a position of superiority.

"This is a surprise. How can I help you?"

"Actually, you can start by forgiving me."

"For what?"

"After we talked, I realized that you had been stonewalled by my staff when you telephoned with concerns about Father Corrigan. I could claim ignorance and just say that I wasn't told—all of which would be true, incidentally—but I am the bishop and, as Harry Truman would say, 'the buck stops here.' You were placed in an untenable situation. A situation that might just have turned tragic. I cannot apologize enough."

This was an historical moment. Not only was it the first time a bishop, dressed like an ordinary priest, had come calling on her, but one was actually sitting across from her seeking her forgiveness for something that had gone wrong in the bureaucracy. Patterson was an attractive man with the demeanor of a business executive, albeit a fair and decent one. This was a pleasant change.

"I have to tell you how much it means to hear you say that, your—"

"Skip the excellency routine. I just got back from Rome. It's customary to grovel in Rome and kiss rings and all sorts of other things. Call me Father, please. It's so easy for a bishop to forget that he is, first and foremost, a priest. It is good to be reminded."

"Fine. No groveling."

Patterson laughed. "Have you seen *Spamalot?*"

"No. It's on my list though. I loved the movie."

"I love it when the king hears God's voice and immediately drops to his knees and averts his eyes and the good lord admonishes him about how tiring it is for people always to be groveling. You have to see the play. It's a hoot."

"I've heard."

"The sheriff's office in Jerseyville called. They are still thinking Seamus walked into the river."

"Yes. I heard."

"Do you think that's true?"

"It's the only thing they have to go on apparently. I have no information to the contrary."

"I have read the horror stories, the legal documents in our attorney's office, and I wouldn't be surprised if someone wanted to kill Corrigan. He never should have been sent down here."

"Situations like this have done irreparable harm to the church."

"Tell me about it. And it's not just here, it's everywhere. Ireland, of all places, is reeling. You have to wonder how it all got so bad."

"I can't help thinking that it is something deeply ingrained, and that it has been there for a long time."

"I can't help agreeing with that, Sister. And speaking of that, there are going to be some major reassignments in the diocese in the coming months. I am going to be looking for a new chancellor."

"Father Corredato? He has been chancellor for many years."

"Time for a change. Which is why I am here. You know, Canon law doesn't require that the chancellor be a priest. I could even put a layperson in there if I wanted. Or—a nun."

Margaret grabbed the arms of her chair. She knew what was coming.

"I have been talking with your prioress at Saint Dominic's, and she speaks very highly of you. I am also acquainted with your old boss, Sheriff Hargrove. He wishes he had you back."

"Well, that was a long time ago."

"Which means you are older and wiser."

Margaret laughed. "Older, I will grant that."

"Actually, I play poker with Hargrove. Don't spread that around. He's not catholic so I don't feel bad taking his money. He's a lousy poker player. But to get to the point, would you consider being my chancellor?"

"Oh, Father—" Margaret closed her eyes. "I don't know."

"There's plenty of precedent. Don't worry about that. Plus, you are a woman I think I could trust. At least based on everything I have heard. You are also a woman who won't just go along with every idiotic idea I or the other members of the chancery come up with. I don't want a chancery filled with sycophants. I want people who will tell me what they really think. People of faith, of course, but also people who aren't afraid to speak their mind. From what I have heard, you are definitely not afraid to speak yours."

"Sheriff Hargrove should have told you that I am not good at politics. In fact, when I was his deputy, he had to clean up after some of the decisions I made and had to deal with the political fallout that I did not take into consideration. I don't know that you need that."

"I handle the politics, just like Hargrove. And he told me you sometimes—how did he put it?—made decisions with your heart instead of your head. Frankly, I don't see how the two can be disconnected. Nor do I think they should be. You don't scare me, Sister Margaret. But, hey, I dropped in out of the blue and that's not fair. Will you at least give it some thought before you make a decision? I would really like to have you on board."

"I will do that, Father."

"Good. Now I have to run. I am on my way to St. Louis to have dinner with some old friends. You have to get out of Springfield every now and then. The place will drive you nuts. And the place we're going tonight makes the best manhattans in the midwest."

Patterson stood up and Margaret walked him to the door. He turned around and took her hand in his and squeezed it tightly.

"So, am I forgiven?"

"You had me at 'I'm sorry,' Father."

Patterson laughed out loud. "Renée Zellweger. *Jerry Maguire.* That's good."

"I hate to disappoint you but I never saw it. Heard it a lot though."

"Well, I hope that's the only disappointment you give me. Have a great evening, Sister."

ALICE CAME HOME A FEW hours later in a state of euphoria.

"What are you smoking?" Margaret asked, looking up from her desk.

"The joy of life! Chief Burton came by the restaurant today. Tommy was sentenced to Menard for six years. The judge said he would have to serve at least 5 before he is eligible for parole."

"There is a God."

"Of course there is. Look who's talking!"

Margaret was completing a lesson plan for the upcoming RCIA class. She enjoyed these sessions with persons who were interested in becoming Catholic. The class this year consisted of a man whose wife was Catholic. He had been baptized in the Lutheran church. A woman who had never been baptized in any faith was enrolled as well. Her daughter had encouraged her to come. The other members of the class were either Baptists or Presbyterians who decided, for whatever reason, that they were missing something in their spiritual lives. It was a small class, but then Jesus had begun with only twelve.

She was struggling with the offer that Bishop Patterson had made. On the one hand, she didn't feel it would be a good fit. Ever since she took her initial vows, she had been involved directly with people, first as a teacher in a Catholic high school, then with novices in St. Louis, and now as pastor—and she was the pastor, if not technically at least practically speaking. She didn't really think she would like an office job, and she really had no hankering for the backbiting and politics. The Catholic Church invented politics, and if the faithful delude themselves into thinking that the church is above it, then it's no wonder that they have been able to delude themselves on so many other points.

On the other hand, she felt she would really enjoy working with a man like Patterson. He was unlike any bishop she had ever encountered, and he was a man who seemed hell bent on making a positive difference. He was open and above-board, and didn't seem to rely on his authority to shield the church from accusations of wrongdoing. Such openness had begun to characterize the church in recent years, but it seemed that the new transparency was in part deceiving. She sometimes felt that, while the church would do whatever it took to shield itself from criminal liability, absent such liability it was still an environment where 'what happens in the chancery, stays in the chancery.' What she perceived in Patterson was not PR; it was the way the man intended to run the show. There was an excitement about him, about his charisma and leadership style, that made the offer very attractive.

Teresa Nuñez had not contacted Margaret since the day they spoke at the courthouse. Ann Fisher had called several times after the Bishop's unannounced visit—a much kinder, gentler Ann Fisher—and each time Margaret gave her the same answer. She had heard nothing.

Calls to the sheriff's office went unanswered. Ann Fisher reported the same results.

Margaret told Ann that there wasn't much she or anyone could do. If there were no developments, there were no developments.

Margaret was too busy being a pastor. Life was moving on. The weather was changing, the tourists were not as plentiful, and life along the Mississippi settled into an autumnal routine.

JIM FOGARTY WAS SIXTY-SEVEN and had only been ill a few days in his life. He had quit the farm a number of years back, but his son, Terry, had it now and Jim worked with his boy for as many hours as he did when he farmed it himself. Farming was becoming more and more difficult, and the yields this year weren't going to be as good as the previous year. It had been too wet, and they were late getting the crop in. His grandkids helped out when they weren't in school, and Jim knew that having his old man as an extra hand saved Terry money.

It was raining again. Jim hadn't seen such a wet season in many years, and he was surprised that the river hadn't come up any higher than it had. The highway down at Wood River had flooded once, but so far the river by the McAdams Highway hadn't risen to do any damage. The river was seven miles from the farm, so there was no fear of flooding there. Nonetheless, a flood could do a number on the economy of the whole area. Jim remembered the nightmare that resulted from the flood in 1993. It hadn't happened this year—although he knew it would again someday. It was inevitable. All the rain had done this year was make it tough on the farmers. Today, for example, they should be in the fields. Instead, he was changing oil in the shed behind Terry's brick ranch.

He stood up to walk over to the workbench and suddenly became dizzy. He figured he had stood up too fast. He made it to the bench and leaned on it to catch his breath. He felt composed after a minute, and then reached over to grab the box containing the oil filter for Terry's F100.

He felt the most excruciating pain he had felt in his life. It was as though his chest was suddenly caught in a vise.

He lay on the dirt floor for half-an-hour before Terry came in and found him.

Jim Fogarty was dead.

SUDDEN DEATHS WERE AMONG THE most difficult things Margaret had to attend to. Claire Fogarty had called her as soon as the ambulance had taken Jim to the funeral home in Grafton. The coroner wasn't going to do an autopsy since the death was obviously from natural causes. Margaret sat in the kitchen holding Claire's hand. Claire's eyes were red, but she was holding up quite well.

Their son, Terry, stood near the sink with his arms folded. He wasn't talking much. He had a sister who lived in Springfield, Missouri. Terry had telephoned her soon after they took Jim away, and she and her husband and kids were packing to come home.

"I told him he would work himself to death," Claire said. "But there wasn't a more stubborn man in all of Jersey County. Truth is, though, if he wasn't out there every day he would have died years ago. It wasn't in him to sit around the house. He said I drove him nuts." Claire laughed.

"You drive me nuts too, Mom," Terry said, finally opening his mouth.

"You kids did it to me for years. Consider it payback."

They all laughed.

Margaret visited with Claire and Terry for about an hour. Before she left, she prayed the rosary with them. Their faith had kept them going for as long as they had lived in the county, and it would keep them going now. Margaret told her that she would lead the rosary at the funeral home and arrange for Father Clancy to say the mass, if he was available. If he weren't, she would get someone else. She assured Claire that she would take care of everything.

The Fogartys lived west of the unincorporated village of Beltrees, not far from St. Albans Cemetery. Margaret had tried Eli's residence but no one answered. She decided she would drive by and make the arrangements with him personally.

IT WAS A GRAY DAY AND light rain was falling as she approached the cemetery. She looked over at the graveyard and saw no sign of Eli. She pulled into the drive next to the house and spotted his pickup parked in the back.

She got out and walked to the porch. She rang the bell and knocked on the door. There was no answer. She walked around the side of the house and over by the shed. She stuck her head inside.

"Eli?"

There was no answer. So she walked around to the front of the house, took out a note pad, and left him a note asking him to call her about a burial.

As she turned to go back to the car, she saw something that caught her attention.

Near the drive there was a rusted oil drum that Eli used to burn garbage. Margaret remembered seeing those when she was a kid in Jacksonville. Almost everyone had them in the alleys behind their houses at one time, and when they would rust out, a truck would come and deposit a new one. As strange as it seems now, that was how trash—papers, garbage, just about everything—was disposed of at one time. Now they were only seen in rural areas without disposal service.

Lying next to the oil drum was what appeared to be a book with a red cover. It had fallen out of the drum and was slightly charred. Her curiosity got the better of her. She looked around her, and then walked over and picked it up.

There was writing in the notebook. She glanced at the first page and in a few moments realized what she was reading.

It was a journal kept by someone. She leafed through it and saw on the back the name 'Melvin Barstow.'

She knew she was out of line. She should have simply dropped it back in the incinerator.

Instead, she walked over, opened the car door and tossed it into the passenger seat. Then she started to get into the car.

"Can I help you sister?"

Margaret almost jumped. She turned and saw Eli Barstow standing near the porch. Had he seen what she had done? Her heart raced, and she could feel her face turning bright red. She said nothing, but just stood there.

"I was out behind the shed. Sorry," Eli said. It appeared that he hadn't seen her pick up the notebook.

"Oh, Eli. I am sorry. You startled me."

"I can see that."

"I left a note on your door. Jim Fogarty passed away this morning."

"Aw, gees," Eli said. "What happened?"

"Heart attack, apparently."

"He was a nice guy. One of the best."

"Yes, he was."

She explained that Jim's service would be in three days, and he said he could have the grave ready, assuming the rain let up. Even if it didn't, Eli said, he would get it ready somehow. Jim Fogarty deserved to have things done right. Margaret thanked him, pulled out of the driveway, and drove off.

After she left, Eli walked over to the incinerator. He looked inside for a moment and then glanced down the road. He watched the taillights of Margaret's car until they disappeared over a hill.

Lightning flashed, followed after a few seconds by a clap of thunder that shook the ground. Eli turned and walked into the house. He was softly singing a song by Buffalo Springfield.

"Something's happening here...."

MARGARET KNEW NOW WHAT HAD caused Eli to react the way he did when he first heard the name Seamus Corrigan.

After Alice and the boys went to bed, she sat in the dining room drinking merlot and reading the journal. When she finished she closed it and broke down and cried.

The horror of what she had read threatened to overwhelm her.

She poured another glass of wine, and tossed the book across the room.

The abuse Melvin had suffered was known only to Melvin, and to his psychologist. And Eli. There had been no complaint, no settlement, and no justice. And Seamus Corrigan went on to abuse God-knows how many others. She wanted to throw up.

She knew that the journal, coupled with the revelation that Vergil Atkins was Eli's son, constituted the best motive for murder that she could come up with. Had Eli done something to Father Corrigan? He certainly was more than capable of it. He was angry. He was not a talker. She had been in his presence many times and had only heard him say a handful of words. He seemed the sort who internalized, and she knew that anger internalized was a ticking time bomb.

She really didn't know what to do.

It was about midnight when Margaret walked over to the church. It was dark except for the small pinpoint of light from the sanctuary lamp. She loved being in church after dark. Her head was a bit fuzzy from the merlot, but she genuflected and knelt in the front pew to pray. After a few minutes the sanctuary stopped spinning and she found a moment of peace in which to reflect.

In one more year, her second three-year period of discernment would come to an end. At times she felt like she was ready, but something was still tugging at her. Something was still causing her to wonder whether she would be ready when the time came. Whether she would ever be ready.

She had changed since leaving the motherhouse, and there was no question that the change was for the better—for the most part. She was content in her new position. At times, however, she suffered bouts of indecision and—yes, sometimes—guilt. The Corrigan affair brought it all to a head.

"How could you let those things happen, Lord?" she said aloud. *"In this, the church you founded, how could you allow persons to create such suffering, to do such foul and wicked things to the children? Did not you yourself say that it would be better for such people to be cast into the sea with a millstone about their necks? Yet, how many of them are there? Were there? I hear people say it is between two and five percent, as though that somehow makes it less horrendous. But even one percent is unforgivable. How could your church suffer these people to do what they did? And how many more,*

Lord, are out there under the radar, men who could conceivably show up in another parish and come face to face with unknown victims of their past sins? I don't understand. Help me understand!"

She prayed for all the victims of abuse, for all children who suffered whether at the hands of priests, parents, or other trusted adults. Children came into the world to be loved, yet so many—so very many—were doomed from the start. She tried to pray for the priests who had brought so much suffering. Men like Corrigan. Margaret realized that they had souls too, and that their souls might have suffered similar assaults that they passed on with the mistaken notion that it was acceptable between priest and priest, or between priest and altar boy. Then she remembered that Dante confined betrayers of trust—like the greatest betrayer of trust himself, Satan—to the lowest circle of hell where ice rather than flame imprisoned them for all eternity.

Was Seamus Corrigan in such a place now? In which case, what good are prayers for those in hell?

She had slowly come to realize that her most heart-rending conflict was between the two sides of her personality—the cop and the nun. The cop would have followed up on the information that she had; the nun was compelled to keep confidence. But was the journal she read something that she could, in good conscience, keep to herself? As much as she despised what Seamus Corrigan had done, his death deserved a proper investigation. The victim's merits as a human being should never cause a cop to do less than she should—or a nun from holding out hope for his forgiveness. As distasteful as it was, it was her duty.

But *what* was her duty--to behave like a cop, or like a nun? If Seamus didn't walk into the river, there were two people with motives to kill him. She didn't think it was Rachel—in spite of the absence of an alibi. Her gut told her Rachel didn't do it. Eli, on the other hand, was doubly motivated. Two people. That was it.

Before she stood to leave, she had decided that the journal was a piece of evidence that she needed to share with law enforcement. By the time she poured another glass of merlot in the kitchen before going to bed, she planned to call the sheriff's office the next morning.

As she drifted off to sleep, two things bothered her. One— the opening at the chancery hadn't made her prayer list. And—two—she wasn't quite sure what it was, but it had something to do with the people with a motive for murder.

The only two people who really had a motive.

But she was out before she could develop the thought any further.

THE NEXT MORNING ALICE COULDN'T wake Margaret for the morning run.

"Sister okay?" Erik asked as he passed the bedroom on his way from the toilet.

"Yes. She's just resting. Go back to bed."

"I am going running," Alice said, quietly. "If you wake up before the weekly prayer service, fine. If not, then it's on your head!" Her voice betrayed a real anger. "I'm not coming back up here!"

Margaret awoke later when Alice slammed the downstairs door and started the car to take the boys to school. She made it to the morning service, but her voice was weak and her hair was mussed. Anyone who knew her knew that something was very, very wrong.

MARGARET SAT DOWN JUST AS a glass of tea was plopped unceremoniously onto the corner table.

"What can I get you?" Alice asked. She wasn't smiling.

Margaret scooted over to the middle of the booth seat.

"What's the special?"

"Walleye sandwich."

"Fine."

Alice turned and walked away. Margaret was left with a chilly impression. She knew why. She placed the scorched notebook on the seat beside her. She was going to drive over to Jerseyville after lunch and drop it off at the sheriff's office.

It took five minutes for Margaret's order to come up. Alice walked over and placed it in front of her.

"Thanks," Margaret said.

"No problem." She turned to walk away.

"Alice?"

Alice turned around.

"I'm sorry."

"I'm busy."

Margaret looked around her. There were eleven other customers, all of whom had been served. She nodded her head and Alice walked back and disappeared into the kitchen. By now her appetite had disappeared but she made an effort to eat the deep-fried walleye—which she knew was really pollock. It was one of her favorite dishes at Maybelle's, so her appetite returned after a couple of bites.

After she finished, Alice walked up and placed the check on the table.

"Alice, I know you are upset with me."

"Duhh. Can't talk about it now."

"Can't or won't?"

"Both. Would it do any good anyway?"

"Yes. It would. I know…I know you are upset and I know why."

"So you will stop? Right. Somehow, I have heard that before. It's one thing watching someone going downhill when you are afraid of them, but when it's someone you care about, that's something else again. Look, I can't talk now but you should know. I am looking for another place for the boys and me. We can discuss it later."

Then she walked away.

Margaret felt her eyes well up. She didn't want them to go, at least yet. She had grown to love having them there. She couldn't understand, now, why Alice had turned on her. Especially after what they had been through and after all she had done for them. Where would the three of them find a decent place on what she made? How could she be that ungrateful?

The three of them.

Something clicked as Margaret sat thinking. She remembered something Rachel Atkins had said.

"He has a cousin who stops by occasionally…."

A cousin? Another relative? Margaret had thought that there were only two people who had a motive to do bodily harm to Seamus Corrigan.

What if there was a third?

She left a tip, paid for her lunch, and returned to the car. She wasn't going to Jerseyville after all. Instead, she headed south toward Alton.

She was going to do some reading before she turned the evidence over to anyone.

ON HER WAY TO ALTON, Margaret took a side trip to St. Alban's Cemetery. She hadn't gone in the morning, but decided to stop and check on the progress of the grave. The weather had held up, so she guessed Eli probably had finished by now. There were threatening clouds to the west, but they were apparently holding off. Rain was forecast for the evening, however.

Margaret saw Jerry Crowe getting into his car as she drove over the hill. That meant that the grave was finished. When she pulled up outside the main gate, however, she couldn't see Eli anywhere. She got out and walked down the path to the back of the cemetery. She saw a large pile of dirt and a crate containing the vault. She walked over to the edge of the grave.

When she looked down, she saw Eli. He was still digging. From where she stood, she guessed that the grave had to be a good eight to ten inches deeper than Eli was tall. At one end there was a step stool.

"Morning, Eli."

Eli looked up.

"Morning, Sister. Everything's coming along fine." He set the shovel down, put one huge foot on the step stool, grabbed the edge of the grave and lifted himself out with his giant arms.

"You going to China?"

"Huh?"

"That grave is deeper than the ones I usually see."

"Oh. Sometimes you have to dig a little deeper." He reached over to where his toolkit lay and pulled out a bottle of water. He drank most of it in several swallows and then capped the bottle and wiped his mouth and forehead with a dirty handkerchief.

"Sorry to bother you, Eli. Just stopping by to make sure we were ready to go."

"We're ready, Sister. We'll have it all set up. No problem."

"There never is, Eli. I appreciate that. Eli, can I ask you something?"

"You can ask."

"You knew Father Corrigan, didn't you?"

"Not really. He was in Jerseyville when I was a kid. I wasn't much of a churchgoer."

"I noticed, which is why I am asking. Why did you come to the church that day?"

Eli opened his water bottle and took another swig.

"I guess I wanted to see if it was the same man."

"The same as...who?"

"The man who messed up my brother's life."

This was the most conversation she had ever gotten from Eli Barstow, especially of a personal nature. She realized how tenuous was this connection, and tried to extend it as far as she could. There was a great deal hidden behind his eyes. His life was lived in self-imposed isolation. He had lost contact with people, but had he lost touch with humanity? The glimpse he had given her led her to conclude that this was not the case.

"Your brother—did Corrigan abuse him?"

Eli just looked at her. She knew the connection was broken.

"What's done is done, Sister. It's all in the past. Anyway, we'll be ready tomorrow. Don't you worry about it."

THE ALTON *TELEGRAPH*, WHICH SERVES the community of Alton and several surrounding counties, first started printing in 1836, one year before abolitionist newspaperman Elijah Lovejoy was murdered by a mob in Alton. Lovejoy's newspaper, the Alton Observer, had become a vehicle for Lovejoy's increasingly harsh attacks on the institution of slavery and while Illinois was a free state, Missouri was not. Illinois may have been a free state, but the attitudes of many who lived there were more in synch with their slaveholding brethren from Missouri than with the "radical" abolitionists from New England, where—incidentally—Lovejoy came from.

The bottom of the Mississippi near Alton is littered with parts of several of Lovejoy's printing presses that were thrown in by angry pro-slavery mobs, but the tenacious Lovejoy—former-Presbyterian minister—wouldn't back down. The last press went into the river in 1837, the warehouse it had been delivered to was burned to the ground, and Elijah Lovejoy died of bullet wounds in the street. In a sense, the mob action in Alton was the first conflagration of the Civil War. Part of that printing press was pulled out of the river years later and now sits in the lobby of the *Telegraph*. Margaret read the plaque carefully, thinking of how tenacious evil can be—and how much courage it requires to confront it. Confronting slavery had cost Elijah Lovejoy his life, and eventually required the deaths of more than a half-million Americans on both sides to cleanse the nation of its horror.

The tenacity of the culture within the church that had tolerated pedophilia by priests, covered it up thus allowing it to grow like mold in a basement room, was an evil that still threatened the most vulnerable. Yes, the church was addressing the problem. But Margaret wondered how many other ticking time bombs were there; how many more men whose actions were never discovered could surface like some creature out of *Night of the Living Dead* to confront a person who was once their victim?

Melvin Barstow's journal sat on the table next to the microfilm reader as Margaret scrolled through the August 1968 editions of the *Telegraph*. She read the article about the gruesome discovery by Eli Barstow of the body of Melvin Barstow and his wife Catherine at their home outside of Jerseyville. The article indicated that Catherine had almost been decapitated and Melvin's body had to be identified using dental records. The article mentioned that Melvin Barstow had long suffered from "depression," and that the couple had been in counseling for a while.

Margaret pondered the mystery of human attraction. What had attracted Catherine Earnshaw—that was her maiden name, according to the *Telegraph*— to Melvin Barstow? Whatever it was, it led her to an untimely death. There was some irony in the fact that her name, Catherine Earnshaw, was also the name of Heathcliff's beloved in *Wuthering Heights*—another attraction that was doomed from the start.

As she continued reading, she was looking for references to family. The writer spoke of how the two taught at the Catholic high school in Alton, which is where they met.

Then, she found it.

Catherine Earnshaw had two children from a previous marriage.

She read the rest of the article, and then re-read the entire article. That was the only mention of children.

Catherine's children; Melvin's step-children.

Not cousins. They would have been either niece or nephew to Eli.

Rachel hadn't said whether the "cousin" was a boy or a girl. She pulled out her cell phone. It rang several times. Finally, Rachel picked up.

"Rachel? Sister Margaret."

"Hello, sister."

"Rachel. Quick question. You mentioned a cousin of Eli's?"

"Yes. I guess a cousin. I don't know really. Why?"

"Oh, nothing. I was just curious. Girl or boy cousin?"

"What's going on sister?"

"I am just reading an article about—about the death of his brother and I was trying to make sense of it."

There was silence on the other end of the line.

"Rachel?"

"I don't know, sister. Sorry."

Margaret winced. She was playing cop and trying to elicit information from a parishioner to whom she should be acting as pastor. She felt cheap. She wanted to bang her fist on something.

"Thanks Rachel. I am sorry to bother you."

The line went dead.

"Dammit!"

She kept rolling the tape. A later article indicated that the coroner had ruled the Barstow deaths as a murder-suicide.

There wasn't much here that she didn't know before. Catherine had two kids.

She started rewinding the roll, and before she arrived at the first article, it occurred to her.

The obituary?

She rolled slowly through several days' obituaries. Finally, she came across two for *Barstow*.

She read Melvin's, and then Catherine's carefully. Something in Catherine's caught her attention.

> Her father, Lawrence Earnshaw of
> Carbondale, and a brother,
> Thomas Earnshaw, of
> Bloomington, preceded Catherine
> in death. She is survived by her
> mother, Alicia Earnshaw, née
> Wentworth, Carbondale, and by
> her two children, Paul Richard
> Earnshaw and Teresa Jane
> Earnshaw, Carbondale.

"Anyone seen Teresa Jane?"

Margaret went whey-faced as she recalled her telephone call to the Jerseyville Sheriff's Department several weeks earlier.

"Oh dear God," Margaret said to herself.

Deputy Teresa Nuñez—Teresa *Jane* Nuñez—was the daughter of Catherine Earnshaw.

ALICE WAS OPENING A PACKAGE of pork chops when Margaret walked back into the house. Margaret placed the notebook on the desk and walked into the kitchen.

"Hungry?"

"Not really. I have a rosary at six at the funeral home. But I could eat a pork chop. Where are the boys?"

"Mark picked them up after school and took them fishing. They'll be back by supper time."

"Need any help?"

"You can make the salad. Stuff's in the fridge."

Margaret put on an apron, washed her hands and got the lettuce, tomatoes, onions and cucumbers out.

No cucumbers.

She remembered Vergil's aversion to cucumbers.

"I'm sorry about earlier," Alice said.

"Forget it."

Alice dropped the empty meat package in the trash bin under the sink and turned to Sister Margaret.

"Forget it isn't exactly what I need to hear. I apologize for being rude, but I am still concerned about you. Are you forgetting you were almost raped? You haven't said one word about that. At least not to me. That has to have done a number on you."

"So, you still moving?"

"Why?"

"Just curious."

"I am looking. That is true. Sister, I really don't want the boys to see you like that anymore. It's not fair to them. You have been our rock, and when they see that they must wonder whether there's any hope in life."

Margaret swallowed hard. She stopped chopping the lettuce and pulled out a kitchen chair and sat. She took several deep breaths and broke down and cried.

Alice walked over and took her in her arms.

"Sister, you have been about the best friend I ever had. You should know that."

Margaret stopped sobbing after a few minutes, and got up and walked into the office to get a tissue. Alice stood at the sink until she returned.

"I'm okay," Margaret said.

"You were the one who insisted that Adam see Dr. Rundix, and even though I was never plugged into that kind of thing, I made him go. And it has done him a world of good. You made that happen. Isn't there a phrase from the bible or someplace that goes, 'Physician, heal thyself?' Maybe something like that would be good for you. I know none of this would have happened if you hadn't stepped up to help me. I'm not feeling guilty. I am just facing facts. You were almost raped."

Alice must have forgotten that the reliance on Yellowtail preceded Tommy's attack. That it had made it easier for Tommy to get the better of her. But Margaret knew Alice had a point. She had almost been raped. She had worked with rape victims when she was a deputy and she knew the trauma that followed in the wake of such an attack. She had swallowed her pride in court as intimate photographs of her were entered into evidence and passed around to the jury members. She was lucky. She was a nun and the defense counsel was weak. Some women are made out to be the criminal on the stand. She felt low enough during the ordeal. She couldn't imagine how other women not immunized by religious affiliation suffered through it all.

But the Yellowtail had come into the picture long before that. She was dying for a glass now.

"Okay. You're right. Incidentally, you've been a good friend to me too. People who don't care don't bother to speak their minds. So, about you moving?"

"You are really bothered by that, aren't you? Why do I get the feeling you need me here more than I need to be here?"

Margaret looked at Alice. She could feel her face begin to flush. She didn't say anything.

Alice turned around and began to bread the pork chops.

"Mark and I are getting serious."

"You moving in with him?"

Alice turned around. "No. If I go anywhere, it will be on my own—for right now. But Mark is talking…marriage."

"Oh? Really? What are you thinking about that?"

"I am really tempted. This is the first time I ever let a relationship develop. Before, if I liked a guy it was sack time and then into the trailer, in a manner of speaking. This time, I have really come to know him. It's nice."

"Novel idea," Margaret said. "Getting to know someone before you jump them."

"Well…getting to know them. Anyway."

"Alice, you're being—careful I hope."

"My God! Are you suggesting that I practice safe sex?"

Margaret laughed. "The church teaches…."

"Never mind that. Yes, I am being careful. Enough said."

"Oh. Well, that's good."

They both laughed out loud.

"You're such a hypocrite," Alice said.

"The church teaches…."

"I know what the church teaches. Thanks. Sometimes you have to think for yourself."

Margaret had to agree with her on that one.

"Oh, I forgot. There was a cop here earlier looking for you."

"Bob, or Deputy Nuñez?

"Neither. He wasn't from around here. He was in uniform though. Good looking sucker too. He said he'd drop back by tomorrow afternoon. I told him you would be around."

"Did he leave a name?"

"Yes. Bill. Bill something or another."

"Templeton?" Margaret's heart started to beat a little faster.

"Yeah. That's it. Bill Templeton. Uh, should I ask?"

"No. I mean, yes. He and I used to work together."

"Uh-*huh*," Alice said. "How's the salad coming?"

CLOUDS BEGAN BILLOWING, FOLLOWED BY lightning

and distant thunder around eight-o'clock.

Eli waited until dark. It was starting to sprinkle and the thunder was coming more closely now as the storm approached from the west. He tightened his work boots, threw on a rain slicker and walked to the tool shed with a Coleman lantern.

Inside the shed, he placed the lantern on the workbench and opened the chest freezer. The eyes of Seamus Corrigan were still open, his eyebrows even more frosted over. Eli reached down and grabbed the body under the arms, pulled it out and threw the stiff package over his right shoulder. Then he took the lantern and walked out into the rain, which was getting heavier.

A bolt of lightning lighted up the sky and seemed to come down a mile or so out into the field behind the cemetery and a clap of thunder struck as Eli walked through the main gate of the cemetery. It was completely dark now, and the only light came from the Coleman and from occasional flashes of lightning. The huge man carried the corpse with as little strain as might have been occasioned by a large pillow. The body was stiff, and as Eli walked Corrigan's arms stuck out into the night sky in a kind of fruitless supplication.

When Eli reached the grave, he placed the Coleman lantern at the edge and then unceremoniously dropped the corpse into the bottom. Then he grabbed a shovel, left there earlier for this purpose, and began shoveling dirt on top of Corrigan. Even though it was pitch black at the bottom of the grave, he could feel those eyes staring at him so he threw the first shovel full where the face was. He continued to shovel dirt until he thought he had placed enough dirt over it, and then placed the shovel down and checked his progress with the lantern.

Rain was falling harder now and the ground was slippery. He needed more dirt. As he placed the lantern down and reached for the shovel, lightning struck nearby and the concomitant blast of thunder caught him by surprise. His foot slipped on the mud at the edge of the grave and he fell on top of Seamus Corrigan.

He had to turn over in order to right himself and when he did he found himself face-to-face with the monster in the seven-foot hole. It was probably his own breath, he was shook up by the fall, but he had the sensation that *the corpse was breathing on him*. He planted his hands firmly in order to stand up, and realized that one of his hands was on the priest's face. He moved it, and fell flat down upon the cadaver once again. Then he managed to right himself. Fortunately, the stool was still in the grave. He stepped up on it and before he could grab the edge of the grave, the stool sank into the mud and he toppled back onto the corpse. He had to ram the stool onto the stomach of the corpse to give it the stability needed to finally crawl out of the grave.

He lay on the ground, rain splashing his face, and caught his breath for a few minutes. Then he shoveled in more dirt. He did not want to crawl into that hole again, but he had to in order to smooth the ground over the corpse. Finally satisfied that the body was sufficiently covered, he stepped on the stool and climbed out of the grave. He used a hoe he had brought to hoist the stool out behind him.

In the morning, very early, they would set the vault directly over the thawed corpse of Father Seamus Corrigan.

"Rest in peace, mother fucker," Eli said as he gathered his shovel and lantern and returned to the house across the road.

JIM FOGARTY'S FUNERAL WAS WELL attended, as Margaret had anticipated. The Fogarty family was well liked. Jim Clancy gave a moving homily. He had liked Jim and Claire Fogarty and had been in their home many times. It meant a great deal to Claire to have him say the funeral mass.

The prayers at the cemetery were brief, and the family hosted a luncheon in the basement of the church afterward. It was a feast that Jim Fogarty would have loved—fried chicken, mashed potatoes, sweet potatoes, beans, corn, carrots, roast beef, ham, and naturally about twenty different pies. Cakes were in abundance too. Although it was a sad occasion, people were in good spirits. Fogarty would definitely have wanted it that way.

Claire Fogarty hugged Margaret tightly before she left.

"God bless you, Sister. Jim took a while, but he really came to respect you. Of course, I did from the start!"

THE PRINTER WAS NOISILY KICKING OUT bulletins when a car pulled up out front. She glanced out to see a Sangamon County Sheriff's car sitting there just as the doorbell rang.

When she opened the door, there stood Bill Templeton in full uniform.

"Hi," he said. "I was in the neighborhood and thought I'd drop by."

Bill Templeton had been a detective for the Sangamon County Sheriff's Department when Margaret was teaching at St. Dominic's High School. A former deputy sheriff, Margaret found herself deeply involved in an investigation into the murder of two St. Dominic's students. Templeton was assigned to work with her.

He was a cocky young man and the two didn't hit it off at first. He was a recovering alcoholic with a troubled past, but he was—as Alice had observed—a good-looking guy with a good heart buried under all that attitude. Margaret fell in love with him.

What was he doing here in Grafton? What did he want? She remembered seeing him at Sister Theodora's wake, and how good it felt to hug him. It reminded her of the hours they spent together making love. She often woke up from dreams where they were making love again. As she looked at him now—after more than three years—she still felt that stirring of body and soul. Her feelings for the man still ran deep. She had said good-bye to him to continue her vocation, but her love for him never stopped manifesting itself in quiet moments of reflection. It was, she constantly reminded herself, her cross to bear.

He grinned and it was all Margaret could do to keep from pushing through the screen door and kissing him there on the porch. Instead, she pushed the door open invitingly, trying to ignore the excitement and sense of well being that seeing him aroused in her.

"Lucky for you, I'm a sucker for a man in uniform."

He stepped inside and she threw her inhibitions aside. She put her arms around him and squeezed tight. When she was finished, she backed away.

"Okay. I'm good. See you later," he said with an impish grin. She slapped him on the shoulder.

"Not so fast, deputy. Get in here."

They walked into her office. Paper was still coming out of the printer.

"So, you're the head honcho here, huh?"

"Something like that."

"Guess it's better than filling out a job application and writing 'nun' down for experience."

"I can see you're still a smart ass."

"Part of—"

"Your charm. I know. Sit down. What in heaven's name are you doing here?"

"The sheriffs' association is meeting in Alton and I am here for one more day. Hargrove asked me to attend in his stead."

"Impressive. Don't tell me you are getting more political in your old age?"

"No. He used to ask Ernie Jones to go for him occasionally. But Ernie's gone now."

Ernie Jones had been chief of detective for Sangamon county and Bill's boss when Margaret first met Bill.

"Ernie's gone? Don't tell me—"

"Yep. He's running that bait shop in Louisiana he always dreamed of."

"But who is chief of detectives now?" Her eyes went wide. "You—?"

"The one and only."

"Bill. I am so happy for you. Really. That's great. Hargrove knows talent when he sees it."

"He and I still have our days, but he's fair. I'll give him that."

"Yes. He is fair."

"Anyway, I know it's late in the day, but I was wondering about lunch."

Margaret was about to explode from the food she ate at the luncheon.

"Great. I know just the place."

WHAT APPEARED TO BE ABOUT a twenty-year old river catfish was staring at Bill through the aquarium glass, wiggling its whiskers. Margaret and he were sitting in a booth at the Fin Inn.

"Uh...do you really get used to this?"

"After a while you learn to ignore them."

Bill turned and looked deeply into the giant cat's eyes.

"Can you, like, order lunch out of the aquarium?"

"You're gonna need a bigger doggie bag if you order that old beast."

They both laughed. It felt great to laugh again, Margaret thought. She couldn't express the joy that she felt just having him sitting across from her.

Bill ordered catfish, and Margaret ordered a house salad with Italian. She figured she could manage that on top of the fried chicken, potatoes, beans and chocolate pie she had finished only an hour before. She didn't care. Indigestion was a small price to pay to spend time with Bill again.

There were so many things Margaret wanted to know. There wasn't a wedding ring on his finger, but was he seeing someone? Of course, it wasn't her business. Still, she wanted so badly to know who—if anyone—had replaced her when she chose to remain in the convent. But they kept to safer topics and eventually got around to the situation in Grafton.

"Any news on that priest that disappeared?"

Margaret took a sip of water. "That's a long story. Don't you have to be back for a conference or something?"

"They can carry on without me for a while. They're discussing new techniques in detection. I know all that stuff."

Margaret laughed out loud. "Oh, yeah! I forgot! You know all that stuff."

Bill stopped eating to laugh with her.

"Anyway. The priest?"

Margaret explained everything that had transpired, and then discussed her take on the case, carefully avoiding anything told to her in her role as spiritual advisor. She said it bothered her that the Sheriff's office seemed to be hanging everything on a suicide by drowning and not following any other leads. Finally, she told him about the notebook and her discovery that Teresa Nuñez was closer to the situation that she had let on.

"Oh man," Bill said. "She should have recused herself."

"My point exactly. But she didn't."

"So—you're thinking that she is somehow involved? Covering something up?"

"I'm not a cop any more. There's not much I can do. But if there was any way to find out a few things, I might have a better idea."

"Well, I happen to have some connections. What do you need to know?"

"The night Corrigan disappeared, he got here late for

confessions. He said he had been pulled over by a cop for speeding. He referred to the cop as "she." Now, Grafton has a woman who works the evening shift. I am guessing it wasn't in town, but outside of town and that would have been Jersey County. There are two females on the force, Nuñez being one. There is an outside chance it might have been a state cop. If we could narrow it down, that would help."

"How about I make a few inquiries? Sangamon County has an interest here, since Corrigan lived in Springfield. Let me see what I can find out."

"That would be great."

"Margaret, I heard through the grapevine that you had—some trouble."

Margaret sat back. She didn't really want to go into this.

"It was nothing, really. Where did you hear that?"

"Stuff like that comes across. One of the deputies in Sangamon County told me. Margaret, they said you had been attacked."

Margaret closed her eyes. "Almost attacked. Fortunately for me a couple of Bikers for Christ were whizzing by and took the guy out."

"Bikers for Christ! What kind of place is this down here?"

"It's absolutely charming. You would love it. One of those bikers is a former convict who turned his life around."

"So a former convict rescued you from an attempted rape. Okay. Sounds charming. Absolutely. Are you okay?"

Margaret didn't answer right away.

"I don't know, Bill. I don't know any more. Yes, I was almost raped and everyone keeps asking me how I am handling it and the truth is—I don't know. It is supposed to leave me shaken, or at least that's what everyone assumes. I always expected that result from women when I was a cop—and I frequently witnessed it in victims. But, in truth, that hasn't happened. I don't know whether it's just a delayed reaction or if—"

Bill leaned across the table.

"If what?"

Her lip quivered. "Or if I'm just—numb. Can you get that way, Bill? Can you get numb to the pain you should be feeling?"

"Why are you doing this to yourself?"

"Doing what?"

"Margaret, do you think at some level that you are wasting your life? What are you doing?"

"No, Bill. I don't think that."

"Then what is it you don't know? What are you talking about?"

"Okay, it's like this." She looked over to the aquarium for about half a minute and fidgeted with the napkin with her right hand before turning back to face him.

"This might sound like a stupid question, but—*how did you know you were an alcoholic?*"

Bill sat back and placed his hands flat on the table. The waitress brought their orders. Margaret blessed herself and quietly said grace while he sat with his head bowed and one hand on the napkin.

"This looks good," Bill said. He then turned and addressed the black river cat that was still staring at him through the glass. "This is you some day, pal."

The fish, as if understanding the comment, suddenly turned and went to the other side of the tank to watch someone else.

"To answer your question," Bill said, "I didn't. That was the problem. Everyone else could tell me I was, but I didn't think there was a thing wrong. I was just fine. No sir-ee, nothing wrong with me."

He took a drink of water and noticed that Margaret wasn't eating.

"They say a family history of alcoholism is a trigger too. But, if I remember, you didn't have that problem. And a general feeling of powerlessness. Powerlessness over your fate, your self-esteem, what have you."

"Your brother?"

"Something like that."

Margaret remembered that when Bill was a child his younger brother had drowned in a pond the two were swimming in. His father had struck Bill when they discovered the body and never quit blaming him for the younger boy's death. Bill carried that guilt with him for years until he found the strength to let it go. Margaret had made that possible.

"Why do you ask? What's up?"

"I'm not focused lately, I guess. Too many things floating around in my mind. Too many—feelings."

"Any of them for me?"

"You know there are. They never went away."

"Well, for God's sake why have I not heard from you, except

when someone dies?"

"Because this is the life I have chosen."

Bill wiped his face with his napkin. "Bullshit! It doesn't have to be that way. You are the one who is making that choice."

"Because I think it is the right choice."

"But now you're not sure? Is that what you are saying?"

"Please, Bill! Please. This is getting out of hand, off track. Please. Just let me speak."

He dropped his fork on the table and sat back. "I'm sorry. You have no idea how it felt when you walked out on me. I haven't been with—I haven't even had a date since then. I just didn't want to. You have no idea how many times I have wanted to call you—wherever you were—or drive down to St. Louis, or here. I wake up sometimes and imagine you are next to me. I dream that you are, and then I wake up to find that you are gone. Oh, hell! I'm sorry. I didn't mean for this to happen. Please—forgive me, okay?"

"Bill, you should have moved on."

"I did move on. I plowed into my work, and I received several commendations and now I am chief deputy in charge of the detective unit. That's how I moved on."

"You moved from alcohol addiction to process addiction. Bill, listen to me, please."

"I'm listening. Go."

"Bill, I really *do* need you now. But not in that way."

"In what way do you need me?"

"Bill, if I ever needed you to be a friend, I need it now."

He reached over and placed his hand over hers. He always loved looking into her eyes, seeing how they stared intently, clearly, intelligently and crossed ever-so-slightly as she honed in on his gaze. It troubled him now to see that her eyes seemed slightly unfocused, and her overall appearance seemed, somehow--malnourished. Yes. Malnourished. That word seemed apt.

"If you need me to be a friend, I will be a friend. If you need me to be a stepstool or a whipping boy, I will be either of those. I will be whatever you need me to be, whenever you need me to be it. Because, Margaret Donovan, I haven't stopped loving you for one minute."

Margaret could feel her eyes begin to fill until tears flowed down her cheeks. Bill pulled a handkerchief from his pocket and handed it to her.

"Thanks," she said. She wiped her eyes and then blew her nose.

"You can…keep that," Bill said.

Margaret looked at the handkerchief and then she laughed. "Oh. Yeah. Sorry."

"Well, at least I will leave you smiling. Guess we better get back." He took a credit card out and placed it on the tray with the bill.

"You said you needed me to be a friend. Okay. What can I do for you, *friend?*"

MARGARET POURED A TUMBLER OF merlot after Bill dropped her off at the rectory. She had wanted so badly to kiss him, to hold him—and, yes, to go upstairs and make love with him. Instead, she had taken his head in her hands and kissed him lightly on the cheek.

"I pay for lunch and that's all I get?" Bill grinned.

"I had a house salad. That's about what it's worth. And I didn't eat that."

She stood on the porch long after his car turned onto Main Street.

Later she sat staring at a tumbler filled with wine. She picked it up and walked upstairs. Something Bill said at the restaurant was working on her. "

They say a family history of alcoholism is a trigger too. But, if I remember, you didn't have that problem."

In her bedroom she changed into jeans and a sweatshirt and hung up her skirt and blouse. As she did, she saw the large box on the top shelf of the closet that contained papers, pictures and letters that she had found in her father's house after he died. She had glanced through them a dozen times since her father died, but there were so many letters and cards that she browsed selectively. Some were from relatives she barely knew, and so paid little heed to them. She reached up and pulled it down.

Sitting on the bed, she started to go through them. She had looked through them a few times after her dad passed away, but had never taken the time to organize them. There were many things she had never paid attention to at all.

She found a picture of her father—and her mother. It was a black and white and appeared to be a photo done by a professional photographer. Patrick Aloysius Donovan was a good-looking guy, with ample dark hair—although it was starting to recede already when this picture was taken—an impish Irish grin, a determined jaw and eyes that drew you in. Looking now at the picture of her mother, Alexandra, Margaret could see a reflection of herself. Margaret had her dad's chin, but everything else was Alexandra.

Margaret never knew her mother, or rather couldn't remember her. She had died in a fiery crash south of Jacksonville when Margaret was very small. Underneath the picture, she found a sheet of black construction paper on which an article was pasted from the Jacksonville *Journal-Courier*. The date at the top was May 3, 1976 and the headline, "Jacksonville woman killed in car-truck collision."

> **Jacksonville** – A head-on collision on Route 67 south of Jacksonville resulted in the death of a Jacksonville woman Tuesday afternoon around 3:30. The car collided with a semi-trailer truck driven by John A. Stevens of Murrayville. Stevens was taken to Passavant Memorial Hospital where he was treated for minor injuries and released.
>
> The driver of the car, Alexandra Donovan, was pronounced dead at Passavant Hospital. She had suffered massive head injuries.
>
> According to Stevens, the car driven by Donovan suddenly crossed the centerline and struck his truck before he could react.
>
> Alexandra Donovan is the wife of Morgan County Sheriff Patrick Donovan.
>
> The cause of the accident is under investigation.

She swallowed some merlot, and sat lightly brushing her fingers across the black and white face of her mother. How can you miss someone you never knew, yet she had missed her mother her whole life. Her dad did everything he could to make sure that Margaret was loved and cared for, sacrificing his own happiness along the way—or so it seemed to Margaret. Patrick could have had any number of women, and she remembered him dating a few. But his life was wrapped up in the daughter who was a living image of the woman he had loved. Between loving Margaret, and serving the people of Morgan County as Sheriff, his life was quite busy.

She pulled out more articles and letters, this time reading everything carefully. After she was finished, as she started to close the book, she noticed something.

One of the pages was fatter than the others. She ran her finger across it and realized that it wasn't one page but two. The pages were stuck together and something was wedged between them. She found the edge of one and started to pull it back. As she did, she discerned that the pages had been glued together. Pieces of the page she pulled adhered to dried glue. When she separated the pages she found a letter in an envelope addressed to her father. The ink was faded. She looked at the return address and saw that it was from her aunt—her father's sister, Bessie Marquardt—who lived in Olney, Illinois. Margaret had never seen it before. When she opened it, she saw that it was dated June 25, 1976—two months after her mother's accident. It was a three-page letter on lined paper. Bessie wrote with a red pen and the ink had faded somewhat.

The letter talked about how sad she was over Alexandra's death, and how much she hoped that Patrick would be able to cope with raising "little Maggie."

God almighty, Margaret thought. She was glad that nickname hadn't stuck.

She was about to put the letter back in the envelope, but something about the penultimate paragraph caught her attention. She pulled the letter close and read it.

> I know how long you have lived with the possibility that something like this could happen, Pat. I know, also, that you tried to get Alex the help she needed. I also know how you suffered so long, sometimes not knowing where she was, sometimes having to carry her to bed. She was a damaged soul, Pat, and now she is with God who can heal all our hearts. That accident

was the inevitable result of her drinking. It's an
awful thing to live with, but it's a fact. Thank
your lucky stars that she hadn't taken Maggie in
the car with her.

Margaret felt the room begin to spin. She was starting to shake, and some of the wine from the glass spilled onto the bedspread. Why hadn't her father told her? Then she realized why: her father would never want Margaret to think ill of her mother. Her father had been gone almost twenty years without ever telling her. Was this what her mother meant in the dream? "Look to me."

"Thank your lucky stars that she hadn't taken Maggie in the car with her."

Margaret threw the glass against the wall, and it shattered and splattered wine in all directions.

"You didn't have to leave me, damn you!" Margaret screamed. "God damn you! You could have been here. You could have been with me when I needed a mother. But you were a fucking drunk! Daddy, why in the hell didn't you tell me? Why did you keep it from me? Damn you to hell!"

She fell to her knees, placed her head against the mattress and sobbed. Her tears were spawned partly by guilt. Somehow she had always known—or at least suspected but never would have admitted it even to herself. Honesty with oneself is a crucial as honesty with others.

But she didn't want to know. Her rage was misplaced. And she knew it.

What had Bill said about family history? Alexandra Donovan had been a drunk. Margaret was almost forty, and she was heading in the same direction. That direction could only lead to ruination or to a fiery collision somewhere along a lonely blurred highway to nowhere.

Suddenly, Alice was there. Margaret hadn't heard her come in the front door. Mark was standing in the hallway. Alice knelt next to her and took her in her arms.

"My God! What's wrong? What in the hell happened?"

Margaret didn't answer. She couldn't answer. Instead, she buried her head in Alice's lap and cried until she couldn't cry any more.

Alice got her onto the bed, removed her shoes and threw a light blanket over her. She kissed Margaret on the forehead, and looked up at Mark. She shook her head. She was about at the end of her tether. She walked out and pulled the door to, and left Margaret to sleep it off.

Margaret dreamed about Dean Martin and Ricky Nelson and John Wayne and watching videos with Pat Donovan, the father she had loved more than anyone else in the world.

MARK HAD BEEN DRIVING SHEETROCK screws for over an hour and was well into the rhythm of it. Jack was laying tile in one of the bathrooms and Bobby was tightening up plumbing. This house had to be finished in two weeks, and it was going to be close. They would have been closer, but Bobby made Jack tear up the tile in one of the upstairs bathrooms because it wasn't "right." It was costing Bobby money, but he had come to care more for his reputation than for the few dollars he would save. This was one of the reasons that Grayson Builders had a waiting list.

There were two other men finishing drywall in the other rooms upstairs. They were new hires. One wasn't out of prison for too long, but that didn't bother Bobby as long as they worked and could be depended on. So far both of them had worked out. Bobby always stayed close, however, and when he had to leave he put Mark in charge.

Bobby had given chances to more than a dozen ex-cons. Four of them took advantage of the opportunity and went on to become quite successful in their own right. Sadly, most of the others were back in prison. "It's a game of numbers," Bobby always said. "But some of them are worth the risk."

Mark loved his dad, and Bobby had been a good father after he came out of prison. Mark's mother, Beverly, was a tough cookie, a biker girl with the tattoos to show for it; but she was a decent sort who loved Bobby enough to stick with him through the tough times. When Bobby got out, he had changed. He never talked about what happened there, but he turned his life around. He had found religion. He raised Mark in the local Baptist Church, sent him to Sunday school and to Vacation Bible School, and was hard on him because he didn't want Mark falling into the same pit he had fallen into as a young man. Mark knew not to mess with his dad, and knew that he would rather face prison time than have to deal with his father's anger over him messing up. So Mark managed to stay out of trouble. The longer he did, the easier it became. He had a good job working for Bobby in a business that would someday be his, and life was good.

Girls had come and gone. Several of them he suspected of caring more about being with a guy who had a good job than being with him, *per se*. It wasn't him, but the opportunities he afforded that attracted him. He could sense that after a while, and when he did he would break it off. He had almost given up when he met Alice. Alice liked him for him. And he had slowly grown to love her very much.

Her kids weren't a concern. In fact, he looked forward to spending time with them as much as he did with Alice. They had planted their tentacles deep into him and now he couldn't imagine not having them to go fishing with or just to hang with.

"Well, I guess Beverly has changed her mind," Bobby said as he sat down with Mark over the noon hour and started opening his sandwich.

"What else is new?" asked Jack.

"She wants a two-story now. So I guess I am going to have to finish up her dream home and sell it and start all over again."

Bobby and Mark had been working on a story-and-a-half near the river in their spare time, which is what Beverly said she always wanted. Apparently, "always" was a word that slipped easily in and out of her vocabulary.

"Why do you put up with that, Bobby?"

"Because I love the woman, Jack."

Mark chuckled. "And she would knock him senseless if he didn't do what she wanted."

"Got that right."

Mark sat quietly as Bobby and Jack sparred over this and that. After he crinkled up his trash, he turned to Bobby.

"Hey, Pop? Think you might be interested in selling that house to someone in the family?"

Bobby and Jack stopped eating and just looked at Mark.

"Who-hee!" said Bobby, after regarding his son for a few seconds. "I do believe that Whitaker gal has you pussy-whipped boy."

"Dad?"

Bobby grinned, a broad grin that spread from cheek to cheek.

"You by-God better believe I would, boy! I'll make you an offer you can't refuse!"

ON WEDNESDAY, MARGARET SAW BOB Burton at Maybelle's. He was paying his bill.

"How you doing, Sister?"

"Fine. You had lunch, obviously?"

"Yep. The fried chicken. It's to die for."

"Deep fried. Sure is! You got a minute?"

"Sure"

"Let's sit."

ALICE TOOK MARGARET'S ORDER AND joked with Bob Burton a few minutes. He asked about the biker guy.

"Mark is great. We're still dating."

"Seems like a nice young man," Burton said. "His dad is okay too. He really turned into a solid citizen."

When Alice walked away, Bob looked at the slightly charred red book that Margaret had placed on the table.

"Looks like you pulled that out of the flames."

"Sort of. Bob, you remember the day Corrigan disappeared? It was a Saturday."

"Sure."

"A cop pulled him over just outside of town for speeding. Didn't ticket him. Apparently just gave him a verbal warning. I doubt it was Clair, but could it have been possible?"

"*Where* outside of town?"

"Not sure."

"Why. What's up?"

"I am just trying to figure something out, Bob. Something doesn't add up."

"You playing cop again?"

"Okay, look. I'm sorry, but the investigation seems to be stalled at the county. They are waiting for a body to turn up down river. Maybe it will. But there are just things that I can't help wondering about. Nuñez hasn't been real informative, either with me or with the diocese. I haven't spoken with her in quite some time. The diocese keeps calling me. I got to thinking—what if it wasn't a cop who pulled him over? What if it was someone playing cop who was just trying to get a fix on Corrigan and what he looked like?"

Margaret didn't want to tip her hand as regards her suspicions of Nuñez, so she was trying a subterfuge.

"Okay. I'd have to go back to the office and check the logs, but thank God for cell phones."

He dialed a number.

"Clair? Bob. The Saturday that Corrigan went missing. Did you by any chance pull him over anywhere in or near town for speeding?"

Margaret bit her cuticles and watched passersby through the window.

"Okay. Thanks."

Burton clicked his phone off.

"Wasn't Clair."

"Okay. Thanks."

"You know, Nuñez has some problems."

"What kind of problems."

"A month ago she was diagnosed with an aggressive form of breast cancer. She has been trying to work, but frequently misses because of her treatments. They are doing a number on her. That may be why she isn't really on top of this."

Margaret remembered the last time she had seen Nuñez. She had seemed a bit drawn, and her hair seemed a bit thin.

"Oh, dear. I had no idea."

"Yeah. It's a shame. She's been a damned good cop for a long time. Not sure how much longer she is going to be able to hang in there."

Alice sat a plate of fried chicken, mashed potatoes with white gravy, green beans and a large dinner roll in front of Margaret.

"Enjoy your starch and cholesterol," Alice said.

"Oh, I will. I definitely will."

ON HER WAY HOME FROM lunch, Margaret received the call

she had been waiting for from Templeton about the afternoon Seamus had been pulled over. There were only two females on the Jersey County force—Deputy Mary Clark and Teresa Nuñez. Templeton learned that Clark had been on vacation that whole week. He also checked with the State Police, and it wasn't one of theirs. And Bob Burton had ruled out Clair.

The next day, Margaret placed a call to the Jersey County Sheriff's office and asked for Deputy Nuñez. The man who answered said that she was on duty, but she wasn't in the office.

"Please ask her to call Sister Margaret Donovan." She gave the deputy the cell number. "It is imperative that I speak with her. Tell her that I have evidence in the Corrigan disappearance and she must see it."

"Will do."

"Officer. This is urgent."

MARGARET WONDERED WHETHER SHE WOULD get a call back. It was around two in the afternoon when her cell phone chirped.

"Sister Margaret."

"Sister, this is Deputy Nuñez."

"Deputy, we need to talk."

MARGARET AGREED TO MEET NUÑEZ at an Arby's in Jerseyville around three-thirty. When she pulled into the parking lot, she saw the county car parked near the front of the restaurant. When she entered, she ordered a coke at the counter and then walked back to where Deputy Nuñez was sitting at a booth near the back. There were no others in the restaurant.

"How are you?" Margaret asked. She could definitely see signs of pain in Nuñez's face, and her hair had thinned even more. Her color wasn't good. Her face had an odd pallor to it. She was in a struggle for her very life.

"I'm okay," Teresa said, showing no expression.

"I won't waste your time," Margaret said. "I have some evidence that I thought you should have." She pushed the charred red notebook across the table.

"What's this?"

"I pulled it out of the incinerator at Eli's house one day when I was out there. It could very well constitute a solid motive for murder."

"Corrigan's death?"

"Yes."

"Eli?"

"Did you ever talk with Eli about any of this?"

"Been meaning to. The fact that he was Vergil's father certainly makes him worth following up."

"Why haven't you?"

Nuñez's eyes flashed.

"I've been a little busy. Besides, all indications are—"

"That he walked into the river. Right?"

"Look, I've known Eli for a long time. He's no killer. But I will follow up. Did you come here to give me information or criticize my investigative procedures?"

Nuñez suddenly winced, and then placed her hand on her chest.

"Deputy Nuñez, Bob Burton mentioned your condition to me."

"He did, did he? He always did have a big mouth. Yeah. The radiation burns on my chest look like I have been deep fried in oil. It hurts like hell. I don't want to—don't intend to—give up any sooner than I have to. I hope you will forgive me if my investigation isn't going as quickly as you would like. But we'll get to the bottom of it. Don't worry. You're not a cop anymore, Sister. Don't forget that."

"You're right."

"So, what's in the book? Give me a quick summary."

Margaret sipped her coke, and then looked Nuñez directly in the eye.

"You know damned well what's in there. It's about the suicide of Eli's brother, Melvin, back in 1968. He poured gasoline over himself and went out in a blaze of glory. Not before, however, he killed his wife Catherine with an axe.

"You know. Because Catherine was your mother. *Teresa Jane.*"

Nuñez went whey faced. Then she closed her eyes.

"Okay. Yeah. But what's that got to do with anything?"

"I can't believe you are asking me that question. You're a cop. From everything I have heard, you are a good one. You have no business running this investigation, especially since you yourself have a motive for murdering Corrigan. Corrigan abused Melvin Barstow when he was a kid and screwed him up pretty bad. Sure, Melvin suffered abuse at the hands of his father and was probably messed up to begin with. But Corrigan betrayed him—and probably hundreds of other boys—by using his power, his authority, and his sacred relationship to seduce rather than help him. This journal was Melvin's and Eli probably got it from Melvin's place. You must have seen it at some point when you were at their house.

"You pulled Corrigan over the day he disappeared. I know it was you because the other female in the sheriff's department was on vacation that day, there were no state cars in the area, and it wasn't Clair Peterson.

"Why'd you stop him? Did you get his plate number and wait for him to come to town and pull him over just to get a look at him? Just to make sure you could identify him so you wouldn't go after the wrong priest? A prosecutor could make a good circumstantial case out of this. Eli told you he was devastated to learn that Vergil was his son, that Corrigan had abused Vergil, and that was the straw that broke the camel's back. That sent you over the edge. Not only had Corrigan set the sequence of events in motion that led to the death of your mother, but he also abused a boy who was the only son of a man you felt a kinship with because of your mother. Body or no body, with a little digging they could make it stick."

"You go to hell. You don't have the slightest fucking idea what you are talking about."

"Don't I? If you weren't involved in some way, why would you insist on heading this up? The only reason I can think of is to keep the investigation away from *you*—or Eli. *Or both of you.*"

"Eli isn't a killer."

"Are you?"

Nuñez stood up and slid the book across the table.

"Go fuck yourself, Sister. That's probably how you spend your time anyway, isn't it?"

With that, Nuñez walked out of the restaurant, got into the cruiser, and pulled out of the parking lot.

MARGARET POUNDED ON THE STEERING wheel several times during the drive back to Grafton. She had taken a shot, and still she wasn't any more certain than she had been before. She had a theory: either Eli had killed Corrigan, and Nuñez had covered it up; or, more likely, Teresa Jane lost it, killed Corrigan and disposed of the body. She knew the whole county and could easily have made a body disappear. Or, there was even a third possibility: Teresa Jane and Eli had both been in on it. Who better to help make a body disappear than a gravedigger?

But supposition was all that Margaret had going for her. Who could she tell? Not the sheriff. Nuñez had a lot of backing there and that wouldn't go very far. Yeah, Teresa Jane would have to explain why she continued to work the case when she had a stake in the outcome, and would then probably recuse herself—better late than never—but without any direct evidence, the sheriff wasn't going to accept Margaret's theory over the word of a deputy who had spent the better part of her career serving the county residents well and faithfully. Burton wouldn't be much help since it was out of his jurisdiction.

Margaret felt so helpless. Nuñez had hit the nail right on the head: Margaret wasn't a cop any more. The feeling of powerlessness was deadening and she took it out again on her steering wheel, at one point swerving on the two-lane highway going into Grafton.

As she pulled into the drive she remembered something Bill Templeton had said to her at the Fin Inn about the sense of powerlessness.

That feeling had begun to permeate her life. Even prayer wasn't helping. Hence, the Yellowtail. How many bottles had gone into the trash, in Grafton *and* St. Louis? Had she received a dollar for every empty over the past several years, she could probably have afforded a cruise to a Greek island.

Instead, she was on a journey that would take her somewhere she didn't want to go, unless she found a way to get on another path. Or to find again the path that, somewhere along the way, she had lost.

When she got back in the office, she flipped open her cell phone and dialed a number. She got a recording.

"Bishop, this is Margaret Donovan. I am calling about your visit a few weeks back. Please call me when you get a few minutes. I need to come to Springfield and talk with you about that.

"And some other things."

IT WAS UNSEASONABLY WARM IN Springfield as Bishop Greg Patterson pulled into the parking lot at *Fast Tony's*, a popular restaurant in the north end of Springfield. He opened the door and lit up a cigarette as Margaret got out of the passenger side.

"Go on in and get a seat," Patterson said. "I'll be there after a few drags. Tell Tony the bish is here!"

"You know, those things will kill you," Margaret said.

"It's okay. I work out."

Margaret rolled her eyes and walked into the diner. She spotted an empty booth in the far corner. It was about the only place available. The place was crowded—it was a little past noon—and three waitresses were bustling around trying to keep up. A short, slim man with thinning hair and a gray beard got up off the stool and walked toward her. He wore a black shirt with the name "Tony" on it.

"Hey guys," Tony said to three elderly men at the lunch counter, "watch your language; we have a nun in the house."

Margaret looked at the man and smiled. She knew him from years before. A former racecar driver, he had hundreds of photos from his racing career hanging on the walls, a variety of toy automobiles on shelves in various spots, and other memorabilia sitting on narrow shelves above the windows. She looked to see if he still had Barbie. Barbie—a doll with a miniskirt—was rigged on a wheel to a wire that ran from behind the cash register running diagonally across the diner to just above the booth by the window. The wire was on an upward slope so that when someone behind the register gave Barbie a push, the doll would traverse up the wire to the opposite side of the room and then come right back where she started from. *Charming,* Margaret thought. But, in truth, Tony was charming, rough edges and all.

Patterson walked up behind Margaret. "How you doing, Tony," he said, extending his hand. Tony took the bishop's hand and turned to Margaret.

"You know, he brings all his women here."

"So I shouldn't get too comfortable, huh?"

Tony guffawed. "I think this one is a keeper."

"Well, you would certainly know about those things," Patterson said, eliciting another laugh from the proprietor. The bishop sat in one side of the booth, and Margaret on the other. Tony scooted in next to her.

"Haven't seen you in a while," Tony said to Patterson. "You still drive that Jap car?"

"Well, my budget isn't as extravagant as yours."

"The women keep draining me dry, that's why. I should have been a priest. You have to be Catholic?"

"Details. We could work something out."

"Did you know this guy used to race?" Tony turned his attention to Margaret.

"Why, no. I didn't."

"I used to race dirt track when I was a kid growing up in Minnesota." He wore a short-sleeved clerical shirt, and extended his left arm and then twisted it to afford a view of the bottom of his arm, below the elbow. There was an ugly white scar that ran from near the elbow to the wrist bone. "Did that when the car I was in hit the wall and flipped over."

"Must have been God's way of telling you something," Tony said. "For some reason, God never spoke to me when I needed him to. Like, to say, 'That woman over there—run for your life!'"

The three laughed loudly, causing heads to turn, just as an attractive middle-aged waitress approached the table. Tony got up from his seat.

"Stay out of trouble," he said.

"See you, Tony," said Patterson.

He and Margaret ordered the special: stuffed peppers and mashed potatoes.

"Still the best place in town for lunch," Patterson said.

Margaret had met with the bishop earlier in the morning, and went to confession. She knew that this was a man she could trust, and so she went into detail about the problems and concerns she had experienced. She noted that, unlike many priests who give you absolution as a matter of rote, Patterson left you feeling truly cleansed. As she watched him finish his lunch, she decided to reach out and get to know a little more about this man.

"I hope you don't mind me asking, but I heard that you were married."

"Yes. For twenty years. Her name was Dorothy."

Margaret sat silently. She didn't know where to go after that. Patterson sensed the awkward silence.

"It's okay, really. She died in a car wreck in St. Paul," he said. "Along with our daughter. She was 18."

"I am sorry," Margaret said, blushing. "I shouldn't have…"

Her sentence was interrupted when a huge plate of stuffed peppers was placed in front of her.

"Get you anything else, guys?" the girl asked.

"This is great, thanks," Patterson said.

Neither talked much while they ate. She noticed that the bishop cleaned his plate in very little time. She was never going to be able to eat everything on hers. The peppers were delicious, but enormous.

"You know, our priest said something to me at the funeral home the night of the wake. It was something he had heard when he was in Italy. *'Love makes time pass, time makes love pass.'* I just looked at him and said, 'Father, I sure as hell hope that isn't true.' Truth is, Sister, I am proud to have been husband to one of the most beautiful and decent women God ever created. It was a wonderful and marvelous experience. Now, I have been given the opportunity to have another wonderful life. God doesn't grant that to too many people."

"You're right about that."

"Of course, I'm right. I'm the bishop."

Margaret laughed out loud. Patterson smiled.

"Corrigan was a priest. He wasn't the only one, as you know. What happened? What brought all this about?"

Patterson scooted back. "We have paid out millions. Some dioceses, as you know, have been forced into bankruptcy. Frankly, that's as it should be. What happened? Boy, that's a good one.

"You studied philosophy. Remember Kant? He said that what distracted us from duty was inclination. He might not have been thinking of original sin—although he grew up in a strict Lutheran family—but that is exactly what he was referring to. You know, G. K. Chesterton said that original sin was empirically provable. And I agree with him. Put humans in a situation where they can do the wrong thing, the majority of them will do just that. Look at Abu Ghraib.

"I do know this wasn't something new. It has been going on for decades. Maybe centuries. Lately, however, I think it has become a cultural phenomenon among certain clerics. Guys like Corrigan were probably looking for ways not to stand out, not to answer the troubling questions about why they never married. Their orientation was something that they dealt with privately, but found a way to cover themselves by going into the priesthood. There they probably found others like them, and they may have convinced themselves that what they were doing wasn't a violation of their vows.

"You know, celibacy means not having sex with a woman or marrying. But somehow helping each other get by was acceptable. In some institutions there was a subculture. I saw it happening among some of the guys in Rome. But Corrigan was a pedophile, which I will never understand. Somehow it got out of hand and, frankly, in many cases the leadership simply did nothing except cover it up, pay off the victims, and sweep it under the rug. Sadly, they shipped the guys out to other parishes to continue their behavior. It is nothing less than a violation of trust on the part of those bishops. Scandal is sometimes a good thing. It keeps things like that from recurring. To the church, scandal was to be avoided at all cost. The result is a lot of damaged human beings and a network of men who would go on doing damage until the public wouldn't put up with any more.

"What bothers me is when people say we need to stop hammering this into the ground. The problem has been addressed. Move on. That ignores the inclination that is always there and does nothing but clear the field. In time, the problem will resurface. I don't intend to ever let this issue die."

"Okay. So Corrigan slipped through the cracks," Margaret said, wiping her mouth with her napkin. "It must have been horrifying for those parishioners to see him in their midst again after so many years."

"Yes. I can't imagine. So what are you going to do?"

"You mean..."

"About your suspicions? Nuñez?"

"I really don't know."

"What if you were still a cop? What would you do then?"

"I would have to report this to a higher authority. My boss."

"And what would he do?"

"Notify the Illinois State Police of suspected irregularities in the Jersey County Sheriff's Department. That would result in an investigation."

"But you're not a cop anymore."

"No, I'm not. And besides, all I have is supposition."

"From what I've heard, your suppositions are better than most that are on the job. I have that from your former boss."

"He talks about me?"

"I think he thinks you're his ticket to heaven. Doesn't help him at the poker table, however. Seriously, what does your conscience tell you about this?"

"My conscience?"

"Yes. That still small voice that speaks to you in the silent moments of your life. I know you have one of those."

"Sometimes you wouldn't know it."

"Nonsense. Seriously."

"My conscience tells me it requires looking into. At least the part I can prove—the fact that Nuñez's mother was murdered by a man whom Corrigan abused."

"Would you be violating anything you learned in confidence?"

"No. Not about that."

"Sounds to me like your conscience is giving you good advice. Margaret, does this place you in any danger?"

Good question. She didn't want to go into the fact that she kept a Sig Sauer in a drawer in her bedroom. She honestly wondered whether she was putting herself in a dangerous position in this whole thing.

"Nothing I can't handle," she said.

"So I've heard."

"Was it any good?" They looked up to see Tony grinning at them next to the booth.

"It was awful, as usual," Patterson said.

"Well, we try to be consistent."

"Don't listen to him," Margaret said, touching Tony's arm as she got out of the booth. "It was wonderful."

"Oh, I like her! If you ever quit the convent, come on back. I'll hire you."

"Then he'd probably try to marry you!"

"That was cold!"

Patterson slapped Tony on the back. "Take care, buddy!"

"You too. Keep bringing the customers in!"

Before getting back in the car, Patterson lit up another Camel.

Margaret stood with him outside the doorway while he smoked it.

"Margaret, you're a brave woman. I will be praying for you through all of this."

Margaret smiled. He wasn't talking about the situation with Nuñez. He was referring to the subject of her confession.

"Those things…"

"Are going to kill me. I know." He put the cigarette butt out in the ashtray. "Let's go. I have a meeting in half an hour. The meetings will kill me long before the cigarettes do."

"Bishop?"

Patterson turned to her before starting up the car.

"I cannot thank you enough. You're a good man."

"And you, Margaret Donovan, are a good woman. When you get your issues worked out, remember there's a place for you somewhere in my office. And I sincerely mean that."

She shook his hand warmly and climbed into her car.

There was one more stop she needed to make before returning to Grafton.

She knew now it was the right thing to do.

TERRY MARSDEN WAS NEARING FIFTY and had been a state cop for almost 25 years. Female troopers weren't a novelty when she enlisted, but one of the first female officers had trained her so she knew well the uphill struggle that women on the force faced early on. In Illinois, female troopers came about as a result of the need for compassion. It had become more and more common for troopers to take their wives with them when they had to comfort bereaved women whose husbands had died in car crashes. In 1963, trooper qualifications for the first time included qualifications for females. By the time Terry enlisted, it wasn't as rough getting accepted but being a female trooper was still not for the faint of heart. She rose through the ranks rapidly and eventually achieved rank of Lt. Colonel. She proved herself and gained the respect of most of her male counterparts, even some who at first resented her presence. She was rightfully proud of what she had accomplished.

She drove up-river from Alton on her way to Jerseyville. She never grew tired of seeing the bluffs and the river under a bright, blue sky. She had, of course, been assigned to help keep the peace whenever the water spilled over its banks, but the eternal beauty of the ancient river dissipated all memory of the havoc it could wreak on a day like this. She loved it.

It was just past noon when she pulled into the parking lot behind the Jersey County Sheriff's Department. Although sunny, there was an autumn chill in the air. She picked up a manila folder, got out and walked to the building and through the glass doors.

"Good morning," said a young deputy who was seated behind a long white counter. "Can I help you?"

"I'm here to see the Sheriff. I'm Terry Marsden, with the Inspector General's office.

"One moment." The deputy picked up a phone and buzzed through to the Sheriff's line. "Inspector Marsden from the Inspector General's office is here. Great."

"Come on back, ma'am," said the young man. He got up and opened the swinging gate for her. Then he led her into a conference room. No one was there. "The Sheriff will be here in a moment. Can I get you something?"

"You can point me to the bathroom."

"Sure. It's right around the corner."

"Thanks."

SHERIFF JAKE COLLINS WAS POLITE but quite obviously nervous. It was cool in the conference room, but Collins was sweating.

"Sheriff, the evidence here suggests that your deputy has a clear conflict of interest. She did not recuse herself, in spite of the fact—if this information is to be believed—she herself could easily be a suspect."

"Nuñez has been with this department for a long time. I have talked with her."

"And she said?"

"Not much."

"Perhaps she will be able to explain it to me," Marsden said. "Is she here?"

"Yes. She's waiting in my office. I...uh...suspended her with pay after I spoke with you the other day. Per your request, she is here to talk with you. Before she comes in, might I suggest that her physical condition might have affected her judgment in this situation."

"I understand that she has cancer."

"Pretty bad. Not a good prognosis. She still refused to give up."

"I will keep that in mind. Let's see what she has to say."

TERESA WALKED INTO THE CONFERENCE room. She was pale and dressed in a white blouse, navy slacks and a sweater. Marsden rose and offered her hand across the table.

"Terry Marsden. State Police. We have the same first name."

Teresa shook the woman's hand and then sat without speaking. Marsden resumed her seat and Sheriff Collins sat next to his deputy.

"Deputy, I assume you know why I am here."

Teresa looked at the charred binder containing the notes, the same binder she had seen in the restaurant when she met Sister Margaret.

"Yes."

"This is an apparent irregularity that we have to look into, deputy. From all appearances, we have a clear case of a situation from which you should have recused yourself. The missing subject, Father Corrigan, may have abused your stepfather. It is possible that you have reason, at best, not to pursue this investigation to its fullest; and, at worst, that you yourself could be a suspect. Can you explain why you did not see fit to turn this over to someone else?"

Teresa looked down and didn't answer. A minute passed. Finally she looked Marsden in the eye.

"I'm a good cop, Inspector. I have not jeopardized this investigation. I have done my job."

"Were you aware of a connection between Corrigan and the man who killed your mother?"

"Not before that document was shown to me by Sister Margaret Donovan." *She lied.* At the last minute, her eyes shifted to the right. *Marsden knew.*

"When you learned of this, did you inform the Sheriff?"

"No."

"Why not?"

"In case you don't know, I am fighting a losing battle with cancer. Perhaps it was an error in judgment not to, but there are many things I am fighting right now."

"Sheriff Collins told me that you have been struggling with cancer, and he also said that you were proud to be able to stay on the job, presumably to keep doing the best job you could. And now you tell me that, in this one instance, you erred in judgment? If so, I must again ask, 'Why in this one instance?' Or, have you also erred in judgment with respect to any other issue?" Marsden glanced at the Sheriff. He was looking down at the table, still sweating.

Teresa didn't say anything. Neither did Collins.

"Deputy?" Marsden persisted.

"I screwed up. I am sorry." She turned to Collins. "I am so sorry I embarrassed you."

Marsden looked at both of them from across the table.

"Do you have anything else to add?"

Teresa shook her head.

"Sheriff, I am going to recommend that you investigate this matter fully. We will also be looking into it carefully. Continuing the suspension would seem to be in order here, at least until we are able to piece together the facts. That will be the substance of my report. Can I count on your cooperation?"

Collins sat up straight. "Absolutely."

"Good." She glanced at Teresa.

"I hope your health improves," she said.

Teresa didn't even look at her.

PREPARATIONS FOR THE ST. ALBAN'S Harvest Festival were in full swing. The week prior had been a busy one. The ladies from the parish were cleaning and decorating the parish hall, and the men were readying the grounds for the children's games and preparing the horseshoe pits. People from other parishes involved themselves in this festival since St. Alban's was the only end-of-year festival in the area. A group of elderly Italian men spent quite some time working out where the bocce ball games should go; a discussion that went on every year, even though—when it was all said and done—the games went precisely where they went every year. It was a happy time, and it raised Margaret's spirits to see such joy and activity. It reminded her once again of the importance of community in a life well lived.

Adam was a changed person. He was not the sullen young man that Margaret had first met, but had developed into a charming and funny young man. He went with Margaret to help arrange the large tables in the dining hall.

"You're pretty strong for a girl," he said, grinning broadly at one point.

"Coming from you, Adam, that's a compliment," she said. "Thanks for calling me a girl."

"Well, I always try to be nice to older women."

"You just blew it, buster!"

They worked for over an hour and then returned to the rectory. Alice had just pulled up in front.

"You two up to no good?" Alice asked, unloading two large grocery bags. Adam ran over and took one from his mom.

"Your son was just reminding me of my age," Margaret said.

"Yeah, well, he's aged me by twenty years, that's for sure. Shut the car door, will you Adam?"

Margaret helped Alice put the groceries away. Adam grabbed a fudge bar from the freezer.

"Hey! Dinner will be in a while."

"Aw, mom."

"Okay, but no more. Where's Erik?"

"He's fishing."

"By himself?"

"Yeah. He can take care of himself."

"Okay."

Adam walked out and bounded up the stairs.

"At one time, you wouldn't have worried about things like that, I guess. Now you don't know who to trust," said Alice as she popped open a can of Pepsi.

"Yeah, I know. But he should be okay."

"I know. Uh...*Sister*, we need to talk."

Margaret gave her a look.

"Okay. So talk."

"You know what I said about moving?"

"Yes. And I can't blame you."

"Well, I haven't moved, right? Truth is, you're like family now.

You don't just walk out on family."

Margaret smiled. That felt good. She was afraid she had alienated Alice who had become one of her best friends.

"So, I need to know if you will put up with us for another three months."

"You don't have to ask. You haven't seen me running ads for another girl with two wild and wooly kids to move in have you?"

Alice laughed.

"But—three months?"

"Better sit down."

"I'm fine."

Alice extended her left hand. A gold band crowned by a single diamond graced her third finger.

"Oh, my God!" Margaret put her hands up to her face.

"It ain't Zirconium, either."

Margaret reached over and grabbed Alice and hugged her tightly. They were both on the verge of tears as they separated.

"Alice, I am so…so happy for you. This is a miracle."

"Tell me about it. You know, I wouldn't have met Mark if it hadn't been for you. I'd probably still be chasing losers and living in their trailers. Instead, I got my prince."

"So, why three months?"

"Well, Bobby has been building a house. He was originally building it for his wife, but she decided that she wanted a two-story. This is a story and a half. Mark asked his dad about it and he said he would sell it to him at a bargain price. When Mark told him why, Bobby said that he would pull out all the stops and have it done by the first of the year. I'm going to have a new house!"

The two hugged once more.

"So, what's up?"

They looked down to see Erik holding a stringer with two good-sized catfish on it.

"That's a surprise, young man," Alice said. "You'll find out in time."

"Mark asked you marry him?"

Alice and Margaret just looked at each other and laughed.

"Oh my God!" Erik dropped the catfish on the kitchen table with a discernibly liquid 'plop,' and ran into the other room and up the stairs.

"Mom and Mark are getting married!!!!"

"Is it true, mom?" Adam was downstairs in nothing flat.

"Yes, it's true!"

"That's awesome!" The boys walked over and hugged their mom.

"So, let's celebrate," Adam said. "Give me another fudge pop!"

THE FESTIVAL WAS PROVING TO be a huge success. By Saturday afternoon, they had run out of pork and several men were sent off to Alton to buy more. The festival wasn't over until Sunday afternoon, and this had never occurred before. The band Friday night had drawn a huge crowd of young people, many of whom weren't from the parish. Bob Burton was on top of things to make sure that nothing got out of hand, and Bobby, Mark, Jack and a few of the other members of the local chapter of Bikers for Christ were on hand to offer their support. There hadn't been trouble Friday night, however. Nor did they anticipate any on Saturday evening.

About 4:30 the parish hall was filled. Mark, Bobby, Jack and two other bikers were chowing down at one of the tables. Claire Fogarty was sitting with them, her face alight with the joy of their company. Claire had always been the life of the festival and was so even absent Jim. Such was the joy that Christ had brought into the heart of this woman that even after the death of her life's love she still found joy in her existence and helped spread it to others.

Beverly sat next to Bobby and was also enjoying Claire's company.

"So, Beverly," asked Claire, "how is it you ended up marrying a wild man like Bobby."

"Actually, Bobby was a step down. The first guy I dated was a Hell's Angel."

"Oh, my," said Claire. "I'll bet that was exciting."

"I'm joshing you, Claire. Ain't never been anybody but Bobby for me, ever since grade school. Right, Bobby?"

"Right, Bev."

"And if you ask him, he will say it was the same for him. That's the kind of incorrigible liar he is!"

Everyone laughed. Margaret walked by and tousled Mark's hair.
"What's so funny?"
"My dad," said Mark.
"Oh, he's a scream," said Jack.
"He does speak," Claire said.
"Not when he's eating."
"Where's Alice?" Mark had been looking around the dining hall.
"She's in the kitchen, stirring."
"She stirs Mark, too," said Jack. Mark just looked at him.
"How are you, Jack?" said Margaret.
"I'm mighty fine. You sure look pretty tonight, Sister."
Bobby slapped him on the back of the head.
"What?"
"Don't you know how to talk to a woman of God?"
"That's okay," said Margaret. She walked behind him, reached down and gave Jack a peck on the cheek. He turned bright red. "You can call me pretty anytime, Jack!"
The table went wild. "I didn't know he could blush like that," Mark said.
"I think he needs to pee," said Bobby.

THE JERSEY COUNTY CAR PULLED into the parking lot south of the church and, after stopping briefly near one of the girls parking cars, simply pulled up next to a telephone pole.
Deputy Jim Fawkes got out and thanked the girl. Fawkes had just turned 25, and his most striking characteristic was his shock of unruly orange-red hair. He wore glasses that seemed thicker than usual, he weighed about 127 pounds—he had just barely made the cut when he applied for the job with the County—and he wore a County jacket.
He walked over to the church and down the stairwell.
"Uh, Jack," said Bobby. "You still have that warrant out against you?"
"Hell, no. I got that cleared up."
"Then why is there a sheriff's deputy looking over this way?"
Fawkes was talking with an older woman who was picking up plates, and the woman was, indeed, pointing to the table where Jack and Bobby were seated. Margaret was still standing at the end of the table. She turned and walked toward the deputy, who was now

approaching her.

"*You're* Sister Margaret?"

"Yes. Can I help you, deputy?"

Fawkes was young and awkward and he spoke rapidly. "Sorry. It's just that—well, I went to Catholic school and most of our nuns looked like a cross between Winston Churchill and W. C. Fields. Oh, sorry. Too much information. I really am sorry."

"Okay. No problem. Frankly, I am impressed that someone your age even knows who either of those two gentlemen were."

"I went to college before—before I, uh, became a deputy."

"Admirable. But can I help you?"

"Actually, uh, sister, I need to see you for a few minutes. Alone."

Margaret touched the boy's shoulder. He seemed so very needy she couldn't help herself.

"Come with me, deputy."

FAWKES AND MARGARET SAT IN the back pew of St. Alban's.

"The sheriff wanted me to bring this to you." He handed her an envelope. She took it, looked at him, and started to open it. Then she stopped.

"What is going on, deputy?"

"Well, actually, I am only relaying the information. I don't know much. But it seems that deputy Nuñez—"

"Deputy Nuñez what?"

"She's dead, sister."

Margaret closed her eyes.

"The envelope contains a photocopy of a letter that was found in her car. The State Police investigator who has been looking into Deputy Nuñez's handling of the priest's disappearance asked the sheriff to see that you got a copy. That's why I am here."

"How?"

"A barge clipped her, and one of the workers phoned it in. She appears to have walked into the river. They don't know for sure, but that's what it looks like." He was getting teary-eyed.

"I'm sorry, deputy."

"No. I'm sorry. She took me under her wing when I joined the force. She was a good cop—and now...."

"She was a good cop, deputy. And you will be too, because of her."

MARGARET PLACED THE ENVELOPE IN her pocket and didn't read it until after the parish hall had been cleaned up, the dishes done, the food put away and the band had gone home. She was bone-tired at midnight. Alice and the kids were zonked, and she sat in the chair in the living room.

Margaret had thrown out seven bottles of wine without opening them. Such had been her resolve. However, she needed reinforcement tonight. She went to the bottom of her dresser drawer, under a box of stationery, and pulled out a reserve. She sat now drinking from a tumbler.

She opened the letter. It was typed on a computer and printed off on plain, white copy paper.

> Jake:
>
> When you find this letter, I will be dead. I would have been dead soon anyway. At least this way, you will know the truth.
>
> I killed Seamus Corrigan. You have the notebook left by the husband of my mother. I stalked him, and then followed him down to the river, and I shot him. I used a pistol that I had kept when I was investigating a series of robberies. It is at the bottom of the river.
>
> I disposed of Corrigan's body. I guarantee that it will never be found. This I do not regret, given the suffering that this man brought to the world under the guise of a holy man. I once read that those who betray lay in the deepest pit of hell, frozen in ice. That is where you must look. You will not find him here.

My long career in law enforcement is undone by
this one act, which was foretold by the murder of
my mother many years ago. I truly regret what I
have done, and now I will go to my maker and
seek his forgiveness—and surcease from the
pain that I have known, both spiritual and
physical, these many years. For any shame or
harm I have brought to you, please forgive me.
You were always a friend. I am sorry that, in the
end, I was not.

Teresa Nuñez

Surcease. Margaret was surprised to see that word. Catherine
Barstow—Catherine *Earnshaw*— had been an educated woman; her
mother had a literary name: Catherine Earnshaw was the doomed
lover of Heathcliff in *Wuthering Heights*. It was ironic that, in her
last letter announcing her demise, Teresa would choose a word that
summoned the specter of Edgar Alan Poe: "surcease of sorrow for
the lost Lenore."

Margaret poured more wine. She had always been fascinated by
the endurance of evil. The last investigation she was involved in,
immediately before going to St. Louis, involved repercussions of a
crime that occurred thirty years earlier. The death of Teresa brought
to an end a web of evil that had been spun over five or six
decades—perhaps longer—involving priests who succumbed to
concupiscence and bishops who shuffled them in and out of parishes
and coughed up hush money to protect the image of the church. It's
no wonder that the writers of Genesis chose the snake as an image of
the demon, for a snake is long and wraps its coils around its victims
repeatedly as it slithers through time. Images of the Piasa bird
flashed in front of her as she began to drift off, clouded by the
anesthetizing merlot.

"You will not find him here." No doubt, Teresa Nuñez knew how
to dispose of a body. Cops learn all the tricks, and if they ever go
bad they are, therefore, a force to be reckoned with.

"You will not find him here."

"...the deepest pit."

Margaret suddenly sat up. The mist seemed to part from her eyes as awareness came upon her.

Suddenly she remembered something. Something that had passed between her and Eli in St. Alban's Cemetery.

The day that she went to check on the preparations for Jim Fogarty's funeral.

MARGARET DROVE UP TO THE main gate of the cemetery and shut off the engine. It was drizzling; there was a chill in the air. She wore a white sweater but the wind from the open farm fields cut right through it. She glanced around and, seeing no one, walked into the cemetery and took the path that led to Jim Fogarty's grave. Flowers were still piled high on top of the grave but no marker had yet to be placed there. Margaret hugged herself to fight off the chill; a chill that grew worse as she contemplated her fears about what—or who—lay in that grave with Jim Fogarty.

"Afternoon, Sister."

Margaret jumped and turned to see Eli standing about three feet from her. He was nowhere to be seen when she came out here, then seemingly materialized out of nowhere.

"Oh, Eli! I'm sorry. You startled me."

"Sorry. It's a bit chilly today. Is there something I can do for you?"

Margaret turned back and looked again at the grave. She didn't speak for a minute or so, and then turned to face Eli.

"The grave was deeper."

"Excuse me?"

"The day I came out here, I remarked that the grave was deeper. It was at least seven feet."

"Yes. Sometimes…"

"I remember what you said."

Neither spoke for another few seconds.

"He's down there, isn't he?"

"I hope so, Sister. I haven't seen Jim Fogarty wandering around lately, have you?"

"Corrigan."

Eli's eyes opened wide and he stepped back. Then he let out a breath.

"Corrigan is probably in the deepest pit of hell as far as I care, Sister."

The deepest pit. She recalled Teresa's letter.

"Eli…"

"You remember that story in the Bible about Abraham and his son?"

"Isaac?"

"Yeah. You see, I read the Bible. Don't go to church, for reasons you can well imagine. But that story always stuck with me. Abraham, who tried for years to have a kid, just picked up firewood and a knife and marched his boy up to this mountain—made the boy carry the wood himself, he did; sort of like Jesus carried his own cross—fully intent on sacrificing his only hard-won son just because God said to do it. That always bothered me. Why? What was the point? Just a loyalty test? Wouldn't an all-knowing God know that Abraham was loyal? Couldn't he read that in his heart? After I found out what happened to Melvin, I couldn't read that story without it making me sick. Sacrifice. God was demanding the sacrifice of a child. Come to find out, people have been sacrificing their children to the church for years and made to feel guilty, somehow, for complaining. How many, Sister? How many more Vergils were out there—*are* out there—living hobbled lives because some priest had his way and then got off scot-free? Things are getting better, they say. Maybe so. But that don't change the damage that was done."

Eli walked closer to the grave, and then spat on it. He turned back to Margaret.

"I don't know where in hell that priest is, and frankly I don't care. You think you know better, there's a bobcat in the shed. Course, poor Jim will have to undergo the indignity of exhumation. *And for what?* Now, is there anything else I can do for you, Sister?"

Margaret was stunned. *Had he just all but admitted what she suspected?*

"No, Eli. Nothing else. I will just stay and say a prayer, if you don't mind."

"Suit yourself," said the gravedigger. Then he turned and walked away, his boots sloshing as his weight pounded on the wet grass, causing Margaret to wonder how he had approached so quietly in the first place.

MARGARET DID PRAY AT THE grave. Prayed for God to release her from her position in the nexus of the mystery surrounding Corrigan's disappearance; but that was wishful thinking. Her thumb was on the pulse of it; the only thing she didn't know was what to do about it. She was all but certain of what lay in this grave along with Jim Fogarty. Oh, she couldn't prove it; but she could raise enough questions, provide Deputy Fawkes with enough trails to follow to eventually provide probable cause.

Probable cause to unearth the remains of Jim Fogarty and look for another body beneath the vault.

And for what?

Eli's taunt came back to her. No one—not even an unremorseful pedophilic priest—deserves to die at the hands of another. Corrigan shared the same inherited propensity to sin as every other human being; the same inbred inclination shared by her. God knows, she had given in to her human nature more times than she could count through the years; she could in no way pass judgment on a Seamus Corrigan, as thoroughly disgusting as his sins were. His sins may have been different by degree, but not in kind, from her own and every other human born into original sin. Although only God knew for certain, it seemed that habituation had slowly sealed off the doorway to redemption for him and many like him. If he was in the 9th circle of hell, in the ice with others who betrayed trust, he had arrived there of his own doing.

Teresa Nuñez admittedly ended the life of Seamus Corrigan. Her pain near the end was unimaginable, and her days on earth were numbered. And the pain of loss, the loss of a mother, had been with her for years before the cancer. The convergence of the physical with a long-standing emotional pain may have clouded her judgment. She had been a good woman, but even good people can kill. Margaret felt certain that she turned to Eli afterward—but how to prove it?

There was still something that didn't seem right. Something she was missing.

Yet, even if she had all of the pieces to her satisfaction, she wondered what she would—or should—do about it. Hadn't there been enough suffering?

She blessed herself and walked through the cemetery and back to her car. As she opened the door, she noticed a Jeep Cherokee pulling into Eli's drive. It stopped behind his Ford F150. Eli walked out onto the porch.

Rachel Atkins got out of the Jeep, looked briefly at Sister Margaret's car, and then walked toward the porch.

Margaret started the car and drove down the road. The sound of the wipers punctuated the silence like a metronome, providing a rhythm to a world out of harmony. She glanced into the rearview mirror and saw something that caused her to pull off to the side of the road.

As she drove away, Rachel and Eli walked into the yard and watched her car leave. Now she saw Rachel turn and watched Eli take her into his arms. The two stood in the drizzle for over a minute clinging to one another. Even at this distance, Margaret could see Rachel's body convulsing as Eli, her long-lost lover and father to her only child, comforted her.

The missing piece.

"Oh my God." Margaret raised her hand to her mouth.

Now she understood. Three lives had been shattered by the sin of one man.

Teresa Nuñez's last act wasn't an act of murder. *It was an act of sacrifice.*

When she walked slowly into the current of the Illinois River, as the water rose and eventually filled her mouth, nose and lungs, Teresa had offered herself as a sacrifice. It was an appeasement, one that—she only hoped—would bring peace to the other victims who had to go on living. *That was what Eli had all but told her.*

It was at that moment that Margaret made the painful but conscious decision that enough suffering had emanated from the evil perpetrated by Seamus Corrigan.

As Teresa Nuñez had reminded her, she wasn't a cop any more. She would leave justice to God, and perhaps to the remorse—if and when it became unbearable—of the woman who murdered Seamus Corrigan.

Teresa Nuñez

I DIDN'T KILL SEAMUS CORRIGAN. I was prepared to. I

wanted to. But I didn't.

Sister Margaret was right. I obtained his license plate number and waited for him for two hours along the highway. When I spotted his car, I pulled him over. I wanted to look the man in the eye. Yes, I wanted to be able to identify him.

I loved my mother more than anyone I have ever loved. She was gentle, loving, intelligent and beautiful. When my father ditched her for a woman who worked in his office, I was shaken, as all children are when something like that happens. But the core of my life, the jewel that held the crown together for me, was my mother. And I still had her.

I still have a picture of the three of us together that was taken when I was ten. Mother is smiling, relaxed in a semi-reclining position, leaning back on one elbow, her other arm resting on her upraised knee. I am on my knees to her side, grinning at the camera. My brother, Paul, sits behind mom, his hand on her shoulder. It was one time when he seemed really happy. I remember the day it was taken. The sun was shining. That moment was washed away by the flow of time, but I still have it. It is framed in my heart.

My brother wasn't as close to mother. But he wasn't close to my father either. I don't think it was possible to be close to my father. I hurt for my brother because he was so sad. He was sad right up until he took his own life. There was a hole where his heart should have been.

But mother and I were so close that I could sense things about her that she didn't say. I knew that she was terribly lonely. I didn't really understand it—a child doesn't know what a woman does—but I sensed there was something wrong.

After several years, mother came home one evening seeming more animated than usual. She was humming to herself and laughing at nothing in particular.

"I have a date," she proclaimed eventually. I tried to share her happiness, but there was a place deep down that made me sad. I didn't want to be selfish—but what are kids that age if not selfish? It's their nature, or so we are taught.

Eventually she brought her beau home to meet us. Melvin was a distinguished looking man who smoked a pipe and seemed affable, if very quiet. He was pleasant, and tried to draw my brother and me into the conversation. He had no luck with my brother, but I decided to bite the bullet and make an effort with him for mother's sake. It seemed to matter to her, because I noticed her smiling at the end of the table as I told Melvin about my schoolwork, my books, and other things that were important to me at that innocent time in my life.

Two months later, mother announced that she and Melvin were going to be married. It was sudden. Very sudden. They had gone out the night before, and the next day the decision was made. There wasn't going to be a big wedding. They were going to have a private ceremony in Alton at a church there, and we weren't invited.

"It's something we haven't planned. I'm sorry dear. It has to be this way."

How could getting married be something you "haven't planned?" That made no sense to me at all.

At that point, I felt the first door close between mother and me. I sensed that it would be the first of many—although I never dreamed that there would be a final one; that after that day, I would never really know my mother again.

I remember Melvin the night mother announced their intentions. He was acting very strangely. He seemed jittery, and he paced about in the living room not focusing on anything in particular and not participating in the conversation about what should have been a very happy thing in his life. My mother was nervous as well.

I have often wondered about that night, about that precipitous decision. With what I came to know later about Melvin's strange religious outlook and his mental condition, I have always surmised that they had succumbed the night before and made love. This created a sense of urgency to a man whose sense of guilt drove him to all sorts of extremes. They had to get married, if I was right, because it was the only way to appease God for their sin. Mother must have experienced awful nights and days following their legitimate lovemaking because I always figured that there was no such thing as legitimate sex where Melvin was concerned.

Life for me changed drastically after Melvin moved in. In time, we moved to his family farm after his mother moved into town. That was nice for a while, but the overpowering darkness that hovered over Melvin made my life unbearable. He wasn't really nice, although he never harmed me. His behavior was erratic. At times, he would be bouncing around the house, expressing excitement over something good that happened to him during the day; but, in a few days, he would disappear into a dark funk and lock himself into their bedroom. On such nights, mother slept on the couch.

"Melvin has a medical condition, dear," mother explained one afternoon.

"Did you know that when you married him?" I asked.

Mother didn't answer me. She just told me to finish the dishes and walked out of the room.

My brother didn't seem to mind, or even notice, Melvin's odd behavior. He pretty much ignored him. I envied that ability to ignore the clouds that hung over our lives. I couldn't.

One night, Melvin began screaming at my mother about something. She had done something wrong—I don't even know what it was.

"Why can't you ever do what you are supposed to do, Catherine? Life must be ordered. Ordered? Do you understand?"

"Do you understand?" That is one phrase that came out of Melvin's mouth so many times I couldn't begin to tell you. I always wondered if he was the one who didn't understand, but was projecting that lack of understanding on mother or on the world as a whole.

What was it he didn't understand?

It broke my heart to leave mom, but living with her was even more painful. She cried and Melvin just sat silently, when I told her that I was going to live with dad. I wasn't close with dad, but when I explained what was happening, he agreed. His new wife was friendly, if not gushy, and she was at least normal. A curtain came down that would never go up again, and I have not stopped feeling empty since.

I visited mother and Melvin sometimes, though not often. I was supposed to spend several weeks during the summer, but I always made up some reason to cut it short. It always left me anxious, fearful, and depressed. Like mother. On one of those visits, I came upon the notebook. It was on a coffee table, sitting open. Melvin wasn't home and mother was in the garage.

I read it. And for the first time became aware of a man named Father C. Seamus. When I lived with mother, we always attended mass. Mother was a devout Catholic. Melvin too. What I read was a tale of horror. I read it several times, just to make sure that I was reading it properly. I was young and sexually inexperienced, but I knew enough to realize what was going on. I also learned about the beatings he endured as a young man. No wonder he was loopy.

I knew that Melvin was sick. I had known it from the start. Underneath his easy charm there was this empty place. Now, I was glimpsing some of what had contributed to his sickness. Not only had he and Eli—his younger brother who, though older than I was, always treated me nice—been abused by their father; but Melvin had been horribly abused by the priest at Holy Trinity.

I never mentioned that book to anyone.

Then, in August, I received the phone call. Melvin's madness had come to an end. And so had my mother's.

I forced my way into the funeral parlor, risking arrest, to see my mother before they fixed her. The image is emblazoned in that part of my brain that stores the horrors. I was screaming as they pulled me away.

Yes, I was ready to kill Seamus Corrigan. The death of Rachel's child—Eli's child—was too much. I stayed around town, hoping, praying that he would leave the rectory for some reason. I had an old .22 caliber pistol I had kept after an investigation years earlier. It was untraceable.

Then, in answer to my unwise prayers, I saw his car pull out onto Main Street. I followed him. He went west out of town, finally pulling off the road on a path that led down to the river. It was a lonely spot. I followed.

I slowed and moved down the steep hill cautiously. Then I saw his car. He was sitting on a picnic table drinking something from a brown paper bag. I pulled up closer to his car, and he turned around. He sat the bottle down quickly and stood up. I got out of the car.

"What'd I do this time?" he asked. He smiled. *He smiled at me.*

"Father Corrigan?"

"Uh, yes. Are you going to read me my rights?"

"No. Just ask you a question. Do you remember Melvin Barstow?"

The priest looked at me strangely.

"What is this?"

"*Answer me!*" I screamed.

"Look, if I have broken some law arrest me. *But I won't be talked to that way.*"

Then, I pointed the pistol at him. He seemed to look beyond me, however, as though seeing a spirit descending from above. He raised his hands.

"What—?"

I started to squeeze the trigger. I was within a centimeter of an ounce of doing it. I was perspiring, shaking, nauseous. The gun was shaking in my hand. I knew I couldn't just kill another human being. It wasn't in me.

I let my arm drop, and started to turn and walk away.

That's when I heard the explosion. I dropped to my knees, and turned to see the horrified look on Corrigan's face. Blood was leaking onto his black clerical shirt. He looked down at himself, then up toward me. And then he just dropped.

I turned and saw what he must have seen when he looked over my shoulder.

About six feet from me, slightly above me on the incline, stood Rachel Atkins. She was still holding the pistol in her hand. Then she dropped to her knees.

I rushed over and removed the gun from her hand. She wrapped her arms around me and I hugged her.

"Oh dear God," she said. "Oh dear God."

Then I made a decision that left the disappearance of Seamus Corrigan the mystery that it became.

"Rachel, you've got to help me."

"Help you do what?"

"Just do what I say."

I opened the trunk of my car and took out a box of latex gloves.

"Put these on."

"Why?"

"Look, just do it!"

I looked around. There were no cars nearby. We were at the bottom of a hill. There wouldn't be boats about at this time of year, but we had to move quickly.

I couldn't risk putting Corrigan in Rachel's Jeep, in case the investigation somehow steered in her direction. *I knew then I would have to make certain that never happened.* I popped the trunk of my cruiser, took out two boxes of report forms, and then had Rachel help me lift the lifeless priest into the trunk. I lowered the lid.

"Now, listen to me," I said. "You go home. You go home and go to bed. This never happened. Do you hear me?"

She shook her head. She turned and walked back to the car.

"Rachel— is this gun traceable? Whose is it?"

"It was one my husband kept in the basement. He got it years ago. I don't know where. It's not one that I have ever used."

"Good. Now go."

The gun later made its way into the Illinois River when I crossed on the Brussels Ferry over to Calhoun County.

Corrigan made it to Eli.

Eli was horrified at first. He wanted nothing to do with it, until I explained what had happened. He had lost the son he never knew to Corrigan, and a brother as well. When he realized that he could lose the woman who gave birth to that son he softened.

He helped me carry the body to the shed behind the house. He rolled it in turf. He said he would take care of it the next time there was a funeral. I knew he would.

I was dying. I was in pain most of the time. That pain was made worse by knowing that I violated every principle I stood for all those many years. But I would not allow Eli or Rachel to suffer more than they have already. I was dying anyway, and sooner rather than later.

The river is so beautiful. It is the same at its source as it is at the mouth, and yet it is different. It is eternal. Only Rachel,

Eli and I—and God of course— will know for certain what happened on its banks. That is as it should be. We three have been bonded in blood since the nineteenth of August in 1968. That day led to this, and will haunt their tomorrows.

There has been too much pain.

Now the pain is over. For me, there are no more tomorrows.

I see the river now. I am hovering over it. I expected to be somewhere else, somewhere unpleasant; instead I am hovering now between heaven and earth in a queue of wraithlike souls that snakes its way through the clouds to the final quietude. Waiting.

Perhaps God heard the words I spoke as the water reached my nose and as I slipped at last, losing my footing, feeling my lungs fill and seeing the light as I drifted away. Perhaps it was those words that I spoke.

I cannot but wonder whether Seamus Corrigan, as he looked down at the hole in his chest, before the darkness overwhelmed him and he fell to the ground, spoke those same words. As strange as it seems, I am certain that if he had, God would have heard him too, perhaps to show him pity.

Oh my God, I am heartily sorry for having offended Thee.

And I detest all my sins because I dread the loss of heaven.

And the pains of hell.

Epilogue

Sonny Corredato

THE GENTLE, ROLLING HILLS OF Kentucky are healing balm for a troubled soul. For hours each day, I walked them, stopping to pray along one of the low walls, at the base of a statue, or by the lake at sunset. When Bishop Patterson suggested that I take a retreat in order to think through my life's choices, he asked where I would like to go. There was only one place that came to mind: the Abbey at Gethsemani, Kentucky. I spent two weeks there in almost total silence and rediscovered my vocation.

It was not the first time I had been to the Abbey. When I was a senior in high school, I happened to pick up a copy of *The Seven Storey Mountain*, a spiritual autobiography of Thomas Merton. Merton—a Columbia University scholar-turned-Trappist monk—put Gethsemani on the map after his book became a bestseller. He also became one of the flag bearers—together with Flannery O'Connor—of the Catholic literary renaissance of the mid-twentieth century. After I read this book, Merton became one of my most admired men. He was a man of deep spirituality who, like me, fought sexual drives (albeit with a different orientation) almost until the last day of his life. My pastor, a good man who sensed that I was considering a vocation, suggested I take a retreat at the Abbey in the summer between my junior and senior years. After leaving the Abbey that summer, I knew what I wanted to be: a priest.

How did I get so far off the path? Had my success, my selection to go to Rome, and my placement in the chancery clouded my mind and fed my arrogance? At what point did I delude myself that what I was doing wasn't a violation of my vows? Celibacy isn't observed just because one does not marry; and that doesn't give you *carte blanche* to satisfy your lust in other ways. Father Seamus and others lived in the shadows of misconception, and some of them did a great deal of harm. True, I never would have married even if I hadn't chosen the priesthood. *Had I chosen this life simply because I feared my true nature would be exposed? I honestly don't think so.* In truth, I believe the choice had more to do with a love of Christ that my parents had instilled in me. The battle I fought within myself over my "thorn in the flesh" somehow cast a long shadow over my decision, affirmed I am sorry to say by some with whom I came into contact, leading me to a dark place where it all became clouded. *But I made the choices. Not them. And I should never have allowed my judgment to be clouded by those past associations. God forgive me.* There is no delusion like a self-delusion. There is no devil like the one that lives in our hearts and minds and whispers to us in the dark of night, *"It's okay! You're not the only one! There are others here who can help you."*

During those two weeks away from Springfield, I prayed often near Merton's grave outside of the Abbey. I reread his book and a recent biography that detailed his struggles with the flesh, up to and including a love affair he had with a nurse while he was hospitalized shortly before his death. Through it all, he struggled but managed to hold onto his faith and cling to the choice he made when he entered the priesthood. The question I had to ask was, *could I do the same?*

When I returned, I was no longer chancellor. Bishop Patterson spoke with me at length and was pleased to learn that I had come back strengthened in my vocation. My long-term relationship ended. I ended it. It was difficult, but it was the only right thing to do. I still love him and probably will until I die. I pray for him every day. But I had made an earlier, more important commitment years before when I was ordained; and had no right to consider another. It was time to start living up to that earlier commitment. I am, first and last, a priest. I hope to start being a good one.

God is forgiving. All of it, all of the things that I did that had placed my soul in peril, are washed away by God's love. All I had to do was ask. Bishop Patterson made it clear that I can continue to serve in the priesthood, demanding only obedience to my vows. God, he said, made me the way I am and loves me that way. But, he reminded me, "celibacy is celibacy." That is the beauty of my faith. God's grace is there for us, and all we have to do is ask. Having been humbled, I

ALONG THE RIVER ROAD   228

now find that I can ask that much more easily. When you are too important to ask forgiveness, your damnation is all but assured.

I will soon be assigned to a parish. Ironically, Patterson is sending me to Calhoun County, not far from the River Road. He also suggested that I serve as Moderator at St. Albans in Grafton, working closely with Sister Margaret. "You can learn a great deal from that woman," he said.

Perhaps I can. Perhaps I will learn to be a good priest. Which is, somehow, all that I should ever have wanted to be.

My life is not over. There is much yet to do. With God's help, I will do it well.

———

THE CLOCKS WERE SET BACK a week after All Souls Day; how appropriate that darkness comes into the world after ghosts and goblins wander the earth. A slight drizzle had dampened the highway and the damp pavement reflected back at her as she wended her way to Jerseyville. She was anxious. She was a bit frightened about the implications of what she was about to do.

She was meeting Bill Templeton.

She had prayed about this, cried about this, and finally gave in to what she knew—deep in her heart—was the only thing that she could do if the rest of her life was to have any real significance.

Alice had hugged her before she left the house. Alice knew. She approved.

"Focus on the road," Margaret said to herself at one point when she caught herself thinking about it too much.

"Sometimes, you think too much," her father used to tell her. She never really understood how someone could think "too much." But, her father was right. Sometimes she did.

She reached Jerseyville a few minutes before seven, drove down the main street and, towards the outskirts of town, pulled into a parking lot. Her heart had begun beating rapidly. She looked for Bill's car; there were about a half-dozen parked there.

Finally, she saw it.

She swung in next to it. She took a deep breath and then shut off the engine. Bill, seeing her, opened the car door and got out.

Margaret got out and walked over to Bill. The drizzle was lighter now, and seemed barely a mist. There was something cleansing about it. She looked up at him. He opened his arms, ever so slightly, and she reached out and hugged him.

"You ready?"

Margaret looked up at him. "Yes. Thank you."

"Don't thank me. I love you, remember?"

She smiled. She loved him too. She knew that now. Perhaps that was one of the reasons she had to be here. She also knew that, after tonight, he couldn't be here anymore. He could only open the door, and then someone else would have to step in for her. It had to be that way.

They walked across the parking lot and entered a double door. They walked down a set of stairs and down a long corridor, past a rack of folding chairs and a stack of long tables. Finally, they came to a doorway that stood partially opened with a hastily scrawled note on lined paper taped to the doorjamb.

They walked in. Seven other people—two women and five men—stood as they entered.

"Please, join us," one of the men said.

Margaret and Bill chose empty chairs and sat down. She reached over and took his hand, squeezing it tightly. The others resumed their seats.

The man who welcomed them was a gaunt, gentle man with a thick head of salt-and-pepper hair. His eyes were kind, but at first glance his face conveyed a sense of hurt long suffered. Then he smiled. When he did, his eyes shone bright blue, the crevices etched in his face from a life of alcohol and chemical abuse dissipated as though bathed in a new, brighter light: a light of hope.

"Welcome," the man said. "My name is Ezra. Please, introduce yourself."

Margaret felt a tear well up behind her eye that finally breached and began to slide down her right cheek. She squeezed Bill's hand tighter, and he gave a reassuring squeeze in return. At last she stood up.

"Good evening," she said. "My name is Margaret.

"I'm an alcoholic."

About the Author

Isaac Morris, a native of Iowa, holds a masters degree in religion from Butler University and Christian Theological Seminary and currently teaches philosophy and religion at Lincoln Land Community College. He lives in Springfield, Illinois. *Along the River Road* is his second novel. His first novel, *The Absence of Goodness* (iUniverse Corporation, 2009), introduced the character of Sister Margaret Donovan—a nun like no other you have encountered in fiction!

CPSIA information can be obtained at www.ICGtesting.com
Printed in the USA
LVOW072159270412

279524LV00007B/108/P